Shameless

A Bitter Creek Novel

Joan Johnston

DELL • NEW YORK

A Dell Mass Market Original

Copyright © 2015 by Joan Mertens Johnston, Inc.
Excerpt from *Surrender* by Joan Johnston copyright © 2015 by Joan Mertens Johnston, Inc.

Published in the United States by Dell, an imprint of Random House, a division of Penguin Random House LLC, New York.

DELL and the HOUSE colophon are registered trademarks of Penguin Random House LLC.

This book contains an excerpt from the forthcoming novel *Surrender* by Joan Johnston. This excerpt has been set for this edition only and may not reflect the final content of the forthcoming edition.

ISBN 978-0-8041-7868-6
eBook ISBN 978-0-8041-7869-3

Cover design: Lynn Andreozzi
Cover illustration: Alan Ayers

Printed in the United States of America

randomhousebooks.com

9 8 7 6 5 4 3 2 1

Dell mass market edition: January 2016

Praise for Joan Johnston

"Joan Johnston does short contemporary Westerns to perfection. —*Publishers Weekly*

"Johnston warms your heart and tickles your fancy." —*New York Daily News*

"Bless that Joan Johnston and her scheming ways!"
—*USA Today*

"Joan Johnston continually gives us everything we want . . . fabulous details and atmosphere, memorable characters, a story that you wish would never end, and lots of tension and sensuality."
—*Romantic Times*

"A master storyteller . . . Joan Johnston knows how to spin a story that will get to the readers every time." —*Night Owl Reviews*

"Johnston has a keen eye for quirky circumstances that put her characters, and the reader, through a wringer. Laughing one moment and crying the next, you'll always have such a great time getting to the happy-ever-after."
—*Romance Junkies Reviews*

"Johnston is a writer who can combine romance side by side with tragedy, proving that there is magic in relationships and that love is worth the risk." —*Bookreporter*

This book is dedicated to
Michael J. Ludvik,
a writer and prolific reader.

Prologue

PIPPA GRAYHAWK WAS the best horse whisperer in Australia. She'd spent most of her nineteen years taming brumbies—wild horses—on her father's remote cattle station in the Northern Territory. She was so good with animals that the wildest stallion was soon gentled and eating from her hand. But when it came to men—or rather, one particular man—her instincts had utterly failed her.

Pippa whimpered as she pressed a frigid bag of ice against the painful bruise high on her cheek. She'd made a terrible mistake, but one she would never make again. A flush of shame heated her face. How gullible she'd been! How naive! She gritted her teeth to still the quiver in her chin. From now on, she would know better than to trust. She would know better than to give her heart so freely. No man was ever going to hurt her again.

Pippa's heartbeat ratcheted up a notch when she heard a knock on the door. No one knew where she was. Two days ago, she'd run away from home with one of her father's wranglers, Tim Brandon. They'd checked into a hotel room in Darwin, which was when Tim had shown his true colors.

Pippa stared at the door, wondering if it was Tim, returning to apologize. He'd walked out in a huff an hour ago—after slapping her hard enough to cause the bruise on her cheek.

"How the hell did you get pregnant?" he'd ranted. "You told me you were taking precautions."

"I did," she'd protested. "I was sick in the middle of the month, remember? I couldn't't keep anything down. The pills must have come back up with everything else. What does it matter?" she'd said. "We're going to be married anyway."

"No, we're not."

Pippa's heart had nearly stopped at Tim's announcement. Before she'd given herself to him the first time, he'd told her he loved her. He'd told her he couldn't wait to marry her so they could start a family together. Was he really taking it all back? "What do you mean?"

Tim stuck his balled fists on his hips and shot her an irritated look. "I can't marry you, Pippa."

"But you promised!" she cried, fearful and frantic at his about-face. All the promises he'd made—that he loved her, that he planned to take care of her for the rest of her life, that he would be a wonderful husband, that they would have a wonderful life together—had persuaded her to give him her virginity. She'd waited to part with that precious gift until she'd met the man she planned to marry. She was having trouble wrapping her head around the fact that she'd offered something priceless to someone who'd trampled on it.

And she had no one to blame but herself.

Her father had warned her to stay away from

his hired hands. But Tim had been so friendly—and so good-looking—that she'd spent more and more time seeing him behind her father's back. Being held in a man's arms for the first time had made her tremble. Kissing him had left her breathless. She'd honestly believed that Tim cherished her.

How could she have been so wrong?

She reached out her hands in supplication to the inexplicably angry man standing across from her and said, "I love you. You said you love me."

Tim sneered. "You stupid little ninny. I told you what you wanted to hear to get into your pants. There's no way I'm marrying you!"

"Why not?" she asked, confused and hurt and still unwilling to believe that the man she loved could be so cruel.

"Because I'm already married!"

Pippa's heart had physically hurt, as though someone had punched her in the chest. She thought she literally might die from the humiliation of having been so completely duped. "What about the baby?" she asked past the excruciating lump in her throat.

"Give it away or throw it away. I don't care."

Enraged at how easily Tim had dismissed the child they'd created, she lashed out at him with her palm. He easily ducked so she missed his face, but his hand shot out and caught her cheekbone, causing her to see stars.

Tears of pain sprang to her eyes, joining the tears of distress that had already filled them to the brim. Pippa sobbed as a tear spilled down her stinging cheek.

"Stop your whining! This was supposed to be a holiday. We were supposed to have some good sex and some good grub and that would be the end of it. Now I'm going to have to quit my job and head home to my wife in Sydney, all because you couldn't take care of business."

He'd stomped out, leaving her alone without a single pence in her pocket. Likely he'd returned because he'd realized that she had no money to pay for the hotel, or even her next meal, let alone the trip home. She never wanted to see Tim again, but better that than having to call her father to ask for help.

Daddy is going to be so mad at me for running away. And so disappointed when he finds out what a fool I've been. How can I tell him I'm pregnant? It's a good thing Tim is running for the hills. Daddy would kill him.

Pippa had watched her father punish a wrangler when the man brutalized one of the brumbies. The most terrifying part was that, through it all, her father had never shown any emotion. He'd just done what needed to be done to make sure that that sort of behavior was never repeated.

Tim's attack had caught her off guard because her father had never lifted a hand to her or her six-year-old brother, Nathan. He'd found other ways to discipline them that were especially effective—like the silent treatment her father employed when she failed to live up to his very high standards of behavior.

Pippa set down the bag of ice and rose from the

bed to answer the persistent knock at the door. "I'm coming, Tim!"

She opened the door and gasped in shock. She tried to slam the door, but a large, booted foot caught the door at the bottom and prevented it from closing.

"Go away!" she cried.

"Open the door, Pippa," her father said. "We need to talk."

Pippa could see half of her father's face through the open door: one piercing blue eye, a hank of black hair falling onto his forehead, an angry, flared nostril, and half of a mouth flattened to a harsh, judgmental line. She didn't want to let him in, but there was no way to keep him out. She took a step back, crossing her arms defensively over her chest.

Just as half of his face had been hidden, half of hers had been concealed. When her father stepped into the room, she heard him draw a sharp breath and watched his eyes narrow as he surveyed the bruise on her cheek. She lowered her gaze to the floor, unable to look at him, unable to bear the condemnation she was sure she would see on his face.

A moment later he was standing in front of her, his voice hoarse with emotion as he asked, "Are you all right?"

Pippa couldn't get words past the thickness in her throat, so she just nodded.

His fingertips hovered over the bruise, as though he wished to soothe the hurt, but never touched her face. He dropped his hand and said, "Let's sit down."

It was a good thing he'd suggested it, because Pippa's knees felt so weak she was afraid they would crumple, and she'd land on the dingy carpet. She dropped onto the cheap bedspread, her eyes on her white-knuckled hands, which rested on her jean-clad knees. She felt the bed sink as her father sat down beside her.

"Where's Tim?" he asked.

"He left."

"Is he coming back?"

Pippa was ashamed to admit the truth, but she forced herself to say, "He's gone back to his wife in Sydney."

"Good riddance."

Pippa frowned, because her father didn't sound the least bit surprised. "You knew he was married?"

"Of course."

"Why didn't you say something to me?"

"I told you to stay away from him—from all of my wranglers, in fact. That should have been enough."

Pippa wanted to argue that a heads-up would have been nice. But she remembered all the times she'd snuck out behind her father's back to see Tim. If she hadn't been so secretive, she might have saved herself a lot of heartbreak.

"What happened is my fault," her father said.

Pippa turned to stare at him.

"I should have sent you away to Sydney or Melbourne or Brisbane for school, instead of keeping you with me. Then you wouldn't have fallen for whatever line of bullshit Tim fed you. But . . ."

Pippa knew why he hadn't. He would have been lonely without her. She and Nathan were the only family he had. Her mother had remained a mystery all her life, someone her father refused to discuss.

She had only vague memories of her father's first wife and no idea why their marriage hadn't stuck. His second wife, Nathan's mother, had left her father while Nathan was still a baby, shrieking in a voice Pippa had heard through the bedroom door, "I can't stand to live in this deserted backwater. There are no neighbors. There is no culture. There is *nothing* here except those awful green frogs and a thousand poisonous snakes and a million flies."

She hadn't heard what her father replied. But she'd heard the screamed response. "Keep the boy. I don't care! Just let me go. Please. If you ever loved me. Let me go!"

She'd left, and she hadn't come back.

Her father had been sad for a long time afterward, but he'd never said a word against Nathan's mother. One night, after Pippa had gone to bed but before she'd fallen asleep, she'd heard a glass break in the kitchen. She'd gotten up to make sure everything was all right. When she reached the kitchen door, she saw that her father was staggering, apparently drunk. And he had tears on his cheeks.

She'd quickly stepped back so he wouldn't see her, putting a hand to her heart to keep it from pounding right out of her chest. She'd never seen her father cry. He was her rock. Always steady. Always dependable. He rarely drank, and even then, rarely had more than a single drink. It was terrifying to see him in such a state.

Pippa had hesitated, unsure whether she should try to comfort him or go away and let him grieve—if that was what he was doing. While she stood there, he began to mutter something, and she leaned closer, hoping to hear some explanation for whatever disaster had befallen them to cause such behavior.

Pippa would never forget the malevolence in her father's voice as she listened behind the kitchen door. She had never imagined he could hate someone as much as he seemed to hate his own father. She heard the agony in his voice as he expressed his fear that he might be just like him. She was amazed to learn that he'd run away from home. And that he was never, ever, ever going back.

The fading sunlight hit the bruised side of her face through the hotel window, and Pippa heard her father make an angry sound in his throat. She turned her head away. Matthew Grayhawk didn't need any more villains to hate. He had enough demons from his past to haunt him.

"Are you ready to go home?" her father asked.

"How can I go home? How can I ever hold my head up before our friends and neighbors again?"

"You might think this is the end of the world, Pippa, but it's not. You'll be fine." His hand tenderly brushed through her long blond hair, tucking a bit of it behind her ear. "In a few weeks, or months, you'll move past this incident in your life. Someday, you'll find a nice young man in town who'll love you for the extraordinary person you are."

His gentle voice brought tears to her eyes. He had no way of knowing that in seven months she would have a lifelong reminder of Tim. She had to tell him. There wasn't going to be any "nice young man." Not when the small town of Underhill got wind of the fact that she was unwed and pregnant. Not to mention pregnant with a married man's child. She was going to have to leave her father's cattle station and go . . . where?

Pippa had been homeschooled, but the sole focus of her life had been working with horses. She had no skills that would serve her if she moved to the city. And she couldn't imagine any other cattle station accepting a wrangler with a baby, even if she were the best at what she did.

"No one has to know about this," her father said. "We can—"

"I'm pregnant," she blurted.

Her father let out a long, soughing sigh. "Have you decided what you're going to do?"

"What do you mean?"

"I mean whether you're going to keep the baby?"

Pippa jumped up and turned to confront her father. "Of course I'm going to keep my baby! What else would I do?"

"You could give it up for adoption."

"And have it be raised by strangers?"

"There are a lot of couples out there who would love your child as though it were their own.

And you wouldn't spend the rest of your life paying for one mistake."

Pippa couldn't seem to catch her breath. She'd known her father would be upset when she told him she was pregnant, but she'd never imagined he would ask her to give up her child. "I'm keeping my baby. And that's that."

"Underhill is a conservative town with strict morals. Are you ready to face the scandal of being an unwed mother? Forget the scandal. That will pass. Are you ready to be a teenage mother? That responsibility will never end."

"I'll be twenty when the baby is born," Pippa shot back.

He made a *tsk*ing sound of disgust. "You know what I mean. This is the rest of your life, Pippa. Just be sure you know what you're doing. How are you going to feel about raising Tim Brandon's child?"

Pippa's heart skipped a beat. She already felt an abhorrence for her former lover that knew no bounds. What if the baby was a boy and looked like Tim? Would she be able to separate the child from its lying, cheating, deceitful parent? Would she be able to love her baby when she loathed its father?

Pippa shuddered. She would have to deal with that problem if—or when—it arose. She only knew that she couldn't abandon her own flesh and blood.

She looked her father in the eye and said, "I'm keeping this baby."

He slapped his palms on his thighs as though the matter were settled. "Fine. Let's go home."

Pippa eyed him warily. He hadn't put up much of a fight, but if he thought he could wear her down, he was wrong. She would hold her head high and face the tabbies in Underhill. She would defy them all. And she would prove to her father that this baby was no "mistake." She would love her child despite its father. And she would do it all in the town where she'd grown up.

She nodded to her father and said, "Let's go home."

Chapter 1

"WE'RE MOVING TO America."

Pippa stared at her father with wide, horrified eyes. "Why? What's happened?" *You vowed you would never, ever go back.*

Her father's face looked grim. "I've come to an understanding with my father. He's offered to give me the ranch in Wyoming where I grew up."

Pippa knew there was no way her father would be doing this if it weren't for her. Tim must have told some of his mates that she was pregnant, because, even though her pregnancy didn't show, she'd been treated like a pariah by everyone in Underhill since her return. Her father had ended up thrashing someone who'd made a remark about her, which had caused him to spend a night in jail. He'd said it didn't matter, that the lout had deserved what he'd gotten.

A few days later, she'd been bombarded with rotten fruit by a couple of teenage boys when she'd come out of the grocer's shop. Her defiance had wilted as she swiped at the gooey stuff on her plaid shirt and brushed foul-smelling muck off her jeans.

She was sure if her father could find the culprits, he'd wreak havoc again. And end up in jail again.

There was no help for it. She was going to have to leave Underhill. She'd just been waiting for the morning sickness to pass so she could find a job somewhere in Darwin—and for the right moment to tell her father that she was going.

And then he'd made his grand announcement.

It was impossible to admit that she knew her father didn't want to return to Wyoming, because then she would have to explain how she could possibly know such a thing. She could never tell him that she'd seen him cry. Never tell him that she knew he hated his father and had sworn to stay as far away from King Grayhawk—and King's ranch in Wyoming—as possible.

"You don't have to uproot your life and Nathan's because of me," she said. "I can leave Underhill on my own."

"I have my own reasons for returning home," he replied.

"Such as?"

He cocked a brow. "My reasons are my business."

Pippa was pretty sure his only reason for returning to a place he'd hoped never to see again was to spare her any more pain. "Daddy, please. You don't have to do this."

"It's done. Start packing."

That conversation had taken place a mere three weeks ago. She and Nathan and their father were now settled in a suite of rooms at her grandfather's ranch in Jackson Hole, where Pippa found herself in a situation that was fraught with every bit as much tension as she'd faced back home in Underhill.

Her father had neglected to mention that the ranch house at Kingdom Come was already occupied by her grandfather and his four youngest daughters. Or that King Grayhawk was the richest man in Wyoming. Or that the ranch house, built more than a hundred and fifty years ago, had been expanded and modernized into a home so fantastic it had been featured in several magazines.

More to the point, there had been no joyous homecoming, no delighted welcome for the prodigal son. King Grayhawk's four grown daughters had greeted the invaders with silence and glares.

Her father's half sisters, Taylor, Victoria, and Eve, and their half sister, Leah, bitterly resented her father for laying claim to a ranch that was still their home. Pippa had been appalled when she learned the terms of the "deal" her father had made with King. All he had to do was live for one year—three hundred and sixty-five days—at Kingdom Come, and the ranch was his. Her father hadn't helped matters when he'd ordered the four girls to find another place to live before the year was out, telling them bluntly, "Once the ranch is mine, you're no longer welcome."

No wonder King's daughters hated them!

To say that Pippa felt like an interloper was the understatement of the century. Entering the kitchen for breakfast was like walking into a war zone. The early-morning nausea—from a pregnancy she was determined to keep a secret for as long as she could—didn't help matters. Pippa had decided that eating late at night, when she was less likely to run into one of them, or be sickened by the sight of food, made a lot more sense.

Pippa was peering into the open refrigerator, trying to find something on the shelves that looked appetizing, when she heard a chair scrape behind her. She lifted her head over the edge of the door and discovered the twins, Taylor and Victoria, both wearing pajamas and robes, perched on stools at the breakfast bar.

Her aunts weren't identical twins. Taylor, tall and full-figured, was take-your-breath-away beautiful. Victoria had the same blond hair and blue eyes, but she was more lithe and merely pretty in comparison with her sister. Right now, both girls had a glint in their sapphire eyes that boded no good for her.

"I guess she thinks she's too good to eat with the rest of us," Victoria said to her sister.

Pippa ignored her, turning back to look at the leftovers in the refrigerator. But her appetite was gone, and her stomach was churning.

I will not be sick. I will not give them the satisfaction. And I will not run away. This is my home now, too.

But Pippa could understand their antagonism. She wouldn't have wanted a bunch of strangers making themselves at home at her family's cattle station in Underhill, either. That is, if she still had a home there. The station had been sold. There was no going back.

She chose a plastic bowl containing leftover

fried chicken, closed the refrigerator door, and turned to confront the two young women, swallowing down the bile spilling into the back of her throat. "I wasn't hungry earlier. I am now."

She set the container on the counter and opened the cupboard, looking for the saltine crackers that usually settled her stomach. They weren't there.

"If you're looking for those Australian crackers you brought with you, they're gone," Taylor said. "We had tomato soup for lunch today—which you also missed—and ate the last of them."

Pippa didn't so much mind sharing the last of her Arnott's Salada biscuits—an Australian version of American saltine crackers—but the smug look on Taylor's face, and her vindictive tone of voice, rubbed her the wrong way. She felt her stomach heave and realized she was in no condition to start a fight. She needed a cracker now, or she was going to embarrass herself by throwing up. But the kitchen was huge, and she had no idea where everything was kept.

"Since you've eaten the last of my crackers," she said, swallowing hard to keep her stomach from losing its contents, "perhaps you can tell me where you keep yours."

Victoria threw out an arm and said, "In the cupboard, of course."

Through gritted teeth, Pippa asked, "Which one?"

"What's going on here?"

Pippa whirled and teetered dizzily, grabbing the counter to steady herself.

Her father took one look at her, scowled at the

two women seated at the bar, and said, "I asked a question."

Pippa didn't want to be the cause of any more dissension between her father and his sisters than already existed. "I'm looking for some saltines," she said. "Victoria was going to point me in the right direction." She met Victoria's gaze with a lifted brow that suggested discretion in this situation was the better part of valor.

Victoria ignored the suggestion, rising to confront Pippa's father. "Well, Matt, it's like this. Taylor and I were wondering why your precious daughter can't be bothered to eat with the rest of us."

It felt odd to hear her father called by his first name. Unfortunately, the attempt at familiarity did nothing to soften her father's response.

"When or where or how or what my daughter chooses to eat is none of your damned business," he retorted.

Pippa had one hand over her mouth and the other hand over her unsettled stomach. She wanted to run from the room, but it felt too much like giving up and giving in. She'd promised herself she would never let anyone ride roughshod over her again. She had to stand her ground.

Her father must have divined her problem, because he started opening cupboards and slamming them closed until he found a box of saltines. He yanked it out and pulled it open, tearing into a sleeve of crackers so it spilled across the counter.

Pippa grabbed for a saltine and began chewing, her back to the two young women, letting the salt and soda crackers do their work. She was focused on keeping her stomach from erupting, but she could hear her father arguing with his sisters.

"As far as I can see, you two have been living high on the hog here with no responsibility for anyone or anything. You're twenty-eight. You should be out doing something with your lives. On March 31st of next year, Kingdom Come will be mine. Find yourselves another place to live, because I have other plans for this ranch."

"Like what?" Victoria asked.

Her father ignored the question. "And if I see you bothering Pippa again, you'll find yourselves out in the cold a lot sooner than that."

"You can't kick us out!" Taylor shot back.

"Watch me."

"Daddy will never let you do it," Victoria said.

"I wouldn't count on that," her father threatened.

Pippa heard scraping chairs and then an ominous silence. She concentrated on what turned out to be a futile attempt to swallow the dry saltines. She gave up and dropped a half-eaten saltine on the counter, searched for and found a glass, and filled it with water. She took careful sips, worried that her stomach wouldn't tolerate the liquid. She closed her eyes and leaned over the sink until she was sure it would stay down, then took another sip.

She'd been so focused on not vomiting that she didn't realize she and her father were alone until she heard him say in a surprisingly gentle voice, "Are you all right, Pippa?"

She opened her eyes and found him standing

beside her. She leaned her head against his chest and let his arms close around her. "That was awful," she said against his shirt.

"They're just spoiled rotten. I think the sooner they're out of this house and on their own, the sooner they'll grow up. I know how it is, because I've lived here with King for a father. He's worked his way through four wives, who've given him eight children, including your aunts' half sister, Leah. None of those wives were around long enough to become much of a mother to any of us."

This was all new information to Pippa, who was astonished at what she was hearing. Her father had never been forthcoming about his family, and none of her aunts had been friendly enough toward her during the three weeks she'd been at Kingdom Come to encourage questions.

"King was far too busy to spend any time with me, either, when I was growing up," her father continued. "It doesn't look like things have changed much in the twenty years since I've been gone."

Pippa leaned back and looked at her father with wide, assessing eyes. She quickly did the math and said, "You left home at seventeen?"

He nodded.

Pippa blurted the next thought that came into her head. "So my mother was an American?"

She felt her father's body stiffen. He was silent so long she thought he wasn't going to answer. At last he said, "Yes. She was."

"Did she live here in Jackson Hole?"

He nodded.

Then it dawned on her that he'd used the past tense. "What happened to her? Did she die?"

"She moved away."

Pippa was trying to work out what might have happened to her mother, but she didn't have enough facts to make sense of the situation. "It's been twenty years since you left home. I'm nineteen. Does that mean I was born here in the States before you left home?"

He nodded.

"Why didn't my mother come with you to Australia?"

Pippa didn't think she'd ever seen her father's blue eyes look so bleak.

"It's a long story, Pippa." He took a deep breath and let it out. "Your mother and I were never married."

"Oh." Pippa's active imagination went to work making up a story from the information her father had revealed. Obviously, her mother hadn't wanted to keep her. That thought caused a sharp ache in her chest. It was one more reason to keep her child—so it would know it was cherished.

Had her father had his heart broken when her mother rejected him—and his daughter? Was that why his first marriage hadn't worked out, and why he'd waited so many years to marry Nathan's mother? Or had Pippa's birth been an "accident," the result of sex with some stranger? Maybe the reason her father had never spoken of her mother was that he hadn't known her well.

Pippa had questioned her father about her mother many times as a child. His reaction had always been so agitated, and his answer so brusque, that she'd stopped asking. Since her mother hadn't lived nearby, there was no chance she was ever going to run into her, so she'd let it drop.

But here she was in Wyoming, where her mother had come from. Should she try to find her? Or just leave well enough alone?

"Is your stomach feeling better?" her father asked.

Pippa managed a weak smile as she stepped back from his embrace. "Yes."

"I presume that's why you haven't been joining us for meals."

She nodded. "I've felt nauseated. Or I haven't been hungry."

"If you want to keep this pregnancy a secret, I suggest you do a better job of showing up at the table. I still think you should—"

"Don't say it, Daddy. Please."

He shook his head in what she presumed was disappointment, which she didn't think was fair, considering the startling new information that she was a child born out of wedlock. But maybe he didn't want her to have to go through what he'd been through, trying to raise a child on his own. She could still remember a time when they'd moved around a lot, a time when she'd been both cold and hungry. But that was all so far in the past she'd almost forgotten about it.

It was hard to imagine why her father should have struggled so much to survive when he was the son of such a wealthy man. Which made Pippa wonder what King Grayhawk had done to his son to make him run so far from home and stay gone for so long.

She was here now, where her mother and father had met, where her father had lived until he was seventeen, where her grandfather still played lord of the manor, and where she had four aunts who presumably knew some of the family history her father had never shared. Before her child was born, Pippa intended to have some answers.

Chapter 2

"I CAN'T BELIEVE you're eating that disgusting stuff for breakfast," Eve said.

Pippa's hand trembled with rage and frustration as she listened to the youngest of the four Grayhawk sisters ridicule the Vegemite she was slathering onto a piece of burned toast—burned because one of them had changed the dial on the toaster to its highest setting without telling her. Pippa had lived too frugally all her life to throw away the burned toast, so she'd scraped off the charred parts and resigned herself to a less-than-perfect breakfast.

Granted, Vegemite was an acquired taste. The dark brown Australian food paste, made from leftover brewer's yeast extract and various spices, was salty, slightly bitter, and rich in a substance similar to beef bouillon. But to her, it was comfort food, a reminder of the home she'd left behind.

Pippa's father had eaten breakfast and left the house at dawn, and her little brother was still sleeping, so she was on her own with King's daughters. "Silly galahs," she muttered under her breath, likening them to an Australian bird known for its crazy antics. She was out of patience with the whole bunch of them. She drank tea rather than coffee, and began pouring boiling water from the electric teapot over the Earl Grey teabag she'd put in her cup.

She clenched her teeth to hold back an oath as coffee, instead of hot water, came out. She set the teapot down carefully, unwilling to add a burn injury to the insults she'd already suffered. She heard a snigger from one of the sisters but refused to be drawn into the brawl she could tell they hoped to provoke.

She had to get out of here. Now. Before she exploded and said or did something that would make her life here even more unendurable than it already was. Her stomach roiled. She'd been feeling crook ever since she'd woken up, and she fought back the nausea that rose in her throat. Heaven only knew what sort of gibes she'd fall prey to if they learned she was unwed and pregnant. She dropped the burned toast and left the ruined tea behind as she marched across the kitchen, grabbed her jacket from an antler coatrack, and headed out the back door.

Tears welled in her eyes as she stepped off the covered porch and hurried across the enormous lawn, which showed patches of spring green. She shivered from the cold in her light Australian jacket and wrapped her arms around herself in an attempt to stay warm. The chilly April spring in Wyoming was similar to the April fall in the Northern Territory, but at least there was no snow on the ground right now, and the sun was shining. She wasn't about to go back into the house to retrieve a warmer coat.

Pippa had no destination in mind but soon found herself inside the stable. The familiar smells of leather and manure and hay soothed the awful ache in the back of her throat.

She was homesick. And lonely, which surprised her. She'd never had a lot of friends, yet she'd never felt alone. Why was that? The answer was simple. Spending her days gentling wild horses had made her life meaningful and given her something to care for and to love.

But there were no brumbies to tame here.

This nightmare is all my fault. If I hadn't been so gullible, we would still be in Australia. There would be no resentful relatives to make my life hell.

Pippa moved from stall to stall caressing velvet noses and feeling the solace of welcoming nickers. She missed her favorite mount, Beastie. He'd been the most challenging brumby she'd ever tamed, but he'd been a sweetheart ever after. Sadly, Beastie had been sold along with her father's cattle station.

The ache in her throat was back with a vengeance.

Pippa scrubbed away the tears in her eyes and saw that the horse Leah usually rode was missing from its stall. That explained why the eldest Grayhawk girl at Kingdom Come—the one who'd been five years old when King married her mother— hadn't been at breakfast. Leah had been tight-lipped whenever Matt or Pippa was around, but it was King she blamed—and gave the cold shoulder—for offering Kingdom Come to his prodigal son.

Leah had frequently shown her disapproval of her younger sisters' behavior toward Pippa with a sharp look or a lifted eyebrow that usually nipped it in the bud. It hadn't taken long for Pippa to realize that Leah was more a mother than a sister to her mother's three daughters with King. It was a role she'd apparently taken on at ten years old, when their mother had run away with one of King's cowhands.

Pippa quickly saddled a horse and rode out, determined to spend the day as far from her aunts as she could. Every story she'd heard about the four women since she'd arrived at Kingdom Come was fraught with calamity. That, combined with what she'd experienced herself over the past three weeks, made it easy to see why the locals had labeled her grandfather's four youngest daughters "King's Brats."

Still, she couldn't help feeling sorry for them. No wonder they'd turned out as they had, abandoned by their mother and with a father who'd apparently left the parenting to an older sister and the servants.

Pippa shook her head. Her sympathy was misplaced with those she-devils. The fact was that she'd always been too softhearted. Which made no sense when she'd grown up with a father who didn't give second chances. She'd never understood how her dad could be so ruthless. But meeting her grandfather, dealing with his children, discovering their sense of entitlement, their arrogance, and their pride, she was beginning to see why her father might have turned out as he had.

Pippa caught her breath when she came around a bend and was greeted by the nearly fourteen-thousand-foot Grand Tetons. She loved the Australian Outback, but these majestic, snow-tipped mountains had to be one of the most beautiful sights in the world. She joined a trail that led along the edge of a forest of spruces and pines, feeling her body—and her soul—warm as the sun and her surroundings did their work.

She spied Leah in the distance, but she wasn't alone. Pippa shaded her eyes to see if she could identify the other person on horseback riding with her aunt. She was shocked when she recognized the man. It was one of her father's four Flynn cousins. She'd met two of them, Aiden and Brian. The Flynns lived on a large ranch that bordered Kingdom Come. If she wasn't mistaken, that was Aiden Flynn. And he was . . . Oh, my God. He was leaning over to kiss Leah! At the last instant, Leah reared back out of reach.

Pippa realized she must have been mistaken in what she'd surmised. The first thing she'd learned when she'd arrived at Kingdom Come was that Grayhawks *hated* Flynns—and the feeling was mutual. The feud had started when King divorced his first wife, Jane Flynn, who later died of an overdose of barbiturates. In the aftermath of her death, Jane's brother, Angus, had done his best to make life miserable for King Grayhawk, and once they were old enough, Angus's sons and King's daughters had joined in the fray.

Pippa couldn't imagine why Aiden and Leah would be out riding together, much less kissing. As she watched, Leah and Aiden rode away in different directions. Leah must have accidentally run into Aiden, and they'd exchanged rancorous words. That must have been what she'd seen.

Pippa saw Leah turning in her direction and quickly angled her horse onto a narrow path that led into the concealing forest. The last thing she wanted was to run into another Grayhawk girl. She kicked her mount into a trot to take her farther away from her aunt and disappeared into a lush, evergreen wonderland, an ethereal world lit by dappled sunlight.

A half hour later, she passed through a gate set in a barbed-wire fence and emerged onto a blindingly bright, breathtakingly beautiful meadow decorated with white, yellow, and purple flowers. A herd of Black Angus cattle was scattered across it, munching grass.

In Australia, her father had raised Brahman cattle, and the sudden bawl of a calf searching for its mother brought a wistful look to her face. She watched as the cow and calf were reunited and the calf took suck. And felt all the sadness of being alone in a strange place well up inside her again.

She kicked her mount into a lope, following a creek that flowed along the lower end of the meadow, determined to outrun the feelings that were so unfamiliar to her. She tried to remember the last time she'd laughed. Too long ago, for sure.

Pippa firmed her jaw. She wasn't going to let these Grayhawks get her down. She was going to make the best of her situation for herself and her child. Which reminded her that she needed to find a doctor in town and get a checkup. She'd been putting it off, wondering if she could trust a small-town doctor—and his nurse and receptionist—to be discreet.

Pippa was so caught up in her thoughts that she was nearly upon the other rider before she was aware of him. He pulled up his mount at the same time as she did.

Her heartbeat stuttered as she registered the fact that she was completely alone in the back of beyond. Common sense came to her rescue. The stranger was dressed like one of King's cowhands in a buff cowboy hat, blue chambray shirt, fleece vest, jeans, chaps, and boots. His presence made perfect sense, considering the fact that she was riding across a meadow filled with cattle.

Then he smiled, his gray-green eyes crinkling at the corners, his lips uptilted more on one side than the other, and Pippa felt all the tension ease out of her.

"Good morning," he said in a rich baritone voice. "What brings you here?"

Pippa realized she was smiling back. Her smile broadened as she said, "I'm just enjoying the sunshine."

"Me too." He held up a paper bag, then gestured toward a large pond surrounded on three sides by budding aspens and vivid evergreens. "I was going to eat breakfast. Want to join me?"

Pippa realized that her morning sickness had

passed and that she was ravenous. A little tucker sounded wonderful. "Sure."

He kicked his mount so they were riding side by side as they headed for the idyllic spot. "You must be one of the new arrivals from Australia."

Pippa cocked her head. "How did you know?"

He laughed. "Your accent gives you away. I like it, by the way."

Pippa liked his laugh and his smile. She liked the fact that he'd offered to share his breakfast. She liked the easy way he sat in the saddle and how one large, callused hand held the reins while the other rested on his muscular thigh. She especially liked the day-old beard on his jaw and his warm, moss-green eyes.

Pippa felt a surprising frisson of physical awareness skitter down her spine. She stared, wide-eyed, at the stranger beside her, suddenly breath-less, conscious of a strong desire to know more about him. Pippa warned herself to be careful. She had no intention of letting another man into her life right now, especially one as charming as this cowboy.

They'd reached the pond, and he dismounted and tied his reins to a budding aspen branch. He crossed to catch the reins by her horse's mouth as she dismounted and then tied her horse off next to his. Then, without making any attempt to touch her, he headed toward a broad, flat stone, the per-fect height to sit on, at the edge of the pond.

"King had this stone put here," he said as he dropped onto it.

"Why would he do that?" Pippa asked as she joined him on the sun-warmed river rock.

"I think he used to come here to be alone and think."

"And he doesn't anymore?"

He shot her a wry smile. "Nobody ever comes here these days but me and those cows."

Pippa leaned back on her palms, inhaling the crisp scent of the pines and listening to the jays calling to each other in the evergreens as she watched two white trumpeter swans glide across the pond. "That's a shame. It's beautiful here."

"You're beautiful."

Pippa sat up, startled by the compliment, and her eyes locked with the stranger's.

He must have sensed her sudden wariness, because he grinned and added, "You fit right in with the mountains and the columbine and the pond and the forest."

She exhaled with relief that he'd simply been comparing her looks with the beauty of their surroundings. She didn't want to be admired as a woman. She wasn't looking for another boyfriend. What she really needed was a friend. She hoped she could steer this chance meeting in that direction. "It's all very breathtaking, isn't it?"

Instead of answering, he took his hat off and laid it crown down on the rock behind him, thrusting his fingers through sun-shot chestnut hair that fell over his brow. Then he opened the bag and pulled out two items wrapped in tinfoil. He handed one to her, then unwrapped the other and took a big bite of what turned out to be a biscuit with ham.

Pippa unwrapped hers and took a small bite, unsure how her stomach would react. But everything tasted wonderful.

"I could have eaten this at home this morning," he said, "but you have to admit there's something about eating outdoors that makes everything taste better."

He was smiling again, and Pippa felt herself smiling back again.

"How do you like living at Kingdom Come?" he asked.

She opened her mouth to admit the truth and shut it again. King's Brats were mean as cat's piss, but they were also her aunts. She didn't want to bad-mouth her family to a stranger, especially one of King's cowhands. She settled for saying, "It's not what I expected."

"Better? Worse?"

She shook her head, unwilling to be pinned down. "Just different."

"Everyone is curious about how you're getting along."

Pippa stiffened. "Why is that?"

"It's common knowledge that Matt brought a grown daughter home with him, but nobody's seen hide nor hair of you in town."

"I haven't had any reason to go to town." And having grown up driving on the opposite side of the road in Australia, she was still leery of traveling on the highway.

"To be honest, I don't go to town much myself," he admitted.

"Why not?"

He shrugged. "Prefer my own company, I guess."

"Oh." She felt surprisingly disappointed. Did that mean he wasn't interested in making a new friend?

He lifted a brow and said, "What?"

She had nothing to lose by admitting the truth, so she said, "I was hoping we could be friends."

He reached out and brushed a callused thumb across her lower lip. "Biscuit crumb."

The explanation came too late to keep her entire body from surging to fiery life at his touch. Unsettled, Pippa rose to her feet, crushing the foil into a ball in her hand.

He rose as well, replaced his hat, tugging it low on his forehead, and then held out his hand. "I'll take that."

She dropped the foil into his hand, careful not to touch him.

"I've never had a female friend," he said, looking directly into her eyes. "Sounds like something worth exploring."

Pippa's heart began racketing in her chest as though she were facing some feral animal. She knew she should run for the hills, but her feet refused to move. Then it was too late. He'd already turned and headed toward his horse. He untied and mounted it, then rode back to where she still stood by the stone.

"I come here now and again. Guess I'll see you

when I see you." He touched a finger to his hat brim and said, "So long for now."

"Hooroo," Pippa called after him.

He glanced back over his shoulder, grinning at her use of the Australian goodbye, then turned and kicked his mount into a lope across the meadow in the opposite direction from which she'd come.

Pippa felt both excited and anxious as she watched the stranger ride away. He'd given her no way to contact him. She didn't even know his name! What were the chances she would ever be here again at exactly the same time as he was? Slim to none.

And yet, he'd offered to be her friend, when a *friend* was exactly what she needed in this new home. She knew he came here in the mornings. Maybe it was time she started eating her breakfast far away from King's Brats.

Pippa looked at her watch and then raced for her mount. By now Nathan would be up and hunting breakfast. At least for the short term, her little brother was her responsibility. There was no telling what kind of trouble he would get into if she wasn't there to keep an eye on him.

Pippa felt happy—and hopeful—as she headed back into the forest. Next time she would ask the stranger's name. And find out who he was and where he lived. And she would ask him all the other things she'd forgotten to ask because she'd been entranced by a lopsided smile and a pair of mesmerizing green eyes.

Chapter 3

PIPPA RACED HER mount across the meadow in the moonlit darkness as though the hounds of hell were after her. She replayed the terrible conversation with her father in her head as she made her way toward the retreat where she'd found peace over the past week. She'd escaped every morning to the pond, hoping to meet her new friend again. But the stranger had never returned.

Dinner had replaced breakfast as the worst part of her day, and tonight she'd reached her limit. Her father had merely asked Eve to move her herd of mustangs off land that he needed for quarter horses he'd purchased. Instead of saying, "Okay," Eve had accused Pippa's father of being heartless and demanded, "How can you be so cruel?"

Pippa had responded to the attack before her father could. "My dad doesn't want anything to do with you Grayhawks. We had a great life in Australia until *he* showed up and lured my dad back here." She'd jerked her chin toward her grandfather, then lurched to her feet and snarled, "I can't wait till this year is up! Maybe then you'll leave us alone and stop making my dad so sad."

Her father hadn't looked anywhere but at his plate. "Sit down, Pippa," he'd said quietly, "and finish your supper."

"I'm not hungry." She'd thrown her napkin halfway across the table and marched out of the dining room, her stomach threatening to erupt.

Several hours later, hunger had forced her out of her room. Her father had caught her by the stairs on her way to the kitchen and said, "I can fight my own battles, Pippa."

"You can, but you don't," she shot back. "How can you let them speak to you like that?"

"Lower your voice," he hissed. "Do you want the whole house to hear?"

"I hate it here. I want to go home!"

"You know why you can't do that."

"It's not as though I've committed some heinous crime. I'm just pregnant."

"With a married man's child!"

Pippa had been struck dumb by the ferocity of her father's voice. And the blame she heard in it. "I loved him," she'd replied softly. "When I ran away with him, I didn't know he was married. He lied to me."

He'd tipped her chin up with a forefinger until he could look into her eyes and said in a heartbreakingly sad voice, "The gossip would never have died. You'd have been an outcast the rest of your life."

She couldn't remember exactly what else he'd said, but his point was clear. There was no going back.

"You can start over here," he said.

"And do what?"

"Whatever you want. You can give up the baby for adoption and—"

Pippa had jerked her chin free, her heart clutching at the thought of giving up her child. "Stop right there. Is that what you thought? That I'd give up my baby so no one would ever know what a shameless bitch I am? Think again! I'm having this baby. And I'm keeping it!"

She never heard the rest of what he'd said. She was already running. She'd grabbed her coat and left the house, muttering angrily to herself that she would love her child no matter who its father was. But all the while, she felt chilled to the marrow of her bones at the thought that it simply might not be possible to separate her loathing for Tim from the child he'd sired.

She'd saddled a horse and galloped away, wishing there were some way she could keep on riding and never come back.

But she had nowhere to go.

Except the refuge she'd found where the ever-constant wind rustled in the evergreens and the elegant white swans came during the day to glide silently by. She wondered where the stranger was and what he was doing. And why he'd never come back to see her.

The pond seemed different at night. Eerie and fantastical, as though there were ghosts in the shadows. She stepped off her horse and tied the reins to a nearby pine, then headed for the perch where she'd first sat down with the stranger. She shivered as her jean-clad bottom hit the cold stone and wrapped her arms around herself to stay warm in her fleece jacket.

She put a hand to her belly and murmured to her unborn child, "I will find a way to put the past behind me. And I will love you with all my heart and soul and mind."

But she wasn't going to be able to live at Kingdom Come any more than she'd been able to stay in Underhill. Here everyone would know she was an unwed mother. She needed to go somewhere else. But where? And how?

Tears stung her nose and one fell onto her cheek. She angrily brushed it away. Tears solved nothing. She had to start planning a life for herself and her unborn child. But the enormity of the task ahead caused more tears to well in her eyes. Pippa covered her face and sobbed for her lost dreams of a husband who would love her and a child who would laugh and play in their happy home.

She heard a low growl and froze. She'd been warned that gray wolves stalked these mountains, along with cougars and bears. She'd felt safe riding through the forest during the day because she always made plenty of noise, knowing the wild animals would do their best to stay out of her way. She'd hardly given the danger a thought when she'd left the house tonight. She regretted that now.

She had no weapon with her. She was totally defenseless. She rose slowly, backing toward her horse.

She heard the growl again, louder, more threatening, and stopped where she was.

Behind her a familiar voice said, "Hello again."

"Be careful!" she said. "There's something—"

The growl came again, right beside her. Pippa saw the wolf's eyes and its sharp teeth reflected in the moonlight and struggled to hold her ground against the wild beast, when every instinct urged her to flee.

"Don't move," the stranger said, his voice filled with enough warning to raise the hairs on the back of her neck.

"Stay back," she whispered.

"Wulf," he said. "Sit."

To Pippa's amazement, the wolf licked its chops and then sat down meekly in front of her.

Pippa felt a hand on her shoulder and, with a sob of relief, turned and threw herself into a pair of strong, waiting arms. Her whole body trembled with relief as she clutched the stranger around the neck. "I thought I was done for!" she said in a strangled voice.

She felt his hand on her back pressing her snugly against him as his deep, male voice offered soothing words of comfort. She held on tight as her heartbeat slowed, accepting the solace she'd sought when she'd come here. It felt so good to lean on someone, to be held close and know she was safe.

Pippa gradually became aware of her surroundings. Of the wind rustling the trees. Of the stranger's warm breath against her cheek. Of an owl hooting in the distance. And that the man holding her had become aroused. She fought against the urge to arch her body against the hard length she could feel pressing against her belly.

Instead, she slowly freed herself from the stranger's embrace and backed away, staring warily at the man before her. The stranger's eyes gleamed with desire in the moonlight. She hitched in a breath of fear, aware that she was alone in the wilderness with someone she barely knew. He'd seemed friendly enough, but she had little reason to trust any man right now.

The wolf must have sensed some threat in her, because it was suddenly on its feet again, growling low in its throat.

Pippa took a deep, calming breath. What had happened was the natural result of a man and a woman being in close proximity. It was a struggle not to let her bad experience with Tim—and her fear of trusting another man—influence what had just happened. She wanted to believe the stranger had only good intentions.

She held out a hand to the wolf and said, "It's all right, Wulf. I'm not going to hurt him." She met the stranger's gaze. "And he's not going to hurt me."

Then she reached down and scratched the wolf behind his ears. The animal sat and licked her hand, at which point Pippa dropped onto her knees beside him and ruffled the fur along his back. The wolf, it seemed, was no threat, but she still wasn't sure about the man.

A moment later the stranger was beside her again. She glanced up and saw a look of awe on his face. "How did you do that?"

"Do what?"

"Lay hands on Beowulf without getting bitten."

"I thought he was tame," she said, still clutching a handful of the wolf's fur.

"Far from it," the stranger said. "He's been willing to share my company and obey a few commands. But Wulf's never let anyone except me touch him. What did you do to him?"

Pippa felt the stranger's hand grasp her elbow to help her up as she let go of the wolf and rose. She realized her knees were still weak and sank onto the stone again with a laugh of relief that neither the stranger—nor his pet wolf—had turned out to be dangerous. "I guess animals know when someone likes them."

"I've raised Wulf from a pup, and I can tell you he's nearly taken my hand off enough times that, even though I like him just fine, I have a healthy respect for the fact that he's a dangerous predator."

"How did you end up with a wolf as a pet?"

"I heard a gunshot where no one should be hunting and found his mother dead. When I tracked my way back to the den, the single pup I found was too young to live on its own, so I took him home with me. I'm not sure I made the right decision."

"It sounds like Wulf wouldn't have survived without your help."

He shrugged. "Likely not. But he's a fish out of water now."

"What do you mean?"

"He's too wild to be around people, but he's lost his fear of humans, so he can't go back to the wild. There are enough ranchers around here who don't like wolves preying on their cattle that he'd end up getting shot for sure."

Pippa felt sorry for the wolf's plight. "Come here, Wulf." The wolf rose and crossed to her, sticking his cold nose into her open palm. "I think Wulf's lucky you came along." She scratched his soft ears again as she looked up at the stranger, then gestured with her chin toward the other side of the stone and said, "Come join me."

A moment later he was sitting beside her, cutting off the bitter wind. He was dressed much as he had been the last time she'd seen him, except he'd lost the chaps and had on a shearling coat.

"What are you doing out here in the middle of the night?" he asked.

"It's a long story."

"I don't have anywhere else to be."

Pippa opened her mouth to speak and shut it again. She couldn't tell this stranger she was unwed and pregnant. And she didn't want to relive her trials and tribulations with her aunts and her father. Instead, she said, "I'd rather talk about you. To start with, what's your name?"

The lopsided grin that she'd found so charming the first time she met him reappeared. "I was afraid you were going to ask that."

"Afraid? Why?"

He took a deep breath and said, "I'm Devon Flynn."

Pippa gasped. The man she'd thought was one of her grandfather's cowhands was actually the youngest son of King's mortal enemy, Angus Flynn.

Chapter 4

Devon had known from the first moment he laid eyes on Philippa Grayhawk exactly who she was. He should have told her right away that he was one of "those awful Flynn boys" who were the bane of her aunts' existence. But he'd been entranced by her compelling gray eyes and an air of loneliness that he understood far too well, since he lived in a secluded cabin in the woods, with animals rather than humans for company.

So he'd kept his identity secret. He'd stayed away from the pond because he'd known that any relationship with her—even a friendship—would be fraught with difficulties because of the isolated life he preferred to live and, of course, the feud between their families.

Not that her father was part of that feud. In fact, in the last year of her life, Matt's mother, Jane, had lived with Angus and his sons, and sixteen-year-old Matt had been a constant presence at the Flynn supper table. Jane's death, which Angus blamed on King's treatment of her during their marriage, had created a hate in Angus that had survived—and thrived—for twenty years. In return, King had blamed Matt's disappearance on Angus—and Angus had never denied it. Devon had been only eight at the time, but that was old enough to know that seventeen-year-old Matt had been sullen and short-tempered in the months and weeks before he'd departed.

Now Matt was back with a daughter who had to have been born before he'd left. Was Pippa the reason he'd disappeared?

Devon eyed the extraordinary young woman askance. She must be something special for Wulf to have given her his trust. He wondered what burden she was carrying that was making her so sad. She reminded him of one of the wounded animals he was forever rescuing, desperately in need of a safe haven where she could rest and heal.

He just wasn't sure he was the right person to help in this particular case. With his injured animals, he was always careful to keep his distance, to let them remain the wild creatures they were, to stay carefully detached so that he could let them go when they were ready to leave his care. It was how he'd always lived his life where humans were concerned as well. Disconnected. Separate. Alone.

From a very young age, Devon had felt like he didn't belong in the family to which he'd been born. He didn't look the same, and he didn't like doing the same things as his three older brothers. He'd been six years old when he'd heard his father utter the words "He killed his mother, or she'd be with us here today. He looks just like—"

Devon knew he wasn't supposed to be listening, because when his father caught sight of him, he'd cut himself off. Devon had asked his eldest brother, Aiden, what their father meant.

"He doesn't mean you actually *killed* her. It wasn't anything you did wrong. He just means that Mom died when you were born."

But how could he not be responsible when she'd died giving birth to him?

Dad blames me for killing my mother.

He'd felt guilty and ashamed. And despite Aiden's dismissal of his responsibility for their mother's death, he couldn't believe his brothers didn't blame him just a little. If not for him, their mother would still be alive.

Devon was a little older, maybe twelve, and learning genetics in biology class, when he'd first focused on the physical differences between himself and his brothers. Every one of them had black hair and blue eyes, like their father. And they were broad-shouldered and narrow-hipped, where he was more long and lean-bodied. He was the only one with eyes a different color.

Devon had been surprised, when he started looking for a picture of his mother to compare his eye color to hers—expecting to find that she had eyes of either gray or green, since his looked gray in some light and mossy green in others—to suddenly realize that there were no photos of her around. When he dug up a photograph at last, he knew why they'd all been hidden.

She was looking back at him with very beautiful, very *blue* eyes.

He'd questioned his biology teacher about recessive genes, wondering about the probability of two blue-eyed parents producing a child with mostly green eyes. It was pretty much impossible.

Devon had remained in shock for several days. And then had come to the only conclusion that seemed to make sense.

Angus Flynn is not my father. At last he had a reason that explained everything. Why he felt different. And why his "father" treated him differently than his other sons.

He couldn't believe that his "brothers" had never put two and two together and figured out that he wasn't "brother" number four. To be fair, none of them, not Aiden or Brian or Connor, had ever treated him as anything other than another brother. But because he was two years younger than the next youngest of his brothers, he was often left out or left behind.

From that point on, every variance in Angus's behavior toward him, as opposed to his brothers, was magnified a thousand times. Over his lifetime, the slights had occurred in subtle ways that folks wouldn't have noticed if they weren't the person being snubbed. Like giving his brothers their own horses when they were six while withholding that gift from Devon until he was eight. Or missing Devon's track meets at school but making his brothers' football games.

Worst of all was the way his father had made fun of Devon for bringing home so many injured wild animals and nursing them back to health. It was Angus's contention that nature decided which animals should live and die, and Devon had no business getting involved. "In this dog-eat-dog world, it's survival of the fittest. Remember that, Devon."

There didn't seem to be anyone he could blame for his plight—except his mother. She had cheated on his father. She had been bad, and he was paying for her mistake.

Devon had grown up keeping his mother's dark secret. What if his father didn't *know* his mother had cheated on him? What if he only *suspected*? Or what if he'd never suspected at all? What if all this supposedly different treatment from Angus was actually the result of the fact that Devon had stolen his mother's love and companionship from his father by causing her death when he was born?

Whenever his father had made some snide remark about Devon's interest in treating wounded animals, behavior foreign to the rest of his family, Devon wanted to confront him and say, "What do you expect, when I'm not your son?"

But he'd never spoken to Angus and demanded the truth. What would be the point? His "father" hadn't thrown him out, so obviously he was willing to raise him in the same home with his other children. Then again, maybe Angus didn't want his friends and neighbors to know that his wife had cheated on him.

Or maybe Angus didn't know the truth himself. After all, Devon had the same chestnut hair as his mother. And his moss-green eyes looked gray often enough that he might be mistaken for one of Angus Flynn's blue-eyed sons.

But if the reason for being treated differently was that he'd killed his mother, and not that his mother had cheated, why hadn't Angus—not once in Devon's entire life—called him "son"?

Ever since he'd figured out the truth about his birth, Devon had spent many hours wondering why his mother had cheated—and who his father might be. He'd wondered why a woman who had three sons with one man would betray him with another. He'd never understood his mother's behavior, and he had no one to explain it to him.

He'd understood better how his mother might have done what she'd done once he'd fallen in love himself. It had happened in tenth grade. Melissa Stevens was pretty and smart, and he'd tumbled for her like a ton of bricks. His heart had been in his throat the first time he'd asked her out. To his amazement, she'd said, "Yes."

She seemed to like him as much as he liked her. When they'd been together for three months, he'd told her he loved her, and she'd said she loved him. They'd been dating five months when she announced that she'd met someone she liked better. As simple as that, she'd walked away from him and into the arms of another boy.

He'd felt crushed.

Devon had compared Melissa's behavior toward him to what he thought might have happened to his mother. Maybe she'd met a man she liked better than his father. Despite her vows to his father, she'd indulged that whim, and he'd been conceived.

That single, devastating high school experience had left a lasting impression on Devon. Love didn't necessarily last. He'd learned a hard lesson, but he'd learned it well. He'd dated plenty in high school after that, but he never told another girl he loved her—because he'd never allowed himself to fall foolishly in love again. If the words weren't spoken, there was no opportunity for betrayal later.

As he'd gotten older, Devon had been unwilling to commit, leery of giving his heart to anyone for fear of having it broken. Until at last, it seemed easier to take pleasure from the women who freely offered it and keep his heart to himself.

And yet, he yearned for a woman who would love him, and whom he could love. Someone who would say the words and mean them for a lifetime. He wanted a family of his own. He might be a lone wolf, but he wanted a mate to share his life. He just wasn't sure he would ever find a woman he could trust not to betray him.

His behavior with Pippa had been no different from his usual response upon meeting someone new. As soon as he recognized the depth of his attraction to her, he'd drawn back. A woman like Pippa, a woman to whom he felt such an instant affinity, could steal his heart—and then destroy him. Better to keep his distance. Better not to get involved.

And yet, there was something about her that made him yearn for that emotional connection with another human being that was missing from his life. Maybe Pippa was different. Certainly, his reaction to her had been different.

Devon was tempted to turn and walk away from her, to protect himself from the disappoint-

ment of discovering that she was nothing special
after all. But something kept him standing there,
until at last he said, "You haven't told me what
brings you here in the middle of the night."

She shrugged. "The Brats, of course."

He smiled ruefully. "I have a little experience
with them myself. I remember a long walk back
from the middle of nowhere once when Brian and
I went hunting."

She lifted a questioning brow.

"The twins had put a hole in the gas tank of
Brian's truck."

"Oh, no!"

"We got back at them by letting the air out of
all four tires while they were picnicking at Berry
Creek, one of the more isolated areas of Grand
Teton National Park." He grinned. "They came
back to the car at dusk and didn't get out of there
until midnight."

"I'm surprised you hung around that long."

"Wouldn't have been much fun if we hadn't
seen the payoff."

At least, that was the reason he'd given Brian
for staying put. Actually, he wasn't sure the twins
would have cellphone reception to call a tow truck
to come fill up their tires. There were a lot of bears
and cougars around that season, and he wouldn't
have put it past the two of them to try hiking back
to civilization rather than waiting at their truck
until someone realized they were missing and came
looking for them.

"The first day I saw you here on my grandfather's meadow I thought you were one of his cow-hands," Pippa admitted with a sheepish smile.

He shook his head. "Nope. And for the record, this land borders Kingdom Come, but it's part of the Flynn ranch, the Lucky 7."

She looked startled. "But you said King used to come here."

"He was married to my aunt Jane at the time."

"Oh. Then I've been trespassing all week."

"You've been coming here?"

"Every morning."

He wasn't really surprised. Part of the reason he'd been so leery of coming back was that he'd been aware of the fact that she was as fascinated by him as he was by her. He'd feared that exactly what had happened would happen. He liked her more than he'd liked anyone in a long time. He was atop a slippery slope, and he didn't want to slide down and get hurt.

If she hadn't thrown herself into his arms, he never would have touched her. But once he'd had his arms around her, he hadn't wanted to let go. Their coats had kept their upper bodies from touching, but he'd felt her silky hair against his cheek and her warm breath in his ear. And that was all it had taken for his heart to gallop and his body to harden to stone.

"I was hoping that you'd come back so I could talk to you again," she said, shooting him a look from beneath lowered lashes.

He felt a spurt of pleasure and told himself *Whoa, cowboy!* He'd already had one lesson to-night on how quickly—and with how little effort—

she could arouse him. Not that he didn't want her in his bed. He just had to make sure she understood the rules first. It was sex he wanted, nothing more.

It was like being doused with cold water when she added, "Like I said before, I could really use a friend."

She emphasized the word *friend* in a way that told him in no uncertain terms that she wasn't interested in a relationship that ended up in bed. That was new. That was different. That wasn't the usual behavior from the women he met. He looked at her with new eyes. As he'd told her before, he'd never had a female *friend*. The idea definitely sounded intriguing.

The truth was he had few friends of either sex. He lived alone, away from the rest of his family—and the rest of the world, for that matter. As soon as he'd gotten old enough to leave home, he'd gone. With money left to him by his mother, he'd bought himself an isolated cabin at the foot of some of the most beautiful mountains in the world, began running a few cattle and quarter horses, and continued saving as many wounded animals that crossed his path as he could.

So, yeah. He could use a friend.

But he wasn't ready to give up on the idea of having her in his bed. He didn't want to scare her off by suggesting that he wanted anything more from her than she was willing to give, so he held out his hand for her to shake and said, "Friends?"

She placed her cold hand in his, and he closed

his fingers around it. She met his gaze solemnly. "Friends."

They were still staring at each other, his heart pounding erratically in his chest, when she rose, easing her trembling hand free. She'd felt it too, he suspected. The spark that had leapt between them whether they wanted it to or not. A need to touch that demanded far more than friendship to be satisfied.

He'd wanted to see what she would do, and he'd gotten his answer. She wasn't going to cross that line from friend to . . . something more.

At least, not yet.

He had a sudden thought and asked, "Did you leave a boyfriend behind in Australia?"

She visibly stiffened and responded with a curt "No." For the first time since she'd arrived, she seemed uneasy being alone with him.

His antenna went up. He debated whether to ask her another question about the supposedly nonexistent boyfriend.

Before he could, she pulled her coat tighter around herself and said, "There was someone. But he's no longer in the picture."

He felt relieved that she'd been honest. And then uncomfortable, because it was clear that she'd cared enough—been hurt enough—by whoever it was to want to deny his existence. He wondered if she was still heartbroken, if that was the reason she seemed to want nothing more than friendship from him.

She smiled—or tried to smile—and said, "I'd better be getting back."

"I'll ride with you."

She shook her head. "There's no need."

"What about—"

She laid a flat hand on his chest and looked into his eyes. "I'll be sure to make plenty of noise. I'll be fine."

She was right. The bears were barely out of hibernation and still high up in the mountains, and there were plenty of deer, elk, mountain goat, and moose births this spring to feed the mountain lions. And no two-legged villains were likely to threaten her on either Flynn or Grayhawk land.

"When will I see you again?" The words were out of his mouth before he could stop them.

She smiled with obvious pleasure, and his heart jumped. "How about if I bring a picnic lunch here on Sunday afternoon?"

"Sounds great. In case you were wondering, I love fried chicken."

She laughed. "I'll see what I can do." When she ruffled the fur on Wulf's back, Devon quivered, imagining the feel of her hands on his naked flesh.

She mounted, waved once, then rode away without looking back.

Be patient, he told himself as he watched her disappear in the darkness. *She's every bit as wild and wounded as any of those animals you've rescued. Give her time. Give her space. Win her trust. Then you can woo her and make her yours.*

It sounded easier said than it was, because he felt surprisingly impatient. He wanted to taste her lips, to hold her warm, naked body next to his own as he thrust deep inside her.

He was perturbed to realize that he was also imagining the closeness that came from sharing his deepest feelings with someone he cared about—and who cared about him. He knew that picture was false, at least in his experience. He wasn't sure why he thought he could have that with Philippa Grayhawk. But he wanted it so much he could taste it. And he wanted her . . . in his bed. So waiting wasn't going to be easy.

But if Devon had learned anything from the wild animals he'd fostered, it was how to bide his time. And a woman like Pippa was worth the wait.

Chapter 5

EVEN THOUGH THE night air was frigid on the ride home, Pippa felt warm inside. She had a new friend, someone safe with whom she could share her feelings. Someone *safe*.

Pippa realized she was lying to herself even as she thought the word. Oh, Devon was no physical threat. But emotionally? In the past few months her whole world had been turned upside down, and she desperately needed someone with whom to have a normal, uncontentious conversation. She needed someone she could confide in, even if she had to be careful what she said. It was no surprise that she'd offered friendship to a perfect stranger.

The problem was whether they could remain merely friends.

Pippa was far more physically attracted to Devon Flynn than she wanted—or had expected—to be. She had the uncomfortable feeling—an honest fear, considering her circumstances—that the spark she'd felt arcing between them could easily be fanned into a fiery blaze. That complicated every-thing. It felt like she was standing on the edge of a high cliff, and that a strong wind was swirling around her, threatening to shove her off.

Pippa felt exhilarated by the danger. She felt excited and alive in a way she hadn't since the day Tim had shattered all her dreams of happiness. So what if she had to walk a tightrope to keep Devon at arm's distance. So what if she had to keep her body on a tight leash when she was near him. She could do it. To start with, there would be no more hugs.

She would miss that closeness. As she'd held tight to Devon tonight she'd relished the feel of his warm flesh under her fingertips and the rough stubble of his beard against her cheek. She'd smelled clean male sweat and pine and wool—scents that she would forever link to him. She was tall, like her dad, but Devon was several inches taller, and his strong arms had held her tight, making her feel protected. It had been wonderful to lean on him, to know he was there to support her.

If not for her experience with Tim, she might have let the embrace continue. She'd known Devon wanted to hold her longer, but she'd backed away to protect them both. She had a secret that made any sort of romantic relationship impossible to contemplate. On the other hand, having a friend would make her life at Kingdom Come so much better—especially a friend who understood how horrid the Brats could be.

She was still reveling in the euphoria of her upcoming picnic with Devon on Sunday when she led her mount into the stable and ran right into her father.

"Where the hell have you been? I was worried sick! Are you all right?"

Pippa was taken aback. "I'm fine, Daddy." She'd lived in the Australian Outback all her life—with some of the most poisonous snakes and spiders in the world—and her father had never sounded as concerned as he did right now.

"When you raced out of the house like that I wasn't sure what you would do." He hesitated and added, "Or where you would go."

She noticed the tightness of his jaw and realized he hadn't just been worried about her safety, he'd been scared that she might have run away and disappeared, as he had so long ago.

"I went for a ride." She would have explained that she'd needed some quiet time to herself, but he never gave her the chance.

"You can't be traipsing around all hours of the day and night in your condition. What if you'd been thrown and injured? You have to think about the baby—and yourself. Anything could have happened."

"But it didn't! I'm not a child. I'm a grown woman, old enough to take care of myself."

"You haven't done such a good job of that so far," he snapped back.

Pippa felt shame wash over her. And responded with defiance. "I won't make the same mistake again. You have to let me live my life."

"It's not just you anymore," he persisted. "There's another life involved here. I know more than you can imagine about what you're about to go through."

"How could you have any inkling of what it feels like—"

"I've been a single parent," he said, cutting her off. "It's harder than you can imagine."

The words seemed torn from him, and Pippa realized he was sharing his own painful experience as a way of expressing his anxiety over what lay ahead for her.

"You mean raising me."

He nodded. "I was younger than you are now, but I knew from the start that you were the most important thing in my life. I wasn't about to let anything—or anyone—get in the way of my taking care of you."

Pippa wondered if King had been one of the people "in the way." Was that why her father had fled his home and stayed gone forever after? Because King didn't think he should be a teenage parent?

She asked the question that had never left her thoughts. "What happened to my mother?"

A look of agony crossed his face.

In the past, she'd let him sidestep the issue, but this time she wanted an answer. "Please, Daddy. I'd like to know."

"You'd better take care of your horse."

Pippa began unsaddling her mount, but she wasn't going to let him get away with distracting her yet again. She glanced over her shoulder and said, "It's time, don't you think?" She tried to sound calm, but her heart was thundering in her chest.

A long breath shuddered out of him, and he

stuck both hands in the back pockets of his Levi's. "We were both too young. Her parents wouldn't let her keep you. So I took you."

She stopped what she was doing and turned to face him. "I presume Grandpa King didn't want you to raise me."

"It wasn't that simple," he said flatly.

Before she could ask him to explain further he said, "Suffice it to say, I know how hard it is to be both mother and father to a child. It's a tremendous responsibility. And it starts with taking care of yourself."

She unlashed the cinch and hauled both saddle and blanket off, intending to lay them on a nearby sawhorse, but her father took them out of her hands.

"I'm not sure you should be carrying heavy stuff like this."

She pursed her lips and stuck her balled fists on her hips. The saddle took effort to lift, but it didn't weigh much more than a bag of groceries. "I'm not sick. I'm just pregnant."

"Have you been to the doctor for a checkup? Have you asked him what you can and can't do?"

She led her mount into a stall and pulled off the bridle, easing the bit out of the horse's mouth, then closed the stall door and hung the bridle on a peg. "Women have been having babies for eons and working in the fields until the day they deliver."

"And dying along with those babies," he interjected. "Pregnancy is serious business. You can't ignore what's coming."

"I'm not. And you're being ridiculous."

He reached out and brushed her long blond hair behind her shoulder. It was the sort of gesture that had been common when she was a child, but which he'd stopped doing once she'd blossomed into a young woman. He looked into her eyes and said, "I don't want to lose you, Pippa."

She took a step closer and put her arms around his waist as she laid her head against his beating heart. "You won't."

A moment later she felt his arms tighten around her. "I love you, kid," he whispered in her ear.

"Love you more," she answered.

"Love you most."

She stayed where she was until her horse whickered, then let go and took an awkward step back. "I need to brush him down."

"I'll do it."

"Daddy—"

"Let me do this for you. You must be tired."

She was exhausted, but she had no intention of admitting it.

"Nathan was asking for you," he said. "I told him you'd give him a kiss good night when you got back."

Her little brother had looked lost ever since they'd moved to Wyoming, but he'd never once complained. Pippa felt a spurt of guilt that she'd missed reading him a story at bedtime tonight, which had become part of their evening routine.

"All right," she said at last. "Thanks, Daddy." She leaned over to kiss his cheek, then hurried from the barn, mulling over the tiny pearl of information she'd gleaned about her mother. If her father had finally answered one question, maybe he would answer others. Was her mother still alive? Did she live here in Jackson? Had her father returned so he could see her again at long last?

Pippa was even more excited about the upcoming picnic now than she had been before the conversation with her father. Maybe Devon knew the answers to some of her questions. Maybe he even knew who her mother was! Pippa couldn't wait to ask him on Sunday.

Chapter 6

MATT WAS BESIDE himself with worry for his daughter, but he had several other desperate irons in the fire as well. He'd had a harrowing meeting with his father tonight, at the end of which he'd headed to the barn for some solitude and discovered that the horse Pippa usually rode was missing—along with his daughter. Thank goodness she'd returned when she had.

As he brushed down Pippa's mount, he replayed the scene with his father, wondering if he could have said or done anything differently to keep the situation from becoming less dire than it was.

King had sent the housekeeper to summon Matt to his office, which had immediately set up Matt's hackles. When Matt arrived, his father said, "Close the door and sit down."

"I'll stand."

"Do what you want. You always did," King retorted.

"Why am I here?"

King fiddled with some papers on his desk, then turned his swivel chair so he was staring out at the starry night sky, his back to Matt. "When are those quarter horses you bought supposed to arrive?"

"You called me in here to ask me that? I told you at supper." Matt felt his blood pressure rising. King had ruled his first three children—Libby, North, and Matt—with an iron hand. He'd kept Libby separated from the love of her life for years. North had moved to Texas to escape their father's influence. And Matt, well, Texas hadn't been far enough. He'd run all the way to Australia. Matt had no intention of letting King fall back into old habits.

He was turning to leave when King swiveled his chair back around and said, "Answer me!"

Something in his father's tone suggested more than just curiosity. Matt hesitated, then turned back, his feet spread wide and his shoulders back. "The end of the week."

"When is final payment due?"

"On delivery."

His father pursed his lips and grunted with disapproval.

"You told me I had free rein to spend whatever was necessary to make this place a working ranch again," Matt said. "Is there some problem?"

"Sit down. Please."

Matt made a face at the two chairs in front of his father's desk, which were purposely set low so that whoever sat there felt like some kind of supplicant to the throne. Then he settled on the arm of one of the two couches on either side of the stone fireplace across the room. "What's going on?"

"That sonofabitch Angus Flynn has me backed into a corner."

That got Matt's attention. Matt's uncle had been trying to ruin King financially for twenty years. According to what Matt had learned since he'd been home, Angus had interfered—or tried to interfere—in every business deal King had gotten involved in. Mostly, his behavior had been a nuisance. But if his father had called him in here to discuss the situation, maybe this time it was more than that. "What's he done now?"

"He's got his big, fat camel's nose under my tent."

"Which affects me how?"

King snorted. "I've invested most of the funds that support the ranch in a venture that turned out to be a bit more risky than I anticipated—thanks to that low-down scheming pond scum."

Matt ignored the verbal castigation of his uncle. Angus could defend himself if it came to that. But he felt a chill run down his spine at what his father seemed to be saying. "How much is at risk?"

"I've got enough money to pay for those quarter horses you bought, but you can't invest in any other improvements until this venture is tied up with a bow."

Matt rose to his feet. "When will that be?"

"The deal will be done when it's done."

Matt took the few steps to reach his father's desk, placing his palms on the battered oak as he leaned across the cluttered surface and put himself nose-to-nose with King. "That's not what we agreed. You offered me free rein here, but that's not going to happen if I can't spend money. I knew I couldn't trust you!" He rose abruptly and snarled, "What am I supposed to do until you—or Uncle Angus—finishes what you've started? Sit around and twiddle my thumbs?"

King met his gaze, his blue eyes flecked with the black in his soul. "I've told you how things stand. What you do is up to you."

Matt's heart was racing as he whirled and strode from the room. His father knew he had him over a barrel. Matt wasn't going anywhere, despite this setback, because he didn't want to uproot his kids again so soon. And besides, where would he move them?

He'd headed straight to the stable, afraid of what he might do or say if he ran into one of his younger sisters before he got out of the house. Thank God Pippa had come home safe and sound so soon after he'd discovered her missing, because he already had enough worries on his plate.

Trust King to screw him! Matt didn't give a damn about Kingdom Come. He planned to sell the ranch the instant the three hundred and sixty-five days he had to live here were done. He'd been making changes because he could see the potential here, and he'd figured he might as well spend the year increasing the value of his property.

And because he would go crazy if he didn't have something to keep his mind off all the other disasters that had occurred to force him back home.

He set down the brush he'd been using to

groom Pippa's mount and slung his arm around the horse's neck, leaning his cheek against the sleek hide, swallowing hard over the painful constriction in his throat, and blinking to stave off tears.

He'd made a real mess of his life.

The horse turned his head around to check on Matt, and he let go and smoothed a hand across the animal's withers. "I'm fine, thank you very much."

He left the stall, but he still wasn't ready to head back to the house, so he walked in the opposite direction. The night was cold, and he zipped up his fleece and shoved his hands into the pockets.

He should have known better than to come here. He should have known King wouldn't honor his bargain. After all, he'd lied to Matt in the past. What had made him think King wouldn't lie to him again?

But he hadn't had much choice. It wasn't only Pippa's pregnancy that had convinced him to accept King's offer. He needed to get Nathan away from his prescription-drug-addicted mother, who was making noises like she wanted Nathan to come spend more time with her in Darwin. He wasn't about to let that happen, especially after what had occurred the last time he'd left Nathan alone with her.

His belly churned as he recalled the moment he'd seen his small, unconscious son in a large white hospital bed. The doctors had wanted to amputate Nathan's right leg. Irene had been so drugged up she'd been incoherent. She'd already told the doctors they could do whatever they thought was best.

He'd arrived in the nick of time and insisted that the doctors set the bones in both of his son's legs, instead of cutting one of them off. It had been touch and go whether Nathan would ever walk again, even with crutches. Matt blamed himself every time he saw his son limp across a room. He should have known better than to trust his child with someone as irresponsible as Irene. Coming to Wyoming was a small price to pay to protect his son.

And Matt had figured he would never have a better chance to make King pay for what he'd done all those years ago. Matt's hate had simmered for a long time, and it hadn't taken much to make it boil over. He knew King believed he would stay the full year at Kingdom Come. After all, he'd sold his cattle station in the Northern Territory. Where else could he go to do what he loved? Ranching was in his blood. He came from a long line of Wyoming cattlemen going back more than a hundred and fifty years. But his hate for his father was far more powerful than his desire to live his life on a ranch he'd grown up loving.

There was a fourth reason he'd returned to America. He'd come to see *her*. The girl to whom he'd given his heart at sixteen.

Matt never let himself think too much or too long about Pippa's mother, because he wasn't sure he had the courage to see her after all this time. Jennie had been a widow for a year. She was finally free. So was he. But all those years ago he'd made a choice, and he wasn't sure Jennie was going to forgive him when he finally told her the truth about what he'd done.

On the other hand, Pippa had never needed her mother more than she did now. So maybe it was time he reached out to Jennie, time he told her that she had a daughter she believed had died at birth.

Chapter 7

"Can you watch Nathan for me today?" Pippa asked Leah, who was brewing a cup of coffee for herself, something she did every Sunday morning after she returned from church. Pippa was bubbling with excitement over seeing Devon again, and it must have shown on her face, because Leah's eyes narrowed.

"What's going on with you?"

"Nothing!" The last thing she needed was a suspicious aunt looking over her shoulder.

Leah eyed the canvas bag Pippa had slung over her shoulder. "What's in the bag?"

"A picnic lunch." She bit back the rest of what she wanted to say. *What business is it of yours where I go or what I do?*

Leah leaned back against the kitchen counter, cup in hand, and said, "Couldn't you take Nathan with you? Shouldn't you take him? That's the loneliest kid I've ever met."

Pippa felt a spurt of guilt. Her brother was all alone at the ranch without any kids his age to play with. However, that situation was no different from his life on their cattle station in the Outback, where he'd managed to keep himself entertained and happy. She wasn't sure why things were different here, but most of the time, Nathan seemed disinterested in—and disconnected from—what was going on around him.

She almost changed her mind and took her brother along, but her relationship with Devon was too new, too fragile, and she didn't want Nathan spilling the beans to her father. Her dad was sure to misconstrue her relationship with Devon as something romantic. Which it definitely wasn't, even though she felt distinctly lighthearted at the thought of seeing her *friend* again.

"I'll take Nathan on a picnic tomorrow," Pippa said. "Can you just watch him for me today?"

Leah hesitated so long Pippa thought she was going to say no. Her heart sank. She'd been looking forward to this picnic with Devon all week. She didn't dare leave Nathan without someone to watch over him, and if Leah wouldn't do it, she wasn't sure what she would do. None of her other aunts were at home.

Taylor and Victoria had flown to Texas on the family jet—Taylor had piloted the plane—and Eve had left Kingdom Come as well. She'd moved in with Connor Flynn to take care of his two young children in exchange for his letting her keep her wild mustangs on his ranch. Eve had apparently rescued her wild horse band from the slaughterhouse, which raised Pippa's opinion of her aunt quite a bit.

Eve's sisters had freaked when it turned out Eve hadn't just moved in with Connor—they'd gotten married! Pippa was completely confused by what her aunt had done. How could she have married one of "those awful Flynn boys" when she and her sisters supposedly hated them? Pippa couldn't wait to ask Devon what he knew about the situation.

Of course, to do that, she needed Leah to keep an eye on Nathan for her. "Will you do it?" She almost said *please*, but that felt too much like begging, and she hadn't sunk that low yet.

"Fine," Leah said. "Be sure you tell Nathan you're leaving. I don't want him to think he's being abandoned. Even if that is what you're doing," she muttered under her breath.

Pippa bit her tongue to stop a retort. She didn't want to take the chance that Leah would change her mind. "I will," she said, hurrying from the kitchen to hunt down Nathan.

She found her younger brother sitting at their grandfather's desk. Nathan spent a surprising amount of time with King. Pippa had seen them mucking out stalls together in the barn, which was as close as Nathan was willing to get to a horse since the riding accident that had shattered the bones in both of his legs.

As she drew closer, she saw her brother was drawing on a piece of paper with her grandfather's favorite fountain pen. "I thought Grandpa King told you he didn't want you in here when he wasn't around," she scolded. Then she saw *what* he was drawing.

Pippa's stomach clenched. Nathan had drawn a picture of a stick-figure horse lying on the ground with a stick-figure child lying beside it, both of the child's legs angled in odd directions. The child's mouth was stretched wide in a large O, as though he were yelling. A stick figure with long, flowing hair was standing beside the horse. Nathan had drawn large, oval tears raining from the female figure's eyes and splashing onto the ground.

Pippa frowned. "How do you know your mother was crying?" Nathan had been unconscious when he reached the hospital, and Pippa had sat by his bed with her father for several harrowing days before he awoke.

"I heard her crying."

Pippa suppressed a gasp. "I thought the fall knocked you out. I didn't know you were awake."

A frown appeared between his six-year-old brows. "I screamed and screamed. Mum kept saying, 'Shush! Shush!' but I couldn't 'cause it hurt so much. Mum put her hand on my mouth, but she covered my nose and I couldn't breathe and then I don't remember anything else."

Pippa was shocked. She'd never heard this story before. She was certain her father hadn't heard it, either, or Irene wouldn't have been allowed near Nathan again. Or maybe he *had* heard it and hadn't wanted Pippa to realize what Irene had done. Had she really suffocated Nathan? Had she been responsible for putting him in a coma? Pippa was shaken.

She took the crude drawing from Nathan. "May I have this?"

He shrugged. "If you want it."

"I do. Thank you." Pippa folded the paper and stuck it in the back pocket of her jeans. "I'm going

to be away from the ranch this morning, so you
need to mind Leah."

"Can I come?"

His voice sounded so hopeful that Pippa's heart
nearly broke. She picked him up out of the chair
and hugged him tight. She nearly changed her plans
then and there, but she couldn't be with him every
minute of every day, and she was pretty sure Leah—
who had the softest heart Pippa had ever seen—
wouldn't leave him alone for long.

"Not today, mate," she whispered in his ear.
She set him down, took both of his hands in hers,
and leaned over to look him in the eye. He looked
back at her with an earnestness that reminded her
of her father, with the same unruly lock of black
hair falling over his forehead and the same striking
blue eyes. "I promise I'll spend all day with you
tomorrow, and we'll do whatever you want."

Nathan shot her a cheeky grin. "Anything?"

Pippa grinned back. "Uh-oh. What have I
agreed to?"

"Tell you tomorrow!" he said as he pulled free
and scampered from the room.

"Where are you going?" she called after him.

He never looked back as he hop-skipped—a
gait caused by having one leg shorter than the
other—from the room. "I'm going to find Leah.
She's always got biscuits! I mean *cookies!*" he
shouted, substituting the American word for the
Australian one as his booted feet thumped down
the hall.

Pippa felt relieved at her brother's youthful resilience. She pulled the drawing out of her pocket

and looked at it again. She wondered if she should give it to her father. He should know what Irene had done. But what would be the point? Irene was in Australia. She could never hurt Nathan again.

Pippa stuck the drawing back in her pocket and headed for the stable. Devon was expecting her. She needed to get her horse saddled and get on the trail.

Once she was on her way, Pippa didn't hurry. The ride through the fragrant pine forest was every bit as enjoyable as she expected her meeting with Devon to be. Besides, it gave her more time to mull over what she wanted to ask when she saw him again.

When she reached the meadow, he waved to her from the other side, a huge smile on his face. Her heart lifted as she cantered her horse the rest of the distance to the pond. "G'day!" she called out as she dismounted. He took the reins and tied her horse beside his.

"G'day to you, too," he said as he crossed back to join her at the stone, where she'd dropped her canvas bag and was down on her knees scratching behind Wulf's ears. Pippa laughed and ducked away as the wolf lapped at her face.

"He looks glad to see you," Devon said. "So am I," he added.

Pippa looked up and caught her breath as she met Devon's gaze. She saw excitement, anticipation, and . . . need. She felt her heart lurch. Felt the blood surge through her veins. Felt an answering need. And reminded herself why anything more than friendship was impossible.

Be his friend. Don't spoil it by wanting more.
"I'm glad to see you, too," she said in the friendliest voice she could muster. She stayed where she was, stroking Wulf's fur, afraid of what would happen if she stood and closed the distance between herself and Devon.

Neither of them said anything more for a while. She waited for him to break eye contact, because she was helpless to do it herself.

"I brought a blanket," he said at last, "so we'd have a little more room to stretch out." He pointed to a patchwork quilt that he'd spread on a flat, grassy spot near the pond.

"What a great idea!" Pippa welcomed the chance to increase the distance between them. She stood and grabbed the canvas bag, then headed for the quilt, dropping onto her knees when she reached it. A moment later, Devon had joined her.

The silence lay heavy between them. Pippa was aware they were sitting on a blanket together, and that it wouldn't take much effort for him to have her flat on her back. What astonished her, what made her question herself, was the knowledge that she would have welcomed the weight of his body on her own.

Are you crazy? What are you thinking? Didn't you learn anything from your experience with Tim?

Pippa reminded herself that she hardly knew Devon Flynn. What if his behavior was all an act? What if this friendship was some bizarre Flynn trick to get back at the Grayhawks through her?

"I wish I knew more about you," she murmured.

"What do you want to know?"

"What do you want to do with your life?"

He laughed. "That's a pretty big question. Right now I'm happy running my ranch. How about you?"

"I worked gentling horses in Australia. I haven't decided yet what I'm going to do here." *Be a mother and then . . .*

"I've got a stud you could help me with. He was abused. Doesn't trust anyone."

"I'd love to help. I mean if you don't mind." She would jump at the chance to have something useful to do in the months leading up to her baby's birth.

"Thanks. I'd appreciate it. When can you come see him?"

"I'm responsible for watching my younger brother, so—"

"Bring him along," Devon said.

"You wouldn't mind?"

"I like kids. I plan to have a few of my own someday."

Pippa felt her heart sink. *A few of my own someday.* Not someone else's. And not right now. Which shouldn't matter, if all she wanted from Devon Flynn was friendship.

"Do you do all the ranch work yourself?" she asked.

He nodded. "I hire a couple of hands during the roundup. Otherwise, I'm on my own. I like it that way."

Pippa struggled to keep the worried frown off her face. He lived alone and liked it that way? How did a woman fit into that intentionally solitary life? "Don't you get lonely?"

He shot her a lopsided smile, the one she found so attractive. "I'm hardly alone. There's Wulf, for a start." The wolf lifted his head from his paws and looked at Devon when he heard his name.

Pippa shivered as Devon stroked the wolf's fur, imagining his hands on her.

"There's also an abandoned fawn, a porcupine with a wounded foot, and a rabbit with a bitten-off ear."

Pippa laughed. "You have a menagerie."

He nodded. "I'm careful not to interact with them, and I reintroduce them to the wild as soon as they're healed. The specific animals change, but there seems to be a never-ending number of wounded beasts that need help."

"Are you a vet?"

"Nope. I do basic first aid and provide a safe place where they can heal. If it's something really serious, I contact the vet in town."

"How do you find all these animals?"

He looked sheepish. "I've gotten kind of a reputation—it started back when I was a kid—for taking in strays. So people bring me wild things in trouble."

Wild things in trouble. Was that how Devon saw her? Was it sympathy he felt when he looked at her? Did he see her as a "stray"? Was that why he'd agreed to be her friend?

Pippa realized that Devon's sympathy or empathy or whatever you wanted to call it might be part of what she felt when she was with him. But that wasn't the only thing. Desire was a part of it, too. She'd seen it in his eyes and felt it when he'd held her in his arms the night he'd comforted her.

So if he preferred being alone, what did he want from her? Most likely what her former lover had wanted. Sex. And he was clever enough to lower her defenses by pretending to be her friend.

Pippa sighed inwardly. She'd found out what she needed to know. Now she just had to resist the lures Devon had set out to trap her into repeating her past mistake. She would keep him at arm's distance and make it clear that she wasn't available for anything except friendship—assuming he was willing to continue the relationship once he realized sex was off the table.

Pippa opened the canvas bag she'd brought and began pulling out the picnic she'd put together. "Are you hungry?"

"Starved," he replied. "What did you bring?"

"Ham sandwiches."

He looked dismayed.

Pippa giggled, then said, "Gotcha! It's fried chicken, of course." She made up a plate of food and handed it to Devon, who took it and sat cross-legged with the plate in his lap.

"This is delicious," he said through a mouthful of chicken.

"Thank you. I wanted to ask if you have any idea what's going on between your brother Connor and my aunt Eve. I thought Grayhawks and Flynns hated each other. Why on earth would they get married?"

"They're calling it a marriage of convenience. He's getting a babysitter for his two kids, and she's getting a place to keep her herd of mustangs. But the way I see it, he used the excuse that he needed someone to take care of his kids to convince Eve to marry him."

"Why would he do that?"

"Truth? Connor's been in love with Eve ever since high school. Somehow he ended up married to Eve's best friend instead. Connor became a widower when Molly died in a car accident last year."

"Do you think Eve has always had feelings for him, too?"

Devon shrugged. "Who knows? It would never have worked between them in high school because things were a lot worse between us kids in those days than they are now. Not that everything's great, but we aren't letting the air out of each other's tires anymore." He made a face. "It's my dad who won't let this feud die."

"So my aunts wouldn't object if they found out we were friends?" Pippa ventured.

He shook his head. "I wouldn't go that far. They'd certainly question my motives for wanting to spend time with you."

"Meaning what?"

"They'd never believe I don't have nefarious designs on your body."

"But you don't!" she protested with a laugh. The sound died when she met his gaze. So she hadn't been wrong. He wasn't interested in friendship, or at least, not merely in friendship.

He didn't say anything, just looked into her eyes as he swallowed a bite of chicken.

Pippa felt a frisson of awareness skitter down her spine as she stared at his mouth. She sat frozen as he leaned closer until his lips were only a breath away from hers.

She could have leaned back. She could have laughed to break the spell, or shoved at his shoulders to move him away. She could have done a dozen things to stop what happened.

But she didn't.

Chapter 8

DEVON KNEW HE was taking a chance kissing Pippa, but he couldn't resist the temptation. When she leaned toward him, he simply closed the distance between them, and their lips met. She tasted sweet. He leaned back and looked into her eyes and saw a myriad of emotions. He chose to focus on the one he wanted to see, the one that invited him to lean in for another taste, another touch. She moaned, and he felt his body harden in response. Her fingertips found their way to his nape as he touched her cheek with the balls of his fingers.

He couldn't catch his breath, couldn't seem to slow his heart, which was galloping out of control. He'd never felt this way toward another woman, and he tried to slow his body down so his mind could consider what he was doing. He'd seen the yearning in Pippa's eyes for that first kiss. He couldn't have been mistaken about that. But she'd been pretty insistent about wanting a friend, not a lover.

And yet, she willingly pressed her lips against his and opened her mouth to the reach of his tongue. He palmed her breast and felt the nipple peak beneath the cloth. She gasped, and her heavy-lidded eyes slid closed.

Devon warned himself to go slow, that he might be making a terrible mistake, but her willingness made it difficult to let her go. "You're lovely," he murmured.

His lips caressed her throat, her cheek, her eyelids, her brows, before returning to her mouth. He pressed her back against the blanket and lay down beside her so he could look into her eyes. She looked back at him with wonder.

"Devon."

He felt his whole body tense when he heard his name spoken. She would stop him now. She would tell him that kissing him had been a mistake.

"This feels so . . . good," she murmured as she stroked his hair. "You feel so . . . good."

"So do you." He slid his arm under her shoulders and pulled her into his embrace, holding her close so they were entwined, his leg between hers, her leg over his hip.

She smiled as she closed her eyes and leaned her cheek against his shoulder. "I don't understand . . ."

Her voice drifted off, and he said, "You don't understand what?"

She looked up at him with troubled eyes. "How this could be happening. How I could want you so badly when I hardly know you."

"It doesn't make sense. But I know what I feel. And I know what I want."

She glanced at him from beneath lowered lashes. "And what is that?"

"You." He tipped her chin up and kissed her,

taking his time, enjoying the thrust and parry of their tongues. His blood heated as he pressed her softness against the hard length between his thighs. He began rolling her over onto her back, but her hair got caught beneath his shoulder.

She cried out in pain as it pulled free. And then froze, staring up at him with wide, dazed eyes. "We should stop this. Now. Before it's too late."

He didn't say a word, just rolled away, covering his eyes with his forearm. He didn't want to acknowledge that the magic they'd just shared was over, so he didn't speak. Then he realized he needed to know what she was thinking and whether it was something he'd done that had caused her to pull away.

He sat up and met her gaze. "Pippa, I—"

"Don't say anything."

For a moment he thought she wanted to prolong their closeness the same way he did. She sat up and thrust trembling hands through her hair, shoving it away from her face. Her eyes glistened with tears. "I'm sorry. I can't be more than a friend. If that's not enough—"

She was already up, gathering together the picnic items she'd brought.

He scrambled to his feet and said, "Pippa, slow down. Tell me what's wrong."

The wind blew her hair across her face, where it caught on the tears streaming down her cheeks. "I don't think this friendship is going to work."

And then she ran.

Wulf had risen to his feet when Pippa did. The

wolf looked from Devon to Pippa and then loped after her.

Devon could understand the impulse. He wanted to chase after her, too. But she seemed to want some distance from him—and the situation—and he figured it was a good idea to give it to her. "Wulf!" he called. "Come."

Wulf looked back at Devon, but he sat down where he was, staring at Pippa.

Devon crossed toward the wolf, concerned that it might close the distance to Pippa's horse, which was already sidling away from the frightening canine, and completely spook it.

"Pippa, don't leave, please," he called to her. "Let's talk. Tell me what's bothering you."

She kicked her mount into a gallop, and Wulf leapt up and started to follow. Devon lunged and caught him by the scruff of his neck. Wulf whimpered and struggled to get free, but Devon held on. He dropped to his knees, then sat back and put his arms around the wolf's neck.

He stared after Pippa, feeling a terrible sense of loss. "She wants to go, Wulf," he said. "We have to let her go."

Devon was angry with himself for being impatient, for not taking the time to be sure that Pippa was ready for more than the friendship she'd said she wanted. For screwing things up royally.

He swore under his breath. Someone wonderful had just walked out of his life. Something wonderful had just been lost. And he had no one to blame but himself.

Wulf made a growling sound in his throat.

"I feel the same way," Devon muttered. He stood and stared across the meadow, where Pippa was just disappearing into the forest. "So what are we going to do to get her back?"

Chapter 9

I SHOULDN'T HAVE *let him kiss me. I should have pulled away. I should have done something to stop him.*

Pippa was halfway home and she was still trembling, still shaken by Devon's kiss. His lips had been soft and supple, and his breath had been warm on her cheek. She'd gasped, and his tongue had slipped inside to taste and to tease. Pippa's whole body had tingled with awareness, and her lips had clung to his.

Her breathing had been erratic when he ended the kiss. Her breasts had felt full and achy, and her heart had caught in her throat. He'd leaned back just far enough to look into her eyes. He must have seen her shock, her confusion, her fear . . . and her desire.

He'd responded by kissing her again, his touch so gentle she felt like crying, and then hesitated, his lips close to hers but not quite touching, waiting for her to make the next move.

Pippa had closed the distance between them, pressing her lips against his, wanting more of the tenderness he'd shown her, both terrified and ex-hilarated by the passion rising between them.

She'd felt his callused fingertips brush her face and reached out a hand to cup his bristled cheek as their mouths meshed again.

And she'd been lost.

Pippa looked up and realized the ranch house was around the next corner. A knot had grown in her throat, and she was fighting a sob of despair. She shouldn't have run away like that. She should have stayed and talked to Devon, explained that her life was complicated, that it wasn't anything to do with him, that she couldn't get romantically in-volved with anyone.

But that would have meant explaining that she was three months pregnant. That she'd been duped by a married man. That would have meant expos-ing her soft underbelly to someone with the power to rip out her guts.

How had Devon Flynn slipped past her de-fenses so quickly? How had he made her care? Why had she befriended him when she'd been so sure, after what Tim had done, that she would never be able to trust another man again?

Why, oh why, had Devon kissed her? They were supposed to be *friends*. There had been noth-ing *friendly* about his kiss. It had been meant to arouse her, and it had done its job.

Pippa moaned. The worst part was, if he hadn't accidentally pulled her hair as he was rearranging their bodies on the quilt, she would have given her-self to him. That moment of pain had reminded her that she was vulnerable, that she could be terribly hurt.

She'd run away, closing the door to any possible relationship. She would never see Devon again. Never share her thoughts with him. Never laugh with him or see his lopsided smile again. She mourned for the lost dream of . . . what? Their *friendship*?

Pippa forced herself to be brutally honest. She'd been as guilty as Devon of wanting more than friendship. She'd wanted the fairy tale, the happily ever after that comes when a knight in shining armor rides up on his white charger and rescues the fair-haired maiden. But her actions in the past— her pregnancy—had made that impossible. Devon must have seen in her eyes what she'd refused to admit to herself. She wanted him.

Why hadn't she discussed what had happened with him, rather than running away? She'd cut herself off from the one friend she might have had in this place. But was there really any way to take back that kiss and be friends again?

Pippa shook her head. She didn't think she would ever forget the first touch of Devon's lips, the feel of the racing pulse in his throat against her fingertips, and the thrumming of her own heart in response. She didn't remember feeling so euphoric when she'd kissed Tim. She didn't understand how kisses from two men could be so different, feel so different.

She groaned in disgust at her behavior. She couldn't believe she'd let down her guard with Devon, couldn't believe that she hadn't stopped him before his lips had touched hers. He wasn't entirely to blame for what had happened. She bore equal responsibility.

Pippa swiped at the tears on her cheeks and eyelashes. She didn't want her father seeing them and asking questions that would require difficult answers.

She crested a rise and was shocked to see red and blue lights flashing on several police cars that were parked in the driveway of the house.

What was going on? What had happened? Had someone been hurt? Had Daddy and Grandpa King had a fight? She'd left Nathan in Leah's care. Had Leah failed to keep an eye on him?

Pippa's heart was pounding against her chest like a trapped beast trying to get out as she dismounted at the back porch, stumbled past the police cars, and crashed through the kitchen door. The two police officers standing at the sink looked startled when they saw her.

"Daddy!" she yelled, moving through the kitchen toward the north wing of the house, where her family had their suite of rooms. "Daddy! Nathan!"

"Pippa?" her father called back.

Pippa caught up to her father in the Great Room, with its cathedral ceiling, river-rock fireplace, and stunning view of the Tetons. She started to throw herself into his arms, but he caught her by the shoulders and held her at arm's length.

"Where have you been?" His voice was harsh, and his face looked ravaged.

"What happened?" she asked, terrified to hear the answer.

"Nathan is missing. He's been gone all afternoon. Where have you been? You were supposed to be watching him!"

"I asked Leah to take care of him while I went on a picnic."

"A picnic? I hope you had a good time," her father snarled. "Because you may have cost your brother his life."

He thrust her away from him as she cried, "Daddy, no! He can't be gone. Where would he go?"

"Your guess is as good as mine. He's been missing for three hours." He thrust a hand through hair that was already standing on end, as though he'd resorted to the frustrated gesture many times over the hours he'd been looking for her lost brother.

"Is a horse missing?" she asked.

He shot her a look that froze her heart. "Nathan hasn't been on a horse since the accident. But the answer is no. No horse is missing."

"Have you searched everywhere in the house?" The house was huge, thousands of square feet, with dozens and dozens of places for a six-year-old to hide.

"We've looked everywhere. I've called out to him. If he were here, he would have answered. I've searched the perimeter of the house and the stables. I've got the police searching the grounds, in case he wandered off and got lost."

Pippa shuddered to think what could happen to her brother if he'd wandered as far as the forest.

He might freeze in the cold at night or fall victim to some marauding predator. He might survive long enough to die of thirst. The Wyoming wilderness was vast and unforgiving.

She sought some other reason for her brother's disappearance and asked, "Is there any chance Grandpa King took him somewhere?"

"King flew down to Cheyenne this morning for some business at the state capitol. He's on his way back now. Nathan isn't with him."

"What did Leah have to say?"

Leah appeared in the doorway to the Great Room, her face bleached white, her blue eyes filled with remorse. "I am so sorry! I only meant to be gone from the house for a few minutes. But there was a problem with one of the studs in the barn, and I didn't dare leave until it was resolved. I swear I wasn't away for more than fifteen minutes!"

"Where did you last see Nathan?" Pippa asked.

"We went through all of this hours ago," her father said irritably.

Pippa ignored her father and said to Leah, "Please, tell me."

"He was sitting at King's desk drawing," Leah replied.

"Did you look behind the curtains?" Pippa asked.

Leah stared at her blankly. "Why would I do that?"

"Why would she do that?" her father repeated.

"He likes to play hide-and-seek. He hides and waits to see how long it takes for someone to notice he's missing and come looking for him."

Pippa saw the stricken look on her father's face, probably because ever since they'd moved to Wyoming he'd spent a lot more time away from the house—and from Nathan—than he used to in Australia.

The three of them hurried to King's office. The curtains were drawn back with ties and pooled elegantly on the hardwood floor at either side. Pippa ran to check one side while her father checked the other, Leah at his shoulder. Pippa lifted the heavy curtain aside and found Nathan lying there curled up, sound asleep. "He's here," she said in a quiet voice. "He must have dozed off."

She bent down on one knee and shook Nathan's shoulder as her father and Leah joined her. "Nathan," she said. "Wake up."

He rolled over, yawning and rubbing his eyes, and smiled up at her. "You found me."

"You're too predictable, mate," she said as she lifted him into her arms and stood. "You need to find a better place to hide."

Before she'd taken two steps, her father had snatched Nathan from her arms and was hugging him tight. Leah held both hands over her mouth, stifling a sob of relief.

Nathan leaned back, put his hands on their father's cheeks, and said, "Were you looking for me, too, Daddy?"

"I was," their father said in a choked voice.

"I'm glad you found me," he said, laying his head on their father's shoulder, his arms around his neck. He yawned again and said, "I'm hungry."

"You missed lunch," their father said, his voice cracking.

"I'll be happy to take him to the kitchen and feed him, Matt," Leah said, reaching out her arms.

"Thanks, Leah."

As Pippa watched, Matt handed Nathan over to Leah. She was surprised to see that Nathan laid his head as easily on Leah's shoulder as he had on their dad's. As Leah left the room, she called back, "I'll take care of sending everyone home."

"Thanks, Leah." Her father followed Leah and closed the office door behind her before rounding on Pippa. "I'd like to know if you plan to pawn off your own child when it's born, the way you did your brother."

"That's not fair! Leah promised to watch him."

"That's exactly my point. Children need constant care and attention. Are you ready for that responsibility? You have no business keeping this child if you aren't willing to take on that obligation. Getting pregnant was your first mistake. Keeping this child—unless you're one hundred percent committed—would be your second."

Pippa was stunned by her father's attack. "You managed by yourself. I can, too."

"That was different. I had no choice."

"That's not true." Pippa was angry enough that she forgot all about protecting her father's feelings. "You could have left me with the Millers."

Her father's jaw dropped. "How could you possibly know about them?"

"I heard you mention the name."

"I would never—"

"You were drunk! I was worried because I heard you crying. I didn't know what to do. Who are they? What do they have to do with me?"

"They were a foster family taking care of you."

"Why?"

"None of that matters anymore," he said flatly. "I came and got you, and that's the end of it. I don't think—"

She interrupted him again, seeing the anguish in his eyes and determined to say everything before she lost her nerve. "You must really regret the choice you made to raise me by yourself."

"Why would you say that?"

"Because you seem so determined to talk me out of keeping my baby. I'm sorry I ruined your life! I'm sorry you made the wrong choice by taking me out of that foster home. But keeping this baby is the right choice for me."

She'd never seen an expression quite like the one on her father's face. He looked stunned.

"You shouldn't judge what you don't understand," he said.

She held out her hands in supplication. "Then explain it to me. Tell me what happened. Why did you decide to come get me? Why did you raise me on your own?"

He opened his mouth to speak but decided against it. He rubbed his fingers on his temples as though his head ached, then leaned his hips back against his father's desk and crossed his arms protectively over his chest. At last he met her gaze and said, "I've never once regretted taking you out of that foster home. But nothing about raising you on my own was easy."

"Then why did you do it?"

His next words seemed to be wrenched from his soul. "Because I loved your mother, and you were all I had left of her."

She'd figured out a long time ago that her mother must be dead, or at least long gone, but that still didn't explain a lot of other things her father had done. "Why did you go so far away? Why do you hate Grandpa King so much?"

"Because he lied to me," her father snarled, rising to his feet. "King told me your mother died when you were born and that you died with her."

Pippa gasped.

"I thought I'd killed your mother by getting her pregnant when she was so young," he said in a harsh voice. "I blamed myself for both of your deaths."

Pippa was speechless. Then something dawned on her. Her father had suffered because he blamed himself for the deaths of *both* mother and daughter. But Pippa hadn't died. Instead, she'd been sent to a foster home. Her hands began to tremble. She clasped them together and asked, "Since I'm not dead, does that mean my mother is still alive?"

For a moment, she thought he wasn't going to answer. Or that the answer was going to be no.

And then he nodded.

Chapter 10

MY MUM IS alive! Pippa had dreamed about having a mother and had imagined many times how she might look. Now, with her father's admission, she realized she might actually get to meet her. The funny thing was there was no one close to her with whom she could share her wonderful, startling news. Nathan was too young, and she wasn't on good terms with her aunts. The only other person she thought might be the least bit interested was her almost-friend Devon Flynn.

But that door had been closed, and she was the one who'd shut it.

Pippa forced her thoughts away from Devon and focused her attention on her father. "Where is my mum? Can I meet her?"

His face looked strained as he replied, "Your mother, Jennifer Fairchild—now Jennifer Fairchild Hart—is living on her grandparents' ranch in Texas."

"How long have you known she was alive? How did you find her?"

"Uncle Angus found her for me a long time ago."

Pippa stared at her father. Her first thought—

along with a spurt of anger—was *Why didn't you say something to me sooner?* But obviously there was a lot more going on here than she'd been told. Maybe there was a good reason why her father had kept her mother's identity a secret all these years. Maybe her mother wasn't someone she would ever want to meet. Or maybe she hadn't wanted to be a teenage mother. Maybe she'd colluded with her parents in the lie about her own and her baby's deaths. Pippa had a million questions, and she wasn't sure where to start.

Devon had admitted her father spent a lot of nights at the Flynn supper table, but it seemed Devon might actually have underestimated the depth of her father's relationship with Angus Flynn. "I didn't realize you and Angus were so close. I mean, that he would go to so much trouble to help you."

Her father's lips twisted sardonically. "I think at the time Angus was more interested in punishing my father than in helping me."

"You'll have to explain that."

"Let's sit down." He crossed to one of the studded leather couches by the fireplace and sat, gesturing Pippa to the couch across from him. She sat on the arm, too excited to settle down.

"Long before you were born, my father told Angus's wife about an affair Angus was having."

Pippa slid off the arm onto the couch. "Holy cow. What happened then?"

"Angus's wife, Fiona, was so upset that she left him for a while. It seems Angus had been waiting for the right moment to pay King back for the trouble he'd caused between him and his wife. Angus told me that King had lied to me, that my child—and my girlfriend Jennie—were both still alive."

"That's unbelievable."

"It struck me the same way at the time," he admitted. "Apparently, Jennie's parents had told her the baby died at birth. Actually, they'd placed you in a foster home in Texas.

"Angus secretly helped me establish paternity so I could retrieve you from your foster family. Once I had legal custody, he helped get both of us out of the country without my father's knowledge."

"Why would he do that?"

He pursed his lips. "To hurt King."

Pippa's brow furrowed as she tried to understand what he was implying. Her father must have seen her confusion, because he continued, "At the time, I was a favorite child. You can imagine my father's agitation—his outrage and frustration—when I simply disappeared. He never knew what happened to me or why." A muscle worked in his jaw before he added, "I wanted him to suffer the way I had when I believed both you and Jennie were dead."

"So to pay him back for lying to you, you left without telling your father where you were going." Pippa met his gaze. "And you stayed gone for twenty years."

Her father nodded. "King had told me more than once that I was too young to be a father. He told me that I was 'lucky' when Jennie's parents disappeared with her and my unborn child. I disagreed vehemently with him about that, and about my ability to be a parent." He made a disgusted sound in his throat. "But I believed he was being honest with me when he told me you and Jennie were both dead. I will never, ever, forgive him for that."

"So why did you come back here? You said it wasn't because of me. So what's changed? Does your decision have something to do with my mother?"

He threaded his hands together so tightly his knuckles turned white. "A year ago Jennie was widowed."

Pippa's eyes widened with sudden understanding. "Do you still love her? Are you going after her? Can I meet her?"

Tears glistened in his eyes as he met her gaze. "She still believes you're dead."

Pippa's jaw dropped. "You took me without telling her that she had a living child? You just *stole* me and ran?"

Her father rose abruptly and paced away toward a picture window that offered a spectacular view of the Tetons. "Her parents hated me. I couldn't take the chance that they would try to take you away from me if I contacted her. I wanted Jennie with me, but it was too risky!"

Pippa tried to imagine what it must have been like for him to make such a choice. But it was hard to feel compassion for her father when she felt so resentful for having grown up without her living, breathing, absent mother. What her father had done didn't seem fair to either her or her mother.

His voice was gruff as he continued, "I was only seventeen. My father had lied to me, so I couldn't turn to him. I had Uncle Angus's support, but that might not have been enough if Jennie's parents went to a judge to try and stop me."

He turned back to face her, his jaw hard. "I had to choose," he said. "So I chose you."

It took Pippa a moment to work out exactly what her father had given up when he'd taken her and fled. And then it struck her. *He chose his child over the woman he loved.* She stared wide-eyed at her father, realizing that over the years he must have reflected on that choice many times—and perhaps regretted it. Maybe, in hindsight, he'd realized he should have chosen Pippa's mother over the child she'd borne him.

What an awful decision to have to make.

Pippa wasn't sure what to think, what to feel. No wonder her father worried about her raising the child of a man she loathed. He'd *loved* her mother, and he'd still struggled with the choice he'd made to raise her on his own.

Pippa felt an ache in her throat. Maybe her father had regrets, but she'd never felt unloved. She'd always been cared for.

She looked at him and saw a great deal that had been obscured before his revelation. Now she understood the darkness in his soul. Now she understood why he'd always worked from dawn to dark, falling exhausted into bed. He'd been exorcising demons, hoping to sleep without dreaming of the woman he'd loved and lost. No wonder both his first wife and Nathan's mother had left. They both must have known that something was missing from his relationships with them, even if they didn't know what it was. Now Pippa knew. Her father's heart had always belonged to his first love.

Then Pippa realized the crux of the problem her father faced. If he was ever going to reconcile with Jennifer Hart, he was going to have to admit to her what he'd done. That he'd chosen their child over its mother. That he'd taken their baby—without telling her it was alive—and run.

No wonder he hadn't told Pippa the truth. He'd known she would want to meet her mother. And there was no telling what her mother would do when she found out how Matthew Grayhawk had betrayed her. How he'd manipulated and deceived them *both,* because Pippa was as much a victim of her father's decision as her mother had been.

Her father had waited patiently without speaking for her to work it all out. She met his tortured gaze and felt her heart squeeze. "And all these years . . . you never told my mother the truth?"

He shook his head.

"Oh, Daddy." She resisted the urge to wrap her arms around him and offer comfort. He'd made the choice he believed was best for her—even if Pippa thought it was the wrong one. But she was pretty sure that her mother would never be able to forgive her father for what he'd done.

Chapter 11

MATT HAD AVOIDED responding to his daughter's question about whether he still loved his childhood sweetheart because he wasn't sure of the answer. How could his feelings for his first love possibly have survived all these years? But his heart leapt at the mere thought of seeing Jennie again. Unfortunately, their love had been doomed from the moment Jennie got pregnant.

Matt's guts were already tied in knots after admitting to his daughter that he'd kept Jennie's existence a secret all these years. He was walking into uncharted territory, and he had the feeling that at any moment the earth could fall out from under him.

"Why are you telling me all this now?" Pippa asked.

"Because I want you to think long and hard about the choice you have to make. Because once you make it, once you decide to keep this child, there's no going back. There's no second-guessing. There's no changing your mind."

"It's obvious what you think I should do," she retorted.

Matt forced himself to stay calm in the face of his daughter's anger. "I worry that you don't realize just how big a job you're taking on."

"You're wrong! You've made your point, Daddy. I wish you would stop harping on the subject."

But he couldn't let it go. How many times in those early days had he felt overwhelmed? How many times had he despaired that he would ever be able to raise a healthy, happy child all by himself? It was hard to believe how naive he'd been, how easy he'd thought fatherhood would be.

Having a mother for his daughter was the main reason he'd married his first wife. He wanted to spare his daughter that sort of mistake if he could. There were so many loving parents who wanted to adopt a child, and she had her whole life ahead of her. "Pippa, you need to listen to me."

"I've heard enough!" She whirled and fled the room.

He started to call her back, but the words died in his throat. He'd hoped that by sharing his own experience he could make his teenage daughter understand the difficulties of being a single parent. The hell of it was he still wasn't sure he'd made the right choice. Could he have made his escape with both Jennie *and* their daughter? Why hadn't he tried harder to make it happen?

How many times had he stopped himself from contacting Jennie to let her know that they had a child, that he still loved her, and that he wanted her to join him? But she'd been a minor, only fifteen when Pippa was born. That was why he'd believed his father when he'd said Jennie was dead. He'd known she was very young to be having a child. That's why they'd both been so careful to use birth control. But no method was foolproof, and Jennie had gotten pregnant.

Matt sank into the chair at his father's desk and steepled his hands against his mouth to keep the sound of anguish from escaping his throat. He didn't often let himself remember how much in love he'd been, because it hurt too much.

The day he'd met her, Jennie had been fourteen. Standing only five foot three, her body had been lithe and athletic, with a tiny waist and small breasts. They'd literally bumped into each other as he was entering the gym at Jackson High School and she was leaving it. He was there for football wind sprints. She was on the girls' volleyball team. She'd looked up at him in the moment of contact, and froze.

Her long blond hair was tied in a ponytail that trailed halfway down her back. A fringe of bangs covered her eyebrows and left him looking down into a pair of soft gray eyes and a cupid mouth rounded into an O of surprise.

He'd put both hands on her arms to balance her until she was steady, then grinned down at her and said, "Why, hello there, little lady."

He'd been charmed by the blush that rose on her cheeks and impressed that she kept looking him in the eye as she said, "You're Matt Grayhawk."

"Guilty. What's your name?"

"I'm Jennie Fairchild."

"Why haven't I met you before?"

The petite girl gave him a cheeky grin. "Because I'm just a freshman, and you've been too busy running after Monica Higgins."

Matt laughed and felt his ears turning red. Monica Higgins was another junior, a girl who everyone agreed had the best body in school.

Jennie shrugged and said, "I can't compete with that."

With the slight movement of her shoulders, he realized he was still holding her and let go. "I don't know about that," he said, doing a quick assessment of her body.

"Hey!"

To his amazement, he felt her hand on his chin, tipping his head up until his eyes focused on hers.

"There's more to me than my figure," she chided.

Matt was astonished that she'd had the nerve to call him on his behavior. He was six feet tall and towered over her, yet she'd very soundly put him in his place.

That simple touch was the moment he fell in love with her. Deep and hard and forever.

He'd laughed. "Point taken. When can I see you again?"

She'd smiled back and said, "I'll see you at the ice-skating rink Friday after school."

That had been the first of many meetings. It had taken him a while to realize that she was always with a group of people, and that they were never alone. But she was so much fun to be with, he never complained. At least, not at first. As time passed, he began maneuvering to get her alone, because he wanted more than a kiss. He wanted to hold her and touch her and put himself inside her.

All of his friends thought he was a stud, because that's what he'd let them think. His sister Libby's experience of being an unwed mother had kept him from having sex because he didn't want to get some girl pregnant. But he'd never loved a girl like he loved Jennie. And he wanted her more than he'd ever wanted anything in his life.

It took him a while to get Jennie to admit that her parents were adamant about abstinence before marriage.

He'd argued, "You're fourteen. I'm sixteen. You're talking about *years* before we're old enough to get married!"

"I agree. Which is why I'm willing to have sex with you before then."

It was the second time since he'd met her that she'd stunned him into silence.

"I don't dare go to a doctor in town for birth control pills, because my parents are liable to find out. So you're going to have to use condoms," she said.

He remembered listening soberly to this speech, but he was afraid that in reality, his jaw might have been hanging open in shock. She spoke so matter-of-factly, as though they were discussing how much homework they had to get done before they could meet up to go to the movies with friends.

"And we'll need a safe place to go. Somewhere with a bed. I'm not going to make love to you for the first time in the front seat of your pickup."

By then he *was* gawking. "You have someplace in mind?" he'd managed to ask.

"Your father keeps a suite at the Wort Hotel for businessmen who come into town. Is there any way to find out when it might be free for us to use?"

"You have some date in mind for this meeting?" he asked, arms crossed defensively, still rattled by how easily she was discussing what he considered a sensitive subject.

For the first time, she seemed uncertain. She put both of her hands on his arms and leaned up on tiptoe to kiss him on the lips. Then she looked into his eyes and said, "I love you so much I almost can't bear it. I want to be with you, to be flesh of one flesh."

It wasn't the first time she'd slipped in some phrase from the Bible when they'd been talking, but nothing she'd ever said had resonated with him as much as those words did. It brought home to him the significance of what they were about to do.

But it didn't keep him from wanting to be with her, from wanting to make love to her.

He cleared his throat, which had swollen almost shut, and said, "I'll check and see when we can get the room and let you know."

Her voice was almost a whisper when she added, "I hope it's soon."

Jennie was nowhere near as calm and collected once they were in the hotel room alone. Her hands were shaking, and she stuttered several times when she tried to speak. Seeing her so rattled made him feel protective.

He pulled her into his arms and whispered in her ear, "It's just me, sweetheart. We have all the time in the world. If you're not ready, we can leave and come back another time."

She'd swallowed and said, "I don't think I'd have the courage to do this again. My parents—"

She cut herself off, but he knew how hard it was for her to go against what her parents had taught her.

"Let's just lie down and hold each other," he said, leading her over to the bed. They climbed onto the bed and lay down with their heads on the pillows facing each other.

"Come here," he said, pulling her into his arms.

She snuggled close, her nose against his throat, and murmured, "I didn't expect to be this nervous."

The truth was, he was every bit as edgy as she seemed to be. He'd experimented plenty, but he was essentially as much a virgin as she was. He knew making love the first time might hurt her, and he wasn't looking forward to that. And he wanted to make it good for her, but he wasn't sure how to do that, either. He felt foolish and fumbling, but he didn't want to expose his ineptness, because the guy was supposed to know what he was doing and lead the way.

Luckily for him, Jennie was a lot smarter than he was about this sort of thing. She made it easy for him by telling him what she wanted, what felt good, and at the same time asking him what he liked.

"Would you touch me here?" she said, moving

his hand lower on her body. She moved her own hand to a similar spot on his body and said, "Should I touch you here?"

Little by little, they began to explore each other's bodies more freely. Clothes came loose. And then came off. Until they were naked and he was poised over her, ready for the final step that would unite them.

"I don't want to hurt you."

"You won't."

"I might not do it right."

"You will."

He'd taken the time to arouse her, and he knew she was wet, but she was small and he could feel from the way she tensed that he was too large and it was hard for her to take him inside. He grunted when he'd penetrated enough to feel a barrier keeping him out. He would have retreated, but he felt her hands on him and her voice urging, "Don't stop. Please, Matt. I want you inside me."

He thrust hard and soothed the small cry of pain with a kiss. When he was seated to the hilt, he met her gaze and saw the light of feminine satisfaction there. And knew it would be all right.

It wasn't all good. It was over too soon, and she bled a bit. But he did his best to comfort her, kissing the tears—of joy or pain or whatever it was she was feeling, he was never sure—from her dove-gray eyes.

They'd learned a great deal from each other over the next few months, always careful to use a condom to protect Jennie from pregnancy. He could still remember the wonder on her face the first time she'd experienced an orgasm. And the joy he'd experienced making it happen again. And again.

And then disaster had struck. Jennie was late.

"Maybe you're not pregnant," he'd argued. "Maybe it's something else."

She'd looked at him with serious eyes and said, "I've been as regular as clockwork from the first time I had a period."

"But we've been careful!"

"Condoms aren't a hundred percent effective."

"But we've been careful!" he'd repeated.

She'd walked into his arms and held him tight and whispered, "What are we going to do? I can't tell my parents. They'll be so angry and disappointed in me." She'd met his gaze with troubled eyes and said, "They'll never let me see you again."

"Wait a minute! They can't do that."

"They can. And they will. I'm fourteen years old. They're my parents. They can do anything they want."

"We'll run away," he said.

"And go where? And live how?"

He'd always admired Jennie's practicality, but right now it was getting in the way of what he wanted. "We'll figure out a way to be together," he told her, holding her tight in his arms, terrified of losing her. "We'll figure out something to make this work."

But he was afraid that she was right. That the adults in their lives would make all the decisions "for their own good," and that they would be separated from each other and from their child. He hadn't planned on being a father so soon, but he figured he could learn what he needed to know. How hard could it be to take care of a baby?

He would ask his father for a loan of enough money to cover living expenses in a home of their own until they finished high school and college. They'd need to pay a nanny while they were in school. Surely his father would bend that far. He never let himself imagine a future that didn't include Jennie and their child, as fantastical as that might seem.

But somehow he never got around to saying anything to his father. He must have known deep in his heart that the fantasy life he'd planned for himself and Jennie was just that. A fantasy. That neither his father nor her parents were going to allow the two of them to "play house."

But he didn't want to face reality. So he kept her pregnancy a secret from his father, hoping that once the baby was born King would see how much Matt wanted to be a father to his child and help make his dream of a future with Jennie and their baby come true.

From the beginning of Jennie's pregnancy, Matt worried about her health. He didn't understand how someone so tiny could throw up so much and survive.

"It's just morning sickness. It'll pass."

It did. She wore blousy clothes to hide the changes in her body. He loved watching their child grow inside her. He was enchanted by the look on her face the first time the baby moved—"Like a butterfly," she said—inside her. Loved the changes in Jennie and feared them. She was getting so big! How could her parents not see the truth? He marveled at how hard her belly was, when it had once been so soft.

Their idyll lasted for six months.

One morning, the principal called him to the office, and Jennie was there with her parents. His insides clenched when he saw the heightened color in her cheeks. She never looked up from her hands, which were knotted together in her lap.

The principal asked him to sit down, but he said, "I'll stand." And he did, his hands stuck in the back pockets of his Levi's to keep anyone from seeing how they were shaking.

"You are not to go within twenty feet of Jennifer Fairchild when she is in school," the principal said. "Is that understood?"

"Who's going to stop me?" he snarled.

Jennie looked up at him with dismay in her wounded gray eyes, and he realized he'd given exactly the wrong answer. He should have been smarter. He should have pretended to agree.

"See what I mean?" Jennie's father said. "He's an animal! I want him expelled."

"I understand your concern, Mr. Fairchild, but since Jennie says the sex was consensual—"

Mr. Fairchild pointed a daggerlike finger at Matt. "He's responsible for this abomination!"

"Daddy, please. It's not Matt's fault!" Jennie cried.

"Shut up!" Her father raised his hand as though to strike her, and Matt lunged for him.

The principal stepped between them, catching

the arm that would have struck Jennie and keeping Matt from reaching her father. "Go back to class, Matt."

"That sonofabitch was going to hit her!"

"I'll take care of it. Go back to class. Now."

Matt leaned around the principal and said, "You better not touch her, you bastard."

"Matt! Leave!" the principal said.

He'd stalked out, determined to see Jennie as soon as she left the principal's office, already planning how they could run away together.

But that was the last time he'd seen her.

Jennie's parents had sent her away somewhere he couldn't find her. He'd gone crazy trying to locate her, but all his efforts had been in vain. He'd gone to his father for help, but King thought things were better left as they were. He'd heard nothing about Jennie for the next three months, until his father told him that she'd died during childbirth, along with their baby. The pain he'd felt was like a blistering fire in his chest that burned down through his gut.

Matt had become a wild child, refusing to follow rules, constantly getting into trouble, not caring whether he ended up in jail. King had made sure none of his troubles came to public light. It was almost a year later that Uncle Angus revealed that Matt's child was alive—and so was Jennie. Angus had found their little girl, but Jennie's whereabouts, now that the baby had been born and supposedly died, remained a mystery. Uncle Angus told him that his father had known all along where Jennie had been taken when she left Jackson, and that he'd lied to Matt to keep him from ruining his life.

Matt could still remember the first time he'd held Pippa in his arms. She'd looked back at him with Jennie's gray eyes, and it had taken all his fortitude not to break down. He'd taken his daughter and gone as far from his manipulative, scheming, controlling father as he could get.

And goddamned if he wasn't back here again. King hadn't changed. He was the same lying bastard he'd always been.

It had taken years more to find Jennie. By then, Matt was married to a woman he hoped would be a good mother for his daughter. It turned out Jennie was married, too, to the junior senator from Texas, Jonathan Hart, living part-time in Washington and part-time on her husband's Texas ranch.

She'd never had another child, which made Matt wonder if there had, in fact, been complications when Pippa was born that made it impossible for Jennie to have any more children. He bore a great deal of the responsibility for that tragedy, if it was true. He was the one who'd gotten her pregnant when she was only fourteen.

They were both older and wiser. He wanted to see Jennie again, to hold her in his arms, to kiss her, to make love to her. And if that weren't possible, at the very least she deserved to know that their daughter was alive and well.

It was that last part he feared Jennie would never understand or forgive. Because of what he'd done, she'd never had a chance to experience the joy of being a mother and raising their child. Matt had stolen that opportunity from her when he took Pippa and disappeared.

He wondered if Jennie had ever discovered the truth. Did she have any inkling that their daughter was alive? Or would Pippa's existence come as a complete surprise to her?

Their daughter had never needed a mother's advice and counsel more than she did now. He shouldn't put off contacting Jennie any longer. After all, reconnecting with her was one of the main reasons he'd agreed to come to America. That and the opportunity to punish King Grayhawk. Thwarting King was the easy part. The hard part was finding the courage to seek out Jennie with the truth.

Chapter 12

PIPPA SPENT A restless night considering everything her father had said, wondering about her mother—and wondering what sort of mother she herself would be. Her resentment had grown overnight. Her father had not only cheated himself when he'd left her mother behind. He'd cheated Pippa as well.

She was having trouble coping with her feelings. Her father had always been her hero, but lately, it felt like he was pressuring her to make the choice he thought would be best for her. The same way he'd made the choice to keep her mother from her. She didn't agree with either one.

She felt confused and unhappy. In Australia she would have taken Beastie and gone into the Outback and let the sunshine and open spaces heal her soul. She'd found a similar escape here in Wyoming at the pond, but she couldn't take the chance of running into Devon. She felt trapped.

She arrived in the kitchen for breakfast and discovered to her dismay that the twins had returned.

"So you've decided to join us this morning. To what do we owe the honor?" Taylor said from her seat at the breakfast bar. She was eating a bowl of oatmeal. Victoria sat beside her with a bowl of strawberries in front of her.

"How was Texas?" Pippa said in an attempt to remain cordial.

"Frustrating," Victoria admitted. "We didn't find out a thing we didn't know before we left."

"What were you hoping to discover?" Pippa asked, her curiosity piqued.

"Why your father left," Taylor said. "And why he came back."

"To what end?" Pippa asked, dropping a slice of bread into the toaster—checking the setting before she pushed down the lever—and then retrieving her Vegemite from the fridge.

"So we can figure out how to get him to leave again," Taylor said.

Pippa immediately felt both alarmed and indignant on her father's behalf. Especially since she now knew that at least one of the reasons her father had returned was to reunite with her mother, a story in which King seemed to be the villain. "Maybe instead of snooping into my father's life you should be examining the actions of someone a little closer to home—like your own father."

"What does King have to do with Matt leaving?" Victoria asked.

Pippa realized she'd opened a can of worms, and that if she wasn't careful they might all wriggle out. The more she said, the more she would be revealing of her father's private business. The last thing she wanted to do was give her horrid aunts ammunition they could use against her dad. What if they pressured King for answers and he gave them?

"Forget I said anything." She got a knife from the drawer, retrieved the toast when it popped up, and began slathering it with Vegemite.

"You brought it up," Taylor said, dropping her spoon on the granite bar with a clatter. "You're the one slinging mud. Finish what you started."

Pippa pursed her lips. *Slinging mud?* There were so many things she *hadn't* said that she wished she could.

"Why can't you just leave me alone?"

"Because you won't leave us alone," Victoria retorted. "You and Matt and your nuisance of a brother are turning our lives upside down."

Pippa bit her tongue. It was bad enough to attack her or her father, but Nathan should have been off-limits. She saw a flash of remorse on Victoria's face when she realized what she'd said, but it was too late. The words had already been spoken.

"Vick is right," Taylor said. "None of you belongs here. This is *our* home. You should go back where you came from."

Pippa gladly would have returned to Australia, but she couldn't. Her home was gone, and she was pregnant. But these two women knew nothing about that, nothing about her or her father or her brother or what they'd been through over the years to survive.

Her hormones were working overtime, and Pippa felt angry tears rising in her eyes. Her throat was swollen with emotion, and she was only a heartbeat away from screaming in rage and frustration. She wasn't about to give her aunts the satisfaction of seeing her fall apart.

She left her toast sitting on a plate on the counter and headed for the door.

Taylor slipped off her bar stool and caught Pippa's arm as she hurried past, stopping her. "Hold on a minute. I'm not done talking to you."

Pippa looked down at her arm and then back at Taylor through dangerously narrowed eyes. "Let go of me." Her father had taught her enough self-defense that she could easily have broken her aunt's arm to free herself.

Taylor held on long enough to say, in a voice more poignant for its quiet intensity, "I just want to know what's going on. We're being thrown out of our home. Can you understand that?"

Pippa understood all too well. But the last thing she wanted to feel was sympathy for her aunts. She jerked her arm free, then met Taylor's gaze and said, "Your father is at the bottom of all this. Get your answers from him. Just stay the bloody hell away from me!"

She grabbed her coat and managed not to run as she escaped out the door. She couldn't spend a whole year with King's Brats. She couldn't spend another minute with them!

Pippa started toward the stable, scrubbing at the tears in her eyes, and stopped in her tracks. If she went to the pond, she might run into Devon, and she was certain that if he opened his arms, she'd walk right into them. That sounded wonderful, but she couldn't accept comfort—or kisses—

from him without telling him the truth. Was she ready to do that? Not now. Not yet.

She wanted more of the tenderness, the kindness, the *friendship* he'd offered, all of which might go away when she told him she was carrying another man's child. But honestly, if she spent more time with him, how long could she hide the fact that she was pregnant? Not long. She felt like an animal on the run, desperate to avoid the perilous, steel-jawed trap that seemed poised to snap closed on her.

Pippa couldn't seem to catch her breath. It felt like she was suffocating. She gasped a breath of air and realized her lungs still felt empty. She sucked in another breath, frightened at how hard it was to get enough air to relieve the pressure in her chest.

She saw her father's pickup parked at the back door and realized she needed to get away faster and farther than a horse could take her. Pippa took a chance that the keys would be over the visor, where he usually kept them. She had the engine started and was ready to slam the truck into gear when she was startled by a knock on the window. She angled her head and saw her father standing there, a worried look on his face.

She debated whether to drive away or open the window.

He knocked again insistently, and she heard him say, "Open the window, Pippa, and talk to me."

She opened the window and asked, "What do you want, Daddy?"

"Where are you going?"

She started to make a flippant response, but she didn't want to argue with him. She just wanted to be gone before he realized how close to the edge she was. "I'm going to town for breakfast."

He frowned, and she realized he wasn't sure whether to believe her.

"The twins are back," she said. "I can't endure any more ear-bashing from them."

He pursed his lips, acknowledging her point. "When will you be back?"

"I'm not sure," she said, irritated that he'd asked, making her feel like a kid with a curfew. He was the one responsible for her being in this situation. If she'd had a mother . . . If he'd sent her away to school . . . If he'd said something about Tim being married . . . This was all his fault!

"King made plans yesterday to spend time with Nathan at the barn this morning," she added. So he couldn't accuse her of shirking that responsibility. "I don't know how long I'll be gone."

"Maybe you should see an obstetrician. At least get an appointment."

Pippa's neck hairs hackled. "Oh, so now you want me taking care of this baby? The one you want me to give away?"

"I want you taking care of yourself," he replied through tight jaws.

"And the baby can go to hell?"

"Don't put words in my mouth."

Pippa felt her face heating and her stomach revolting. "Don't worry, Daddy. I'll take care of myself *and* my baby. You don't have to worry about either one of us!"

She gunned the engine, the tires screeching as she backed the truck, then took off down the drive that led to the main road, scattering gravel and leaving a trail of dust.

As she raced away, she watched her father in the rearview mirror through eyes blurred by tears. She felt another spurt of resentment toward him. Sure he loved her and wanted the best for her, but she felt smothered by his concern.

Pippa was suddenly gasping for air again and quickly pulled to the side of the road. She crossed her arms on the steering wheel and dropped her head onto her hands, choking and sobbing. She wanted to run away. But where could she go? And how would she support herself when she got there?

She felt the urgent need to escape, to run away from all her troubles. But there was no escape from the reality she faced. A child—her child—was growing inside her. In a matter of months she would be a mother.

I want my mother.

She realized that made no sense. She'd never had a mother to seek advice from. Her father had always been the one she'd turned to. But it was her mother she wanted, all the same. She needed a sympathetic ear. She needed a soft shoulder to cry on. She needed someone who would be on her side. She had a mother out there somewhere who could perhaps fill all those needs. The problem was Jennifer Hart might not want anything to do with her supposedly dead daughter—even if Pippa hadn't been unwed and pregnant.

Pippa wasn't sure how long she sat there, but

her stomach growled, and she realized she was hungry. She swiped the tears from her eyes with her sleeve, started the pickup, and followed the road into Jackson.

Staying on the correct side of the road required concentration, which was a blessing, because her mind skittered from one possibility for the rest of her life to the next and the next, without ever settling on one. She had no idea what she wanted to do and no idea where to go from here.

The one thing Pippa knew for sure was that she wanted to meet her mother. She knew her mother's name and that she was living in Texas. Surely she could find her.

Every time Pippa got to that point, she couldn't help wondering how her mother would feel about a long-lost pregnant daughter who showed up unexpectedly. Maybe she should wait until the baby was born. But she was only in the first trimester. Did she really want to wait that long?

Pippa was no closer to knowing what she wanted to do when she reached town than she had been when she'd left the ranch. She parked her father's pickup on the town square, which she found quaint—because each of the four corners had a wide, freestanding arch built entirely of weather-whitened antlers. The nearest establishments were nightspots and art galleries, and she started walking down Cache Street, looking for a café where she could get some breakfast.

She turned left onto Broadway, the main street through town, figuring that was the most likely place to find what she was looking for. Instead she discovered ice cream shops and fashion outlets. She turned right on King Street and found the Sweetwater Restaurant, but it didn't open until 11:30. She glanced at her watch. It was 8:30 a.m.

She was standing on the corner, trying to decide which way to go, when she spied Devon across the street. He was coming out of one of the Jackson Hole Fire Department's open truck bays cradling something in his arms that was swathed in a baby blanket.

Curiosity kept her standing in place. Then he looked up and saw her, and it was too late to escape without being noticed. She blotted her damp eyelashes again with her sleeve, wondering if he could tell she'd been crying.

He seemed as unsure as she was about what to do. Then he crossed the street and headed toward her.

"What do you have there?" she asked when he reached her.

He opened the blanket so she could see inside. "It's a juvenile Great Gray Owl."

Pippa studied the tiny gray-and-white-feathered bird, its yellow eyes sunken in concave circles bracketed by downy gray backward parentheses.

"One of the firefighters found this little one on the ground after they put out a small forest fire. The vet told him it probably wouldn't survive because of smoke damage to its lungs, but it was still alive this morning, so my brother Brian—he's a firefighter year-round and a smoke jumper in the summer—called me to come pick it up."

"Can you help it?"

He covered the owl back up. "I can give it a quiet place to recuperate, and it either will survive, or it won't." He surveyed her face and asked, "Are you all right?"

Pippa flushed at his perusal, knowing she must look like hell warmed over. "I'm fine," she lied.

"What are you doing here in town?"

"Things got a little crazy at the ranch, and I made a break for it."

"Sounds like the Brats have been acting bratty again." He smiled, one side of his mouth tilting higher than the other, his eyes twinkling with mischief.

Pippa suppressed a gasp as her body flooded with desire. How did he do it? How did he make her want him with so little effort? "I'd better go," she said.

"Have you had breakfast yet?"

She thought about lying again but then shook her head. She was hungry, and she needed to eat to keep her stomach from getting upset. "I've been looking for an open restaurant."

"I need to get this owl settled into a comfortable nest. How about coming home with me? I can offer you scrambled eggs and bacon." He must have seen she was on the fence, because he added, "You can meet Satan—the horse that refuses to be tamed."

She was intrigued as much by the chance to see where Devon lived as by the horse that couldn't be broken. Besides, visiting his cabin would keep her away from home a little while longer. "All right," she said. "I'll come."

"Are you here with anybody?"

"I'm on my own."

"Where are you parked? Do you want to follow me?"

She recalled her harrowing trip into town trying to stay on the opposite side of the road from what she was used to, and said, "I'd rather ride with you."

"Fine. Come on."

When they reached his Dodge Ram, which was parked a little farther down the street, he opened the door so she could step up into it. Before he shut the door, he handed the owl to her and said, "Do you mind holding him? He'll do better if he's kept warm."

As Pippa cradled the tiny bird, it dawned on her that in a few months she would be holding her own child in her arms. Assuming her father didn't wear her down and convince her to give it away to a loving family. Pippa bit her lower lip. Surely she had more willpower than that.

She wondered if it might be possible to go live with her mother. She imagined a scene where she introduced herself in one breath and admitted she was pregnant and unmarried and needed a place to stay in the next. Tears rose in her eyes, and she turned away from Devon as she blinked them back. Waiting wasn't going to solve anything. She'd just end up greeting her mother for the first time unwed, homeless, and with a newborn baby in her arms.

"Penny for your thoughts?"

Pippa glanced around and saw they were passing the elk refuge outside of town. She wished she were as free to roam as they were. But she was as bogged down by her circumstances as a calf in a mudhole. Since she wasn't ready to reveal her pregnancy to Devon, she said, "My father admitted to me that my mother is still alive, and that she's living in Texas."

"Wow! That's . . . Wow! Are you going to call her? Maybe go see her?"

She shrugged. "I don't know. She doesn't know I exist. Her parents told her I died at birth."

Devon raised a brow in astonishment. "And no one ever told her the truth?"

"My dad never did. I don't suppose her parents did, either, since they were the ones who lied to her in the first place."

Pippa noticed they'd turned off the state road onto what must once have been a wagon trail bounded on both sides by thick forest. "It looks like you live off the beaten path."

He grinned. "Yep. We have another half hour or so to go to get to my cabin." He hesitated, then said, "I have to admit I was surprised to see you in town."

She sighed. "The Brats aren't the only ones making my life difficult. When I got home from our picnic my little brother Nathan was missing, and the police were there helping to search for him." She saw Devon's alarm and interjected, "We found him and he was fine. But it's my job to watch him, and my dad wasn't too happy with me for delegating the responsibility to Leah. We argued about that . . . and other things."

"So you didn't just come into town for break-fast without the Brats."

She shook her head, feeling her throat tighten-ing again, feeling the crushing weight in her chest that made it hard to breathe. "I needed to get away. From Daddy. From the Brats. From . . . every-thing."

"Then I'm glad I ran into you. You're welcome to hang out at my place for as long as you like."

Pippa caught her lower lip in her teeth. There it was in front of her. A bolt-hole for a haunted ani-mal on its last legs, so exhausted it can barely draw breath. Pippa grabbed at the chance to escape with her life. "Do you have room for me?"

He looked startled for a second, then said, "You mean somewhere for you to sleep over-night?"

She nodded, realizing that she'd misconstrued his offer, but desperate enough that she was willing to accept a bed on the floor if that was all he had. "Anything would do. A pallet on the floor is fine."

He raised a brow at that, and Pippa realized she had to do a better job of hiding her anxiety. She didn't want him asking questions she wasn't yet willing to answer.

"It's no trouble," he said. "I have a second bedroom. I'm just a little . . . I mean, after what happened at the pond, I'm surprised you asked."

Pippa flushed and shot him a look from be-neath lowered lashes. She was the one who'd said she couldn't be his friend anymore. Did she owe him an explanation? She lifted her gaze to meet his and said, "There's a lot going on I can't tell you about. It would mean a lot to me if I could stay with you for a little while."

He shrugged as though it were no big deal, and said, "My house is your house."

Pippa tried to smile in thanks but couldn't manage it. What had she just done? Was she really going to stay with Devon and not go home? Why not? As she'd told her father, she was a grown woman. She could make her own decisions. Right now, space from her father and her aunts was something she needed as much as she needed air to breathe. She felt a fleeting remorse for leaving Nathan on his own, but there was no help for it.

She considered calling to let her father know what she was doing and where she would be staying but decided against it. Knowing how protective he was, and judging by his behavior when she'd taken off with Tim, she was pretty sure he'd insist she come home. She didn't want to have to fight him. She needed time and distance to figure out what to do about her baby. About her mother. About her life.

She'd left the keys in her father's truck, and he could easily find it in town. She'd text him tomorrow and tell him that she was fine and that she'd be in touch when she was ready to come home—if and when that time came.

Pippa felt a niggling sense of unease but tamped it down. She needed the space to breathe freely again. And she was going to do whatever was necessary to get it.

Chapter 13

PIPPA ISSUED AN "Aaah!" of appreciation when she saw Devon's home for the first time. She hadn't expected his cabin in the mountains to look so rustic. The huge logs blended into the surrounding forest of pines and budding aspens and the pitched roof created a cozy porch across the entire front of the house. Scattered patches of snow surrounding the cabin were interspersed with sunlit patches of green growth.

"What a wonderful porch," she said.

"What a *necessary* porch," he replied as he took the owl-in-a-blanket from her. In response to her questioning look he explained, "That's the only way to keep the snow from blocking the front door in the winter."

Wulf came loping around the corner of the house and ran straight to Pippa to be petted.

"Hey," Devon said. "What about me?"

The wolf put his paws on Devon's shoulders and immediately stuck his nose into the blanket in his hands. Devon quickly pressed the blanket against his chest to protect the baby owl. "This is *not* food!"

Wulf dropped to all fours and headed up the

steps toward the front door, where he sat and waited to be let inside.

"I guess he must be hungry," Pippa said with a laugh.

"I keep him well fed so he doesn't turn the local cattle into lunch."

Pippa gestured toward the baskets filled with spring flowers that hung on the front of chest-high pine stumps. The stumps also provided a base for ornamental lamps on either side of the steps. "All of this is lovely."

"And also necessary," he said as he headed up the steps before her, cradling the owl. "It's pitch black out here at night."

The door wasn't locked, and he opened it and gestured her inside. "Welcome to my home."

Pippa shivered as her left breast accidentally brushed Devon's arm when Wulf crowded her as she entered the house. She took three steps inside, then turned in a circle that ended with her facing Devon, who stood just inside the door, which he'd closed behind him.

She smiled. "Your home looks like something from another century."

"I made most of the furniture myself," he admitted. "The buffalo hide I picked up from an estate sale, and I bought the Navajo rug over the fireplace at an art festival in town."

She crossed to a painting on the wall and studied it. She glanced back at him over her shoulder and asked, "Local art gallery?"

"Good guess, but no." He crossed to an empty cage on the kitchen floor, put the baby owl—

blanket and all—inside, and turned on a light above the cage intended to keep whatever was inside warm. Then he took off his coat and hung it on the back of one of the two stools at the cut-stone counter that separated the living room from the kitchen. He immediately began pulling out pots and pans.

"Can I help?" she asked.

He gestured with his chin toward one of the bar stools and said, "Make yourself comfortable. I've got this."

She arranged her coat on the back of the second stool and sat down. "So where did that lovely painting come from?"

"My brother Brian."

"It was a gift?"

"He's the artist."

Pippa swiveled the stool around to look at the exquisite painting again. "Brian the *firefighter*?"

Devon chuckled. "You sound surprised."

She swiveled the chair back around to face him. "I am."

"How do you like your eggs?" he asked.

"Scrambled."

"Bacon? Raisin toast?"

"Yes, please."

He spread a half dozen slices of bacon on a flat skillet and began cracking eggs into a bowl. He dropped four pieces of raisin toast in a toaster and shoved down the lever. Once he had their breakfast started, he began preparing what turned out to be a bowl of food for Wulf, who was investigating the owl with his nose. Pippa was interested to see that the bowl contained mostly raw meat, which finally diverted Wulf's attention from the injured bird.

Devon set down the bowl and continued, "Firefighters have a lot of spare time on their hands at the station. Some of them work out. Some learn to be better cooks. Some read a lot of books. Brian spends his time painting."

She left the stool to take a closer look at the painting of a cowboy in a yellow slicker on horseback, riding along a creek with a single Black Angus cow in the foreground. She studied the cowboy's evocative face. He looked lonely and alone. "Your brother's a good artist."

"Better than just *good,* I think," Devon said. "But Brian refuses to show his art. He gives his paintings away to friends, but only if they promise not to reveal the artist."

"You Flynns are full of surprises," she said with a rueful smile. The smell of frying bacon filled the cabin and made it seem even more homey. Pippa's stomach growled as she studied the delicate spindles on the homemade rocker.

"Wait until you see the painting Brian did of your aunt Taylor," Devon said. "Now, *that's* a masterpiece!"

"How did he paint her?" she asked, sinking into the rocker and rocking a few times, making the hardwood floor creak.

"Stark naked."

She stopped rocking. "Uh-oh. That doesn't sound good." The toast had come up, and she watched him butter it.

"Can I get you something to drink? Orange juice? Milk? Coffee?"

"Milk, please."

He filled a glass of milk for her and poured himself a glass of orange juice. She realized he'd set two places for them at the breakfast bar, including plates, silverware, and napkins.

"Actually," he continued, "what Brian painted was a naked fairy reclining in a forest glade surrounded by wild animals. It looked a lot like an illustration for a children's book—except for the nudity. The fairy just happened to have Taylor's face, and I suppose what Brian imagined Taylor's naked body might look like. It certainly had Taylor's generous curves. Then he donated the painting to one of the charities in town for their silent auction."

"Oh, that's brilliant, in a terrible sort of way."

"Breakfast is served," he said.

She realized he'd retrieved the plates and loaded them with food before returning them to the counter. She settled back on her bar stool and surveyed the huge breakfast. "This looks great. I'm not sure I can eat it all."

He grinned. "Wulf will take care of the leftovers."

As he left the kitchen and joined her at the bar she asked, "What did Taylor do when she saw Brian's painting of her?"

"As you can imagine, she wasn't real happy when she found out about it. Especially since the painting wasn't signed and nobody knew who the artist was. She tried to buy the thing, but someone kept outbidding her, and she lost it." He picked up a slice of bacon, which quickly disappeared, along with a couple of forkfuls of eggs.

"Did she ever find out who ended up with it?"

He laughed. "Brian bought it, of course."

"And she never found out he was the culprit?"

"I didn't say that." He ate a triangle of toast in three bites. "Taylor's pretty resourceful. She offered someone at the charity a big donation if they'd spill the beans. They did. Not just that Brian was the artist, but that he'd bought the painting to keep for himself. Ever since, she and Brian have been scratching and clawing at each other like two bobcats in a gunnysack."

Pippa smiled. "It's hard to think of my aunt as a victim after all the trouble she's caused me and my father since we arrived."

"You must admit King played a pretty dirty trick on your aunts, giving away Kingdom Come to a son who'd disappeared for twenty years without a word."

She drank a few swallows of milk before setting the glass down. "So why not be mad at King instead of my father and me?"

Devon shrugged. "Maybe they hope your dad will pick up and leave. From what I've heard, he needs to stay at Kingdom Come for an entire year before it's his. That gives the Brats a lot of time to make Matt's life hell and hope he heads for the hills."

"They don't know my father. He isn't going anywhere."

He lifted a skeptical brow. "Maybe not, but

I'm afraid your behavior today is only going to encourage them."

"What do you mean?"

"Haven't you just run away? They're going to think that whatever they're doing is working."

She almost blurted out the truth about the biggest reason she'd left the ranch, but the words got caught in her throat. She swallowed hard and said, "There are things going on between me and my dad that have nothing to do with his coming here to live."

A silence fell between them, and she knew Devon was waiting for her to elaborate. She stared down at her plate and realized she'd eaten every bite of the enormous plate of food he'd put in front of her. She looked at his plate and saw it was empty as well. "Since you made breakfast, I should do the dishes."

"The dishes will be fine in the sink," he said, jumping up and stealing her plate and silverware. "I'll stack them in the dishwasher later." The dishes landed in the sink with a clatter. He turned back to her and said, "I want to introduce you to Satan."

"Where are you keeping him?"

"In the barn. Shall we go?"

He helped her into her coat, then put his own on as Pippa followed him out the door. Wulf was on her heels, but Devon said, "Wulf, stay."

He sat down but yelped at being left behind.

"He wants to come," Pippa said, glancing back at the wolf.

Devon firmly shut the door. "I keep my menagerie of wounded animals in the barn—which includes a fawn right now. Wulf would just as soon eat her as look at her."

"I see," Pippa said with a laugh.

When they got to the barn, he led her past several stalls containing horses that thrust their heads out to be petted. Pippa greeted each one—with a pat on the jaw, by scratching behind the ears, by soothing a silken nose—and then reached the last stall, where a coal-black horse was backed up in the corner facing out, every powerful muscle tense, nostrils flared, his ears laid back flat against his head.

When Pippa laid a hand on the stall door, Satan raced at her with a shrieking cry of challenge, teeth bared. If she hadn't stepped back she would have lost her fingers when he snapped at her. Once she was at a safe distance, Satan backed up again into the corner, ready to attack if she tried to come near again.

Pippa stayed where she was, just out of reach of the stallion's teeth, and studied the beautiful animal. Which was when she noticed the scars on his chest. And on his neck. And on his flanks.

"He was beaten!" she said, outraged on the animal's behalf.

"Yes, he was. Repeatedly."

Pippa heard the anger in Devon's voice and asked, "Did you punish whoever did it?"

"I don't know who did it. By the time I got Satan he'd been through several good-hearted owners who wanted to help but couldn't do anything with him." He met her gaze and said bitterly, "I'm one of them." He took a step closer, and the stallion's black body quivered with fury—and with fear. Devon backed up, putting enough distance between himself and the wary animal so that Satan remained in place. "Do you think you can help?"

Pippa observed the stallion's defensive stance, feeling pity well up inside her. "I don't know. I've never seen a horse as damaged as this one."

Devon's shoulders drooped.

She put a hand on his arm. "But I'm willing to try."

Chapter 14

DEVON AND PIPPA had spent the morning on horseback as he showed her around his ranch, where his Angus cows were suckling their spring calves, returning to the house in time for lunch. He'd asked her if she wanted to call her father and let him know that she was planning to stay overnight with him, but she'd declined. He'd taken one look at her troubled face and let the subject drop.

After they'd eaten some sandwiches and chips, she'd insisted on loading the dishwasher while he made some business calls. Then she'd settled into the comfortable corduroy chair in his living room to read some of his ranch journals while he finished up paperwork for his cow-calf operation—and tried to figure out what to do about their sleeping arrangements.

Devon had told Pippa he had two bedrooms, which was true, but he was using the second one as an office. The second bedroom contained a full bath, and he'd put an enormous upholstered couch in the room, which his brothers had told him made a comfortable place to sleep.

While they were having dinner, he'd convinced

Pippa to take his bed while he slept on the couch in his office. She was in his bedroom right now—with the door closed—changing into one of his plaid wool shirts and a pair of long john bottoms he'd provided in lieu of pajamas, which he didn't wear.

He glanced at his watch as he reached for the ringing phone. He'd been expecting this call—and dreading it. Someone was surely looking for Pippa by now. He'd said nothing to his brothers about meeting Pippa at the pond, because he knew they'd give him a hard time about it. But since he was a Flynn, he was as suspect as his brothers whenever there was trouble in Jackson.

As soon as he picked up the phone, Brian said, "Pippa Grayhawk is missing. Matt's crazy with worry. He found his truck abandoned in town. Do you have any idea where she might be?"

"She's here with me."

"You'd better call Matt and let him know she's all right."

"I can't do that."

"Why not?"

"Pippa needs some time to herself. I'm making sure she gets it."

"Are you telling me she's planning to stay there overnight with you?"

"Overnight and as many nights as she wants," Devon replied.

"Holy shit, Devon! What's gotten into you? Have you gone nuts?"

"Pippa's a grown-up. She can decide what she wants to do with her life."

"She's *nineteen*," Brian said. "You're *twenty-*

eight. What are you doing getting involved with a kid like that?"

"She'll be twenty in a couple of months." That response sounded lame even to Devon's ears. "The point is, she's had plenty of opportunities to contact her father, but she hasn't. All I'm doing is giving her a safe place to stay until whatever argument she had with Matt blows over."

"Don't you think Matt deserves to know she's safe? That she hasn't been kidnapped and killed and buried in a shallow grave? You know we had those teenage girls go missing a while back. The ones who turned up dead?"

Devon had forgotten because the culprit had supposedly been caught. That didn't mean there weren't other loonies out there, so he could understand Matt's fear. But surely Pippa wouldn't leave him to worry long. "Pippa asked for my help. I can't refuse her any more than I could refuse to help any creature that needs a refuge."

"What's going on, Devon? Are you infatuated with her or something?"

It was definitely *something*, Devon thought, but he wasn't sure exactly what himself. "I told you, I'm only giving her a place to stay."

"At least let me tell Matt she's safe," Brian pleaded.

At that moment the bedroom door opened and Pippa stepped out. Her eyebrows were raised, as though questioning who was on the phone.

Devon hissed in a breath when he realized she was wearing his shirt but her very long, very attractive legs were bare. The long john trousers dangled from one hand. Apparently, she'd been halfway done dressing when the phone rang. He wondered if the rest of her was equally naked under his shirt. Her long hair had been released from its ponytail and fell over her shoulders like golden silk.

His body responded so quickly that he stepped behind the corduroy chair so she wouldn't see the thick ridge forming in his jeans.

"Who is that on the phone?" she asked.

He responded to the anxiety in her voice by covering the mouthpiece and saying quietly, "It's Brian."

Her eyes opened wide in concern, and her body remained tense as she took two steps toward him. "What are you telling him?"

"I've told him you're here—"

"Oh, no!" she wailed, crossing the rest of the distance between them and flinging the long johns over the top of the corduroy chair behind which he was standing.

He edged his body sideways, aware that it wasn't going to help the situation if she figured out the condition he was in. "Brian won't say anything."

"How do you know that?"

"Because I asked him not to."

"Devon? Are you there?" he heard Brian ask.

He took his hand off the mouthpiece but kept his eyes focused on Pippa. "I was telling Pippa that you won't spill the beans to her father about where she is."

"I think you're making a big mistake keeping her whereabouts a secret from Matt. Tell Pippa how worried he is."

"I don't think—"

"Tell her!" Brian insisted.

He covered the mouthpiece again. "Brian said to tell you that your father's going crazy wondering where you are, that he's imagining you dead in a ditch somewhere."

Pippa winced at the image Devon had described.

"Brian thinks you should give Matt a heads-up so he can stop hunting for you."

Pippa crossed her arms protectively, unintentionally raising the hem of the shirt—and Devon's blood pressure. Then her jaw firmed and she shook her head. "No."

"Why not?" Devon asked, curious as to why she wouldn't want to assuage her father's concern.

"Because Daddy's liable to come here and haul me home like a naughty five-year-old," she retorted. At his look of disbelief she added, "He's done it before!"

Devon felt a pang of misgiving. Pippa had run away before? When? And for how long? Maybe he was making a huge mistake keeping her here without her father's knowledge.

"I'll explain everything to you," she promised. "But please ask Brian to keep my whereabouts secret. Just for a little while."

Her gray eyes glistened in the firelight, and Devon realized he couldn't betray her. He took his hand off the mouthpiece and said, "I'm counting on you to keep what I've told you in confidence, Brian. Matt will just have to trust that his grown daughter can take care of herself."

"All right. I'll keep my trap shut. But I think this is a bad idea."

Devon ignored the warning, focusing instead on his brother's agreement to keep Pippa's presence a secret. "Thanks, Brian."

There was a pause before Brian said, "Be careful, Devon."

He eyed Pippa, who'd retrieved the long john bottoms and was stepping into them. "What does that mean?"

"Don't let yourself get embroiled in something you can't get yourself out of."

"There's nothing—"

"Keep your hands off Matt's daughter," Brian said flatly.

Devon felt himself flushing. "Goodbye, Brian."

"Don't forget what I said."

Devon hung up the phone. He wouldn't forget, because touching Pippa, holding her and kissing her and putting himself inside her, was all he'd thought about all day. He'd been surprised when she took up his offer of shelter, but he'd also been glad. This interlude would give them a chance to get better acquainted, even if it came at the cost of a little of Matt's peace of mind.

Pippa deftly pulled the long johns up under his wool shirt. It came to mid-thigh on her, so he still had no idea whether she was bare beneath his clothes. Once she had the leggings on she said, "Do you have a pair of wool socks I can borrow? My feet are cold."

"Sure. I'll be right back."

He headed into his bedroom and noticed that both a lacy bra and skimpy panties were dripping wet and hanging off the shower rod in his bathroom.

So she *had* been naked under that shirt.

He remembered Brian's warning. He needed to get some answers from Pippa before he let himself get any more involved emotionally—or physically—than he was. How recently had she run away? And why had her father come hunting her?

Devon grabbed a pair of thick, gray wool socks from his top drawer and headed back out to the main room of his cabin. Pippa was sitting cross-legged in his corduroy chair in front of the crackling fire, leaving him the rocker.

He tossed her the socks. "Here you go."

"Thanks, Devon." She uncurled her legs and pulled the socks on, then crossed her legs again.

To avoid staring—he couldn't help noticing that her toenails were painted a delicate pink—he busied himself putting more wood on the fire.

"I was going to bank this for the night," he said, down on one knee by the fire, "but I think we have a little talking to do first." When he was done, he sat down in the rocker and settled one ankle on the opposite knee. "You promised me an explanation. I'd like to hear it."

"I'm afraid what I'm about to say doesn't paint me in a very positive light," she began.

He waited for her to continue, watching as she

played with a loose string on one of the buttons on his shirt.

At last she looked up and met his gaze. She took a deep breath and said, "My father's cattle station in the Northern Territory was about forty-five minutes from Underhill, a town of six hundred people. There was nothing except flies, snakes, green frogs, and roos—that's kangaroos—for three hours in any direction."

Devon had known she'd grown up isolated from civilization, but what she described sounded more remote and exotic than anything he could have imagined.

She continued, "My stepmother—Nathan's mother—ran away when he was just a baby, so the closest female I might have spent time with lived in Underhill. My father went there once a week to shop for whatever we needed and collect the mail. He took me and Nathan along, because he didn't want to leave us alone at the station. Otherwise, I was surrounded, day in and day out, by a dozen young men, all of them my father's ringers—what you call cowboys."

"Your father didn't have a housekeeper?"

"I took care of the house—and Nathan. No woman wanted to live so far away from the world." Her voice was bitter as she added, "Especially Nathan's mother. That's why she left us."

"Didn't any of the cowboys—the ringers— have wives or girlfriends at the station?"

"It would have caused too much trouble to have a few women but not a woman for every man. Besides, the women wouldn't have stood for the isolation. Once a month the hands were allowed to go into town."

"Once a *month*?"

"They tended to drink too much, and they got into fights over the local girls. It was better to keep them at the station. They were allowed two beers every Friday night."

"Two whole beers?" he said sarcastically. "How could they stand that kind of isolation?"

"They didn't for long. You notice I said they were all *young* men. They worked for my father for the adventure of sleeping under the stars in the Outback, which they did during the muster—the roundup—on iron cots covered with mossy nets— that's mosquito nets."

She smiled ruefully and said, "I shouldn't have left out mosquitoes when I mentioned the wildlife in Australia. Anyway, the ringers saved money, because there was nothing to spend it on. When the romance had gone out of being in the Outback, they went home to the city, to their girlfriends or wives."

"Men left their wives behind? For how long?"

She shrugged. "Most never lasted more than a year or two on the station, but there were always other young men eager for a brief escape from the world."

"But you were stuck there."

"I was stuck," she agreed. "To be honest, I loved my life. At least, I did until I got old enough to start wondering about what it might be like to kiss one of those young men who worked for my father."

Devon felt a surge of jealousy at the thought of Pippa kissing another man and tamped it down. She was here now. Those men were long gone and far away.

"I knew it was likely none of them would hang around long enough to become a husband," she said. "I would have been better off looking for a nice young man in Underhill."

She paused, and he finished the thought for her. "But Underhill was forty-five minutes away. And the adventurers who worked for your father were right under your nose."

She grimaced. "Too right."

He wanted to take her in his arms and comfort her, but she clearly wasn't done with her story, and he was afraid if he did, he would never hear the rest of it.

"If I'd had a mother," she said, "or another woman at the station, I might have had someone to confide in when I began to have feelings for one of my father's wranglers. She would have cautioned me, or perhaps even betrayed me to my father, which would have prevented what happened."

He suddenly knew what she was going to say without having to hear it from her lips. "You ran away with one of your father's hired hands."

One of the tears that had brimmed in her eyes slipped onto her cheek. She swiped it away almost angrily. "His name was Tim Brandon."

He wanted desperately to ask what had happened next. Obviously, she hadn't stayed with the man. She was here in Wyoming, and the ringer was nowhere to be seen.

His patience was rewarded when she explained, "Shortly before we moved here, I ran away to Darwin with Tim." She hesitated, then added, "I was head over heels in love with him."

Devon hissed in a breath. That explained why she hadn't wanted to be more than *friends* with him. She was still in love with the other man. That didn't explain why she was here and her lover wasn't. He forced himself to ask, "What happened?"

She untangled her legs and dropped them on the floor, then looked at Devon with bleak eyes. "I'd left a note for my father telling him I was running away with Tim, because I didn't want him to worry. Which was a good thing, because Tim walked out on me when—"

She cut herself off and shot Devon an anxious look. Her gaze remained focused on her tangled hands, and she said nothing more for the next few moments, all the while chewing on her lower lip, as though deciding whether to finish her sentence.

Devon wondered what had caused Tim—what would cause any man—to walk out on her.

She lifted her chin and said almost defiantly, "It wasn't until we'd run away to Darwin that Tim admitted to me that he had a wife in Sydney."

Devon bit back an oath.

"As you might imagine," she continued hurriedly, "I was devastated. When I protested that he should have told me sooner, he walked out, and he didn't come back."

He rose and pulled her out of her chair and into his arms, holding her close and rocking her. He realized he was trembling with rage. "I'd like to get my hands on that sonofabitch."

"My father expressed exactly the same sentiments when he arrived—about an hour after Tim had left." She leaned back and looked up at him. "So you can see why I believe my father might haul me back home if he found me here with you. He would want to save me from myself. He'd think I've allowed myself to be fooled by another young man. He'd think . . ." She focused her gaze on his face, a frown between her brows. "He'd think we're a lot more than friends, when we're not."

Devon edged his hips away, because despite having taken her into his arms merely to comfort her, his body was reacting with a lot more than *friendliness*.

She stuck her nose against his throat and slipped her arms around his waist. "Thanks for listening. And for understanding."

He understood, all right. What he understood was that she'd recently suffered a terrible heartbreak and that despite being abandoned by her lover, she might still have strong feelings for the bastard. He understood that she might not trust any man—not even him—enough to fall in love again anytime soon. And he understood that he might be setting himself up for a lot of pain if he fell any further under her spell.

He should let her go. He should do his best to talk her into calling her father. Instead he hugged her tight and said, "You're safe here. No one will bother you. Tomorrow is soon enough to decide what you want to do next."

Chapter 15

Within twenty-four hours of her "disappearance," Pippa's father discovered—entirely by accident—where she was. Brian mentioned to Aiden at church that Pippa was with Devon—and was overheard by Connor's four-year-old daughter. The little girl then innocently repeated what she'd heard to Matt.

Matt immediately called Devon at home and demanded to speak to Pippa.

"Don't come here, Daddy," she warned him. "If you try to take me back to Kingdom Come, I'll only run again. I need time alone to think." Pippa waited with bated breath, afraid that her father was going to argue, bracing herself for a confrontation.

After a long hesitation, he surprised her by saying, "Fine. I'll stay away if you promise to get in touch if you need anything."

Pippa released the breath of air she'd been holding. She wasn't sure why her father had decided to give her the space she'd asked for without making a fuss, but she was grateful to him for it. She decided to take him up on his offer and said, "I need some clothes and toiletries." She listed them, then finished, "I'd appreciate your having them delivered here."

She hoped that hint would be enough to keep him from bringing them himself, and it was. The next day, one of her father's hired hands dropped off the items she'd requested.

When Pippa opened her suitcase, she almost threw away the note she found inside without reading it. She didn't want to see in writing all the reasons her father thought she should come back home. When she finally opened it, she discovered it was from her brother. It said:

I miss you, Pippa. Come home soon.
                              Nathan

She burst into tears, and Devon came running to see what was wrong. She waved the note and said, "My little brother misses me. We've never been separated before."

He pulled her into his arms and hugged her, which only made the tears flow more freely. Pippa put her arms around him and held him tight. She'd been as much a mother as a sister to her little brother, and it was hard to leave him behind. But she knew Nathan had at least one aunt—Leah— who doted on him, and their father spent as much time as he could with her little brother. Nathan would be fine. It was just hard walking away from someone she loved so much.

She loved her father, too, but he was the one putting roadblocks in her way. Leaving him was necessary if she wanted the space to figure out—on her own—what to do with the rest of her life. She sniffled once, then stepped back.

She swiped away the last of her tears and said, "Thanks for the hug, Devon. I needed it."

"Anytime." He smiled his lopsided smile, and Pippa felt her heart lift and soar like a bird on the wing.

She took another step back and stared at him, wondering what it was about Devon Flynn that made him seem so irresistible. It wasn't just his looks, although his strong, lean body appealed to her, and his face, with its pronounced cheekbones and straight nose and wide-spaced green eyes, drew her gaze whenever he was near. And it wasn't just his smile, although his smile made her smile— inwardly, if not outwardly—whenever she saw it. It was something else . . .

Pippa ended up with far more time to figure out what that "something else" was than she'd ever imagined. What she'd expected would be a few days or maybe a week with Devon quickly turned into three weeks.

Their days developed a "friendly" routine that felt comfortable. Breakfast together, then time in the barn—Devon with his injured wild animals and Pippa with the recalcitrant black stallion. Afterwards, Pippa went along with Devon on horseback as he made sure his fence was secure and checked his cows and their calves and his quarter horses for injuries or death from predators.

Sometimes they took along a picnic lunch. Other times they returned to the house to eat. Pippa often sat beside Devon in the afternoon as he explained how his cow-calf operation worked, how his quarter-horse breeding program was coming along, and how he dealt with the business of running a ranch. She'd brushed his arm with her breast once by accident and heard him hiss in a breath of air. After that, she was careful to keep her distance, but she noticed that the palpable tension never left his body whenever she was near.

She often saw what she thought was longing in his eyes, but he never acted on it. However, that didn't keep her from feeling its effects. She would watch Devon caress the orphaned fawn and the rabbit with the torn ear and shiver as she imagined his hands on her naked flesh.

Pippa did nothing to encourage Devon, but she did nothing to discourage him, either. Whenever they touched, electricity arced between them. She wanted him to hold her and kiss her and put himself inside her. She simply chose not to act on those feelings. For whatever reason, Devon was also careful to limit their physical contact, so the issue of perhaps turning their friendship into something more romantic never arose.

Their evenings were spent in front of the fire talking. That was where Pippa learned that, while Devon wanted to know everything about her, he was reluctant to share anything about himself.

Once she'd asked him, "Why do you live so far from your family?"

He'd merely shrugged.

"I would have given anything to have a sister or brother my own age when I was growing up,"

Pippa said. "Why don't you see more of your brothers? I mean, I've been here nearly three weeks and no one's come to visit, nor have you visited them. As far as I can tell, you haven't spoken to Aiden or Brian or Connor on the phone either, since that call from Brian the day I came here."

He stared at the fire, seemingly lost in thought. A small furrow appeared between his brows before he finally said, "My brothers haven't come to visit because they're busy with their own lives. I haven't called because I have nothing to say."

Pippa hadn't believed a word of it. She was certain his brothers stayed away—and Devon kept his distance from them—because he wanted it that way. But why? What had caused him to become an outcast? She'd asked him the same question on different nights in different ways, but he always managed to avoid giving her a straight answer. It was a mystery she was determined to solve, because she was slowly coming to understand that Devon Flynn lived a very lonely existence, like a wild and wary wolf without a pack.

It was toward the end of her three weeks with Devon that Pippa woke early to discover snow falling in large, gentle flakes. She'd never experienced a snowfall in the tropical climate where she'd grown up, and the idea of romping in fresh-fallen snow was irresistible. She dressed quickly and went to knock on Devon's office door.

"Devon, wake up!" she called urgently.

A moment later he yanked open the door. It was obvious that she'd woken him. His hair stood in spikes, and he was naked and wrapped from the waist down in a sheet.

Pippa stared. In all the time she'd spent at Devon's home, she'd never seen him when he wasn't fully dressed. The sight of his bare chest—with a V of dark hair that arrowed downward, disappearing beneath the sheet—and an abdomen ridged with muscle, caused a stab of desire that made her gasp.

His hand fisted more tightly around the sheet at his waist as he asked, "Are you all right? What's wrong?"

"It's snowing."

He looked confused. He turned to stare out the office window, which bore signs of frost. "I see. What's the problem?"

"I just thought . . . We don't have snow where I come from. I never imagined it was so beautiful when it falls. I wondered if you'd want to go for a walk with me."

His lips tilted up on one side, and she felt her body tighten in response to his warm smile. "Really? No snow?"

She smiled back. "Nope. How about it?"

"Give me a couple of minutes to get dressed. I'll be right out."

She stood there for a few moments after he closed the door waiting for her heartbeat to slow, then turned and headed for the front porch. She immediately saw why the porch roof was so important. Apparently, it had been snowing throughout the night, because there were nearly two feet of the white stuff surrounding the house and beautiful layers of it on the branches of the surrounding evergreens. She heard the front door open, and Devon joined her on the porch.

"It's so quiet," she said, her voice almost reverent. "I'm used to torrential rain and howling winds in the winter. It's a lot noisier than this gentle snowfall. And not nearly as beautiful."

"It isn't always like this. Wait till you see a Wyoming blizzard. But I know what you mean. A gentle spring snowfall like this is pretty amazing. What would you like to do first?"

"Make a snowman!"

He stepped down off the porch and gathered a handful of snow, letting it sift through his fingers. "Too powdery."

"How about a snowball?" she asked hopefully.

"Huh-uh. Same problem."

She felt disappointed, and her face must have shown it, because he said, "How about a snow angel?"

"What's that?"

He held out his hand and said, "Come here."

She came down the steps and took his bare hand. Despite the snow, it didn't feel cold outside. She dipped a boot toe tentatively into the snow and then kicked her way joyfully through it as he led her away from the house.

He found a spot near a snow-dusted pine and let go of her hand. "Ready?"

"What do I have to do?"

"Watch and learn." He spread his arms and fell backward, then waved both arms and legs in the snow, clearing it away. He sat up, looked behind him, and said, "That's a snow angel."

Pippa laughed, then fell backward beside him, creating her own snow angel. "It's cold!" she cried as the snow slid under her collar and melted on the back of her neck.

"Come here," he said, catching her arm and pulling her over on top of him. "I'll keep you warm."

He was smiling up at her, and Pippa laughed as she looked down into his happy face from a mere six inches away. Then she realized that her legs had slid down over either side of his hips, and that a very warm, very hard part of him was pressing against a very soft, very willing part of her.

The smile left her face as she searched his eyes. She saw desire flare and felt an answering response that raced through her body. It was clear he was ready and willing. The decision was up to her. Pippa was tired of resisting. Tired of being sensible. She lowered her head until their lips met.

His lips were soft, but his kiss was urgent. He took her deep so quickly that she was soon panting with need, seeking pleasure by pressing herself against the hard ridge between her thighs.

She put her cold hands against his warm, bristled cheeks as she kissed him, their tongues dueling. She could feel his hands on her buttocks, pressing her against the proof of his need.

Suddenly, something pounced on them.

Wulf apparently thought they were playing in the snow and wanted to join in. He knocked her aside with his shoulder before landing square on Devon's belly with both paws, causing him to issue an inelegant "Ooof!"

"Wulf, get off!" he said, shoving at the heavy animal and trying to sit up. Wulf bounded away, but then returned and knocked Devon back into the snow before returning to lick at Pippa's face.

She pushed the wolf away, laughing. "Cut it out!"

Wulf bounded back and forth, from one to the other of them, spraying snow in all directions, until Devon managed to get to his feet and reached out a hand to help Pippa up. "He's not going to give us any peace until he gets his breakfast."

Pippa let go of Devon's hand as soon as she was on her feet. She felt shy meeting his gaze. What would have happened if Wulf hadn't shown up? Would they have ended up in bed together? They'd certainly been headed in that direction. And then what?

Pippa realized that, as hard as she'd been trying to uncover Devon's secrets, she'd been equally determined to protect her own. He knew no more about what had caused the rift between her and her father now than he'd known the day she'd shown up at his door. He had no idea she was carrying another man's child. And it wasn't fair to either of them for her to allow a romance to develop before she told him that she was pregnant.

Pippa felt ashamed of herself for being Tim's dupe. And angry with Tim for deceiving her. And miserable about hiding the truth from Devon. "We'd better go inside."

"We can take a walk after breakfast, if you like," Devon offered.

Pippa shook her head. She couldn't take the

chance of being charmed again by the snowfall—or by Devon—when she wasn't ready to tell him the truth. She was afraid it would end this idyll.

And she still had no plan for the rest of her life.

Standing at the sink washing the breakfast dishes with Devon, she felt a flutter in her belly like Nathan's eyelashes on her cheeks. She thought the eggs and sausage she'd eaten had upset her stomach, but she didn't feel nauseous, and her belly didn't exactly *hurt*.

Then she felt it again. And realized what it was. "Oh!"

She put a hand on her belly and then pulled it away, afraid of what it might signify to Devon.

"Are you all right?" he asked.

She wanted to howl at the wretchedness of not being able to share this precious moment with him. "I . . ."

She almost told him the truth then and there. But she was too afraid of what he might do—or say—if he found out she was pregnant, especially after what she'd let happen that morning. Although she didn't know where she was going from here, the one decision she *had* made was that she wasn't going back to live at Kingdom Come.

"Hold me," she said instead. "Please, hold me."

He'd been more than willing, and she hadn't let go until she'd realized he was aroused again, and that it wasn't doing either of them any good to lead him on when she was keeping such a huge secret from him.

Somehow her feelings for Devon had become

far more than *friendly*. And she was pretty sure he had the same sort of feelings for her. It was those *romantic* feelings she wasn't sure would survive the knowledge that she was pregnant with another man's child.

After that lovely—and sad—start to her day, Pippa spent the rest of it on horseback, happily helping Devon drop hay at various spots around his ranch to feed his cattle. The two of them had ended up at the barn near suppertime, so that she could work with the stallion and he could check on his menagerie of wounded animals.

"Hey, how's it going with that bad boy?" Devon called from the other end of the barn.

A wild neigh and the thump of trampling hooves provided the answer more quickly than Pippa could. She backed away from the stall as the stallion reared and bared his teeth. She sighed as she turned and headed down the center aisle of the barn toward the animal cages and pens at the other end, where Devon was examining his charges.

"It took Sultan at least twenty seconds longer this afternoon to decide to kill me," Pippa replied.

The first thing she'd done was change the horse's name from *Satan* to *Sultan*. "How can you expect him to behave like an angel with a name like that?" she'd demanded. Devon had laughed at her, but he hadn't called the horse Satan again.

Devon smiled. "Twenty whole seconds? That sounds like progress."

Pippa managed to return his smile, but she was troubled by how little change there had been in

Sultan's demeanor since she'd begun working with him. The stallion remained unapproachable.

Pippa had spent a great deal of time simply talking to the horse, letting him get to know her. She'd also put a single cube of sugar on the top edge of the stall door each time she came to visit. At first he'd knocked it off without seeming to notice it was there. He must have found it after she'd gone, because lately, he was careful to lip the sugar cube and swallow it down before he attacked.

Pippa knew she couldn't expect to change years of poor treatment in a matter of weeks. It was going to take time.

But it was time she didn't have.

The brief movement in her belly this morning was evidence the baby was growing. Pippa had further proof, if she needed it, in the fit of her clothes. Her jeans barely zipped all the way up. Her nearly four-months-pregnant belly was definitely larger than it had been. She wasn't sure how long it would be before Devon noticed she wasn't nearly as slender as she had been when she'd arrived. And the problem was only going to get worse.

She chewed on her lower lip worriedly until she saw Devon notice what she was doing, and then let go.

"This torn ear has finally healed," Devon said as he gently fingered the remnant of the rabbit's ear that had been half bitten off.

As Pippa joined him she asked, "What happens to that cute bundle of fur now?"

"I'll take Peter here a little way into the forest and release him."

"Peter?" Pippa teased. "As in Peter Cotton-tail?"

Devon flushed. "There's usually no one around to hear me talking to these guys."

Pippa laughed. "That's why I didn't say any-thing before now. I didn't want to make you self-conscious. I think it's charming." She took the rabbit from him and checked the ear with her fin-gertips, enjoying the feel of the smooth fur that had grown over the ragged tear, before handing the animal back to him.

He eyed her sideways as he took Peter back into his gloved hands and placed the rabbit back in its cage.

"What?" she asked, wondering about the look he'd given her.

"Nothing." He grinned. "I think you're more in love with Peter than I am."

He was right. She'd gotten attached to all the animals in his menagerie, but she wasn't about to admit it. She couldn't imagine how he could bear to let them go after caring for them day after day, even though she knew they belonged back in the wild. She looked into the owl's nest and asked, "How's Squeaky doing?"

He slipped off the gloves he was wearing and put on a pair that sat on top of the owl's cage, then gently retrieved the tiny bird. He'd moved the owl to the barn when its breathing improved after five difficult days spent under his careful watch in the house. "He's not wheezing anymore, so I'm pre-suming there was less smoke damage to his lungs than Doc Stevens thought."

"How long will you keep him?"

"There's a lady in town who has an aviary. As soon as I'm sure Squeaky's recovered, I'll move him there. She'll make sure he knows how to hunt before she releases him." He returned the owl to the nest in its cage.

Pippa marveled that there was someone who had the willingness—and the financial wherewithal—to spend her time in such a way. "How many people like you *are* there in Jackson?"

He smiled as he pulled off his gloves and laid them on the cage. "Enough to make a difference."

She reached out to him, laying a hand on his chest. His muscles tensed under her touch. She met his gaze and found the kindness and concern of a friend looking back at her from his warm green eyes—and something else that heated her blood and made her body sing. "I think what you're doing is wonderful."

I think you're *wonderful.* She thought it, but she didn't dare say it. She didn't have the right to say it. Devon had been sympathetic and supportive over the past three weeks, but the gap between them was miles wide—a huge crevasse created by the secret she was keeping from him.

Pippa wondered if Devon would be behaving the same way toward her if he knew how she was deceiving him. He knew Tim Brandon had broken her heart, but not exactly how he'd done it. He'd probed for details about her hopes and dreams for the future as they sat in front of the fireplace at night, but Pippa had been necessarily vague, because she had no idea what the future held for her—and the child she carried.

She dropped her hand, realizing belatedly that she was still touching Devon. She turned and headed for the door to the barn, and he fell into step beside her. It was time to leave before temptation caused her to make another mistake. "I need to make some plans so I can get out of your hair."

"You're welcome to stay for as long as you like."

Pippa wondered if she looked as shocked as she felt at Devon's invitation. "I couldn't do that."

"Why not?"

She laughed. "Despite my constant offers to change places with you, you've spent the past three weeks sleeping on a couch in your office."

"It's a comfortable couch. Or we could always share—"

He snapped his mouth shut without finishing. She met his gaze, her body quivering in response to the ardent look in his eyes.

"Are you suggesting we share the bed?" she said with an arched brow.

"It's a big bed."

He left his expression unguarded, and for the first time she realized the depth of his desire for her. Or was it merely the need to be close to another human being? She thought she saw both but struggled to understand why he'd finally allowed her to see his feelings completely unveiled. A moment later his hot green gaze was gone and it felt as though she were staring at a gray stone wall. She was completely shut out, as though he'd suddenly realized he'd revealed too much.

She tried laughing off his comment, but the sound got caught in her throat. She glanced at him sideways. Maybe she wasn't the only one who'd been keeping secrets.

Pippa felt a welling of despair as she tried to imagine what was going on in Devon's mind. What had happened in the snow that morning suggested pretty clearly what Devon might want from her. It seemed he expected her to recover from her heartbreak at some point, so he'd let himself develop much deeper feelings for her than she'd imagined. *Romantic* feelings. She had to nip those feelings in the bud. Or tell him the truth, which would likely accomplish the same thing.

When they reached the front door to the house, she met his gaze and said, "We need to talk."

Chapter 16

WHEN PIPPA SPOKE the dreaded words "We need to talk," Devon knew he'd made a mistake. He should have hidden his feelings a little longer—or maybe a lot longer. But spending the past three weeks with Pippa had only magnified emotions that had begun the moment he'd met her.

The wounded animals he tended allowed him to handle them, but they were still frightened of him, which was why he wore gloves to protect himself when they bit or scratched. With Pippa, they weren't afraid. When she touched them they lay quiescent. The rabbit had twitched when she checked its ear, but otherwise, it had been content to sit calmly in the palm of her hand.

Whenever Wulf entered the cabin, the once-savage beast ran straight to Pippa to be petted. That was another thing. Wulf enjoyed her company, which was further proof, if he needed it, that there was more to her than just a pretty face.

He held the door open for her, but Wulf shoved past them both, once more thrusting Pippa into his arms. He held her close, murmuring, "I need to teach Wulf better manners. Although I can't complain about the results."

She looked up at him, and he saw that, however afraid she was of loving another man, she wanted him. That wasn't nearly enough, but it was a start. She pressed her cheek against his heart, and he felt her arms tighten around his waist. Then she pulled herself free and hurried into the house.

Devon followed her, knowing it was too late to save himself from pain if she walked away. He'd been very careful for a very long time to keep himself from feeling anything for any woman. But there was something different about Pippa Grayhawk—although, even with her, his first intention had been to make sure she knew the rules and then get her into bed.

But she'd been as aloof toward him as he'd been toward the women he dated.

Maybe it was the challenge of getting past that barrier she'd set between them that had caused him to get more and more involved, to ask more questions about her life—most of which she'd avoided answering—making her a tantalizing, mysterious creature with many layers left to be uncovered.

Or maybe it was the simple fact that he'd allowed a woman into his home to become a part of his daily life. If anything, that should have put him off, because there would necessarily be all sorts of changes to accommodate a stranger.

But he hadn't needed to alter his daily routine to include Pippa. She'd fit into his life as easily as a hand into a glove. The best part was, Pippa seemed to enjoy the chores required on a ranch as much as he did. She'd happily accompanied him when he checked on his livestock, and she was as much interested in the progress of his wounded menagerie as he was himself. He was amazed at her persistence with Sultan, when the stallion resisted every attempt she made to reach him.

Every day, in every way, he'd been constantly aware of her. Of the shuttered looks she aimed in his direction when she thought he wasn't looking. Of the tension in her body, like a mare watchful of a stud, deciding whether to allow him to mount her. So far she'd held him at bay.

Today that had changed. Pippa was no longer keeping him at arm's distance. He'd believed his wait was over. Until she'd said those fateful words: *We need to talk.*

In his experience, those words boded no good. He had a horrible, sinking feeling, as he stood and watched her in the kitchen making hot cocoa for the two of them, that this idyll was ending. If he wanted her to stay, he was going to have to fight for her.

She started the conversation facing the stove, where she was setting a pot of milk to warm. "I need to leave, Devon."

He'd expected it, but it still caused his heart to skip a beat. He leaned his hips back against the kitchen counter. "And go where?"

"I've seen signs when we've been shopping for food. They're hiring summer workers in town." She glanced at him over her shoulder. "I think I might be able to get work with one of the outfitters, you know, taking care of their packhorses, or maybe as a trail guide."

"That won't make you enough money to pay rent in Jackson. You'd have to live on the other side of the Teton Pass in Idaho Falls."

"Then that's where I'll have to live. At least, until I can save enough for a plane ticket back to Australia."

Devon felt sick. "You want to leave the States?"

She kept her back to him as she collected the Hershey's cocoa, sugar, vanilla, salt, and marshmallows from the cupboard and set them on the counter. "There's work for me in Australia whispering wild horses."

He grabbed a few marshmallows from the bag and popped them into his mouth. His throat was so tight it was hard to swallow them down. "You could do that here. You've already made a good start with Sultan."

When she turned back to face him, her gray eyes bore the sheen of tears. "I don't want to leave," she admitted. "But I don't have the means to survive here on my own."

"What about your mother? Have you thought about contacting her? Surely she'd want to help."

If anything, her face looked even more troubled. "She doesn't even know I exist. I have no idea whether she'll even believe I am who I say I am, especially since I supposedly died at birth. Besides, I don't want to show up on her doorstep like some beggar needing a bowl of food and a roof over my head. She was a senator's wife. The last thing she needs is—" She cut herself off and lowered her gaze to her knotted hands.

"Then stay with me," he urged.

She met his gaze, letting him see the barely restrained desire that had caused her to initiate this talk in the first place. "You know why I can't do that."

He stuck his hands into the back pockets of his Levi's to keep from reaching for her and forced himself to remain where he was. "I can't say I don't want you. I do."

"This situation—living together, spending every moment of every day together—is dangerous. I don't want to hurt you, Devon. And I don't want to get hurt."

He knew she was right, but he wasn't about to admit it. He'd lived as a lone wolf most of his adult life, and he'd despaired of ever finding a woman he would want to have invading his territory. With Pippa, it felt like she *belonged* here.

She waited for him to concede the truth of what she'd said, and when he didn't, she said bluntly, "I'm not ready to fall in love again."

He'd known it, but it was still hard to hear her say it. He'd been so careful since high school about giving his heart to anyone. With Pippa there had been no choice. Somehow, he'd lost his heart before he'd had a chance to protect himself from the pain it would cause if she didn't return his feelings.

Pippa took a huffing breath. "I'm not sure I'll ever be able to love another man as fully or freely as I loved Tim. But I can't help wanting you."

That sounded promising until she added, "I'm

afraid you might equate that longing with love. I'm not going to fall in love with you, Devon. There are things you don't know about me that make that impossible."

"The milk is boiling." He closed the distance between them, then reached behind her and turned off the stove.

"Don't change the subject."

"Nothing else matters as long as you want me as much as I want you," he said, cutting off whatever excuse she was going to make for why they shouldn't be together. He would settle for making love to her now and hope that by loving her he could make her fall in love with him.

He heard her moan as his mouth touched hers, and he felt her body melt into his as he wrapped his arms around her.

She broke the kiss and said, "Devon, this is—"

He kissed her again to cut off whatever she'd been about to say. *Crazy? Stupid? Risky? Wrong?* He knew all those things, but it didn't make any difference. He wanted her, and she wanted him. He picked her up in his arms, startling a gasp of surprise from her, and headed for the bedroom.

Wulf followed them to the bedroom door and would have gone inside, except Devon turned to him and ordered, "Stay."

The wolf hesitated before sitting. By the time he had his haunches on the ground, Devon was inside the bedroom and had the door closed behind him.

"He's going to howl to be let in," Pippa said.

"Let him." Devon stood her on her feet beside

his log-frame bed. He was watching for any sign of reluctance, any hint that she didn't want to make love to him. But there was none.

She put her hand on his nape and slowly drew his head down until their lips met. "Mmmm," she said, her tongue slipping inside to savor him. "You taste sweet—like marshmallows."

He realized he was smiling. He wanted to touch her—and suited thought to deed. He slipped his hand up under both her unbuttoned plaid wool shirt and the T-shirt she was wearing to feel the smooth skin of her back, and suddenly realized he didn't feel a bra strap.

His hands trailed down her spine and then back up to her shoulders as he held her close and kissed her deeply. Devon was on fire for her, but he knew he had to slow down and allow her to catch up. He broke the kiss and saw her eyes were half lidded, her lips full, and realized she was not the least bit behind him.

Still, he wanted to relish what was finally his. He tugged off the wool shirt she was wearing, then skinned the T-shirt off over her head, gasping at what he found.

Her small breasts were pink-tipped rosebuds waiting to be plucked. He lowered his head and took one in his mouth.

Her fingers clutched his hair, and she made a growling sound of pleasure in her throat as her body arched toward his. She was grasping at his shirt, trying to get it off, and he released her long enough to tear off both his wool shirt and long john shirt before pulling her naked body close. The friction of flesh against flesh was exquisite, and he kissed her again, tasting the sweetness and the goodness of her.

Her fingernails raked their way down his back, raising gooseflesh, until she finally slid her hands into the back of his Levi's.

He freed himself from her grasp and began yanking off his cowboy boots, which he had to rid himself of in order to get his jeans off. She laughed at him, sitting down on the bed to accomplish the same thing—she was wearing a pair of Australian boots—with a lot more grace. He had both boots off, his belt buckle undone, and was unzipping his Levi's when he happened to glance at her face and saw an expression that stopped him in his tracks.

"Pippa? Are you all right?"

The look on her face was so odd he felt cold inside. He sat down beside her, taking her hand in his. "What's wrong? Tell me. I want to help."

She sobbed once, then said, "There's no help for what's wrong with me."

He stared at her, aghast. "Are you sick? Are you dying? What is it?"

"I'm . . ." She swallowed hard, then scrunched up her face and said, "I'm an idiot."

"You're not dying?"

She managed a laugh as she swiped at the tears on her face. "No. But you're going to want to kill me, stopping like this before we really got started."

He pulled her onto his lap, holding her close, aware that he was, in fact, in a very painful condition. "I'm just glad you're not sick or dying or something. Can you tell me what happened?"

She gave a pitiful shrug. "I just . . . I guess I'm not as ready for this as I thought," she said at last. "I'm sorry, Devon."

Devon gritted his teeth against the pain caused by the interruption of their lovemaking. He had no one to blame but himself. He'd pushed and she'd yielded. He still wanted her, but she was no longer willing.

"Let's get you back into some clothes." That would help him resist the urge to reach out and touch again. He stood, dumping her onto the bed, and searched until he found her T-shirt on the floor. Instead of handing it to her, he said, "Arms up!"

She uncrossed the arms that were hiding her naked breasts and held them up so that he could slide the shirt over her head. He quickly tugged it down once her arms were in the sleeves, trying not to look at what he found so tempting. He grabbed her wool shirt from the foot of the bed and held it so she could put her arms in the sleeves. Then he buttoned it up. *Better safe than sorry,* he thought.

Once she was dressed, he sought out his own long john shirt and slipped it over his head, before snapping his jeans, rebuckling his belt, and pulling his boots back on.

All the while, his mind was racing. What had caused her to have second thoughts? Had he done something to trigger memories of her love affair gone wrong? Or was she simply afraid of whatever hurt or heartbreak might ensue from making love to a man she hardly knew, a man she had no reason to believe wanted more than the pleasure they could give and take from each other in bed.

It was his fault this had happened. She'd warned him to keep his distance, and he'd rushed her into bed—or almost into bed—anyway. His heart was set on having her for his mate. He just had to convince her to stay long enough to give him time to win her heart.

The only problem was, he had no idea how to make that happen. He'd never tried to make a woman love him. He'd never wanted to before now. But it was clear that if he wanted Pippa to hang around long enough for him to woo her, he needed to figure it all out.

Chapter 17

WHEN DEVON HAD begun making love to her, desire had risen in Pippa like a dangerous, many-headed hydra, blinding her to everything except the pleasure to be had in his embrace. She hadn't realized just how cheated she'd been by Tim's lovemaking until Devon began kissing and caressing her. With Tim, the focus had been on what she could do to satisfy him. With Devon, every touch seemed to be aimed at increasing her joy.

The amazing thing was, from the avid look in Devon's eyes and his guttural sounds of delight, it appeared that pleasing *her* seemed to bring *him* a great deal of pleasure as well.

Pippa had been lost in a well of sensation from the first touch of his lips, and when he'd sucked on her breast—something Tim had never done—she'd thought she would swoon. Making love with Devon was a more sensual experience than she could ever have imagined. No wonder she'd forgotten that there was a very good reason why she shouldn't be taking her clothes off in front of him.

She'd been holding a boot with both hands, ready to pull it off, when she'd felt that feathery touch inside, reminding her what Devon would see if she stripped herself bare. With a body as lean as hers, she had a definite "baby bump" he was sure to notice when her belly was pressed against his. He wasn't an idiot. He would wonder. And he would ask questions to satisfy his curiosity. And then what would she say?

At that moment, Pippa realized how irrevocably one mistake had changed her life. She was not at all convinced Devon would be willing to raise another man's son. Yes, he rescued wounded animals and nursed them back to health. But he never got attached to them. And as soon as they were well he sent them back where they belonged. That pattern of behavior suggested that Devon was short on long-term commitments. Like raising a child that wasn't his.

Pippa knew she should have told Devon from the beginning that any relationship with her involved a small additional package. She hadn't because she'd never expected to get romantically involved with him. But he'd been persistent, and she'd found herself wanting his kisses and his touches. Until she'd reached the point today where she'd foolishly allowed the situation to get completely out of hand, knowing full well that the longer she kept her secret, the longer she deceived Devon, the more angry and unforgiving he was liable to be when she finally revealed she was pregnant.

She'd been shocked to realize that she couldn't bear to tell Devon the truth—and she couldn't bear to walk away. What kind of person did that make her? Was she really willing to take such unfair advantage of him? He might have forgiven her if she'd told him her secret from the start. But how betrayed was he going to feel when he found out that she'd misled him all along?

The situation would be coming to a head soon, one way or another, because her pregnancy wasn't something she would be able to hide for much longer, even with her clothes on.

Pippa regretted stopping Devon, because now she might never know what it felt like to join her body with his. But guilt—and the fear that her secret would be revealed in such an embarrassing way—had made it impossible for her to go on.

Wulf howled outside the bedroom door, breaking the silence that had fallen between them. It was a truly eerie sound, which Devon had told her upset the horses in the barn and the recuperating animals in their cages. He crossed to the bedroom door and let the wolf in.

Wulf came straight to her and stuck his cold nose in her hand. Pippa brushed her palm down his back, soothing his ruffled fur.

"I'm going to finish up that cocoa," Devon said. "I'll let you know when it's ready."

His voice had sounded curt. Or maybe it was the remorse she felt that caused her to interpret it that way. He walked out, leaving her alone with the wolf.

Pippa nuzzled against Wulf's fur, and he licked her face. She sat up and said, "Yes, I know you were worried about me. I'm all right. Let's go help Devon with that cocoa."

She wasn't going to hide in the bedroom. She needed to talk to Devon and see whether, after what had just happened, he still wanted her to stay.

She hesitated in the bedroom doorway, and he must have sensed her presence, because he turned from the stove to look at her.

"If it's still open, I've decided to accept your offer to stay," she announced. "At least for a little while longer."

The slight frown between his eyes made her wonder if he'd changed his mind. At last he said, "I'm glad." But he didn't sound glad. He sounded troubled. He turned back to the stove, hiding his face—and his feelings—from her. "This is about done," he said. "Grab some cups for us."

Neither of them said anything more until they had their cups of cocoa in hand and were settled in chairs before the fireplace. Pippa realized Devon must have heaped more wood on the fire after he'd left the bedroom, because the flames rose high and fierce. The combination of the heat from the roaring fire and the hot cocoa seemed to warm the cold place inside her.

Devon, who was sitting in the rocker, leaned back and said, "Since you're planning to stay, what would you say to coming with me to an event I need to attend at Kingdom Come on Saturday."

Pippa felt apprehensive at the thought of meeting up with her father. "What event is that?"

"A barbecue and dance."

Pippa made a face. She wasn't in the mood to celebrate. But she owed Devon a great deal, and he obviously wanted her along to share the day with him. "You're definitely planning to go?"

"Along with my whole family."

Pippa gasped. "The *Flynns* are attending an event at my grandfather's ranch?"

Devon grinned. "Yep. Your father agreed to host the event, and your aunt Leah is helping to organize it. Aiden, Brian, Connor and his family, and my father will all be there—along with just about every local rancher and businessman in town. Fur and feathers are sure to fly. I wouldn't miss it for the world."

"It sounds like it might turn into a free-for-all," Pippa said doubtfully. "Who set this up?"

"My sister-in-law." Devon paused and met her gaze. "I think that's the first time I've said that word. It's still hard to believe Connor's married, it happened so suddenly. They just went to the justice of the peace in town without inviting any of us to come. I guess that's what makes it so hard to believe his marriage is real."

"None of my aunts were invited either," Pippa said. "After all the stories I'd heard about the two families hating each other, I was shocked to learn that a Grayhawk had married a Flynn."

Devon snickered. "So were we. My brothers and I decided to commemorate the astonishing event—never likely to be repeated—by holding a shivaree."

"A shivaree?"

"It's an old frontier custom. We turned up at Connor's ranch and made a lot of noise, with the object of interrupting the wedding night. Unfortunately, not only did Aiden, Brian, and I show up, but Leah, Taylor, and Victoria made an appearance—to offer best wishes to the bride and groom."

"Uh-oh."

Devon chuckled. "Uh-oh is right. Connor and Eve made the mistake of inviting all of us inside to quiet us down, since we were scaring Connor's kids. Needless to say, a number of insults got thrown, along with at least one punch—Connor took exception when Brian slighted the bride—before we all left.

"I think I was the only person present who thought Connor and Eve have a chance of making it. Then again, I'm probably the only one who realized how badly he was smitten with her in high school. Anyway, he met Molly—she was Eve's best friend—and that was the end of that."

"Molly's the woman he married?"

Devon nodded. "As far as I'm concerned, Connor and Eve are star-crossed lovers who've finally managed to find their way to each other. It's supposedly a marriage of convenience, but I think both of them care a lot more for each other than either one is admitting."

Pippa quickly swallowed the sip of hot cocoa she'd just taken in order to ask, "How can you know that?"

"Eve was the one who arranged this barbecue and dance at Kingdom Come. She did it to raise funds to support Connor's ranch."

"His ranch is failing? I thought Angus was almost as rich as my grandfather. Can't Connor borrow some money from him?"

"My father cut Connor off when he refused to divorce Eve."

"*Divorce* her? They just got married!"

Devon made a disgruntled sound in his throat. "He doesn't want any Flynn offspring being polluted with King Grayhawk's blood."

"Oh." Pippa felt a shiver run down her spine. If Devon's father was that controlling, what was he liable to say—or do—when he found out that Devon was supporting an unwed pregnant *Grayhawk* woman.

"Besides," Devon continued. "Safe Haven is no ordinary ranch. Connor set it up with his trust fund as a retreat where veterans can enjoy a little rest and relaxation before they return to duty."

"That sounds wonderful!" Then she realized the problem. "Oh, I see. Your father took away Connor's trust fund."

"Yep." Devon blew on his cocoa and then took a sip, licking at the melted marshmallow that stuck to his lips. "That's what this barbecue is all about. Folks who come are being asked to give what they can to help keep Safe Haven up and running. Aiden convinced all of us to throw in some cash, and I don't know how he did it, but he also convinced my father to show up to support Connor—even though he's opposed to Connor's marriage."

"I can see why you don't want to miss it." Pippa sighed. "I guess this is as good a time as any to meet up with my father again." She managed a wobbly smile and said, "My reunion with him should pale in comparison to the fireworks when Angus meets up with King."

Chapter 18

MATT WISHED THERE were some way he could simply shiver his flesh, like some old bull swarmed by flies, and have all his troubles fly away. He'd been in hell for the past month. There was no worse feeling for a father than knowing he'd failed to protect his child. All he'd ever wanted was to ease Pippa's burden, but she kept insisting it was a burden she was willing to carry. Finally, he'd pressed too hard for her to do what he thought was best, and she'd bolted. He blamed himself for that, too.

When he'd found out his daughter was staying with Devon Flynn, he'd been ready to drive over there like a bat out of hell and haul her back home. A warning from Leah had changed his mind.

"Pippa wouldn't take off like that without a good reason. I know it hasn't been easy for her here. If you go after her and bring her back, she'll likely run again. Next time she'll go farther and hide better. At least you know she's safe with Devon. Give her time, and she'll work through whatever it is that's troubling her."

Matt hadn't meant to blurt "She's pregnant!" but the words were out before he could stop them.

Leah didn't look entirely surprised, and Matt figured Pippa's nausea at odd times and naps in the afternoon might have given her away—at least to Leah, who seemed more perceptive to the feelings of others, likely because she was used to watching out for her sisters.

"I presume the father's out of the picture," Leah said.

"The bastard didn't tell her he was married."

"I'm so sorry, Matt. For you and for Pippa."

He scrubbed at eyes scratchy from lack of sleep. "I've been asking her to consider adoption. Maybe pushing too hard to get her to consider it."

"I see. And she wants to keep the baby?"

Matt nodded.

"And you have a problem with that?"

"I've been a teenage single parent. I know how hard it can be."

Leah's eyes widened a little in recognition of what he was admitting.

"She shouldn't be living so far from a hospital," Matt continued. "Hell, I have no idea whether she's even seen a doctor for a checkup."

"Pippa's a smart girl. She'll do what's necessary to take care of herself and the baby. And Devon will watch out for her."

"That's what I'm afraid of," Matt muttered.

Leah lifted a brow. "Devon is your uncle's son. That practically makes him family. Do you really think he would do anything to harm Pippa?"

What Leah said made sense, but Matt wasn't consoled. As far as Devon was concerned, his relationship to Pippa was distant enough to qualify him as a "kissin' cousin." Devon had been a kid the last time Matt had spent any time with him, but Matt had heard plenty of stories about "those awful Flynn boys" raising hell and causing trouble. He was leery of what a grown-up Devon, about whom he knew little or nothing, might do with—or to—his daughter.

Matt rubbed at the lines of worry on his brow and said, "Pippa's vulnerable."

"You don't think she's learned from her mistake?"

He made a frustrated sound in his throat. "I don't know. I just don't want her getting hurt again."

"Mistakes are how we grow," Leah said.

Leah's voice had been both wistful and sad. Matt wondered what painful mistake—or mistakes—Leah had made that had caused her to grow into the generous, unselfish person she was.

"That doesn't give me much comfort," he said at last.

"Trust me. Give her time and space. She'll come back when she's ready."

He'd done as Leah suggested, even sending a hired hand to deliver the items Pippa had asked for, rather than taking them himself to make sure with his own eyes that his daughter was all right. He couldn't count the number of times he'd stopped himself from getting into his truck, driving over to Devon Flynn's place, and hauling her home.

He kept remembering Leah's final warning. *If you bring her home, she's just going to run again.*

Next time she may not end up somewhere as safe as where she is now.

He'd expected Pippa to be gone a week. Or two. He'd never imagined she'd be gone for a month. Or that when he finally saw her again it was going to be in such a public setting.

She was coming to the barbecue being held at Kingdom Come to raise money for Safe Haven, Connor's retreat for veterans. Everyone and his brother from Jackson was going to be there, along with King, Matt's sisters, and every single damn one of the Flynns, from Angus on down to Devon, who was bringing Pippa with him.

Matt stared at his hands, which were shaking. He was a wreck. He hadn't forgotten that nearly the last thing he'd discussed with Pippa was the fact that her mother was alive. Or that she'd been far more angry and resentful than he'd expected about the fact that he'd kept the truth from her.

He'd told her Jennie's full name and enough information about where her mother was living that Pippa could have gotten in touch with her. He wondered if his daughter had found the courage to do what he had not: call Jennifer Hart and tell her she had a living daughter.

He didn't think so, because he couldn't imagine Jennie wouldn't have confronted him if a "dead" daughter had shown up on her doorstep, to demand an explanation for what he'd done. He'd put off seeking out Jennie himself because he'd hoped that any day Pippa would be coming home.

Telling Jennie he'd taken their daughter and run twenty years ago was bad enough. He hated like hell having to add, *Our daughter is alive, but at the moment, she isn't speaking to me. She's chosen to live with a distant relation, a virtual stranger she met a month ago, rather than with her own father. And oh, by the way, I did such a good job raising her on my own that she's pregnant with a married man's child.*

So he'd put off the trip to see Jennie, something he'd pictured many times on dark, sleepless nights and experienced in his dreams before waking up in bed alone. He wanted a fighting chance to get back together with his long-lost love, and he was damn sure their daughter's current circumstances would do nothing to endear him to her.

He was looking forward to seeing Pippa at the barbecue. He hoped to separate her at some point from Devon and have a heart-to-heart talk. He'd promised himself he would listen to her and let her make her own decisions about the baby. He'd done a lot of thinking while she'd been gone and realized he'd been remembering only the hardships of being a single parent, not the joys. Being Pippa's father had been an adventure he wouldn't have wanted to miss.

Matt could vividly remember the day three-year-old Pippa had disappeared and he'd been in a panic to find her. And how he'd finally discovered her quietly sitting at the feet of one of the most explosive brumbies in his corral, feeding it bits of straw, which the enormous beast was gently eating from her hand.

He'd been afraid that if he tried to come near her, the horse—which was still wild—would trample her. So he'd come only as far as the edge of the corral and called to her in a neutral voice, "Pippa. Come here, baby."

She'd looked up, and a glorious smile had curved her lips and crinkled her eyes as she called out, "Daddy!"

He'd gasped as she leapt up, terrified that the startled brumbie would trample her. But she turned to the horse and spoke softly to it, and the wild animal lowered its head so she could pat its nose. Then she'd come running, laughing with delight all the way, her arms outstretched to him. Once she was clear of the brumbie, he'd climbed over the corral and rushed to sweep her up into his embrace.

He'd held her close as he scolded her for leaving the house without telling him where she was going. And he'd warned her that the brumbies were dangerous, and she had to stay away from them. He might as well have saved his breath. The brumbies had been like a magnet to his daughter, and whenever he couldn't find her, he knew where to look first.

He supposed that experience, when she was only three, should have taught him something. His daughter had a mind of her own. She seemed determined to keep her child, and what he had to focus on now was how he could help her to do it.

Matt felt a spurt of guilt and wondered if he'd wanted Pippa to give away her child so it wouldn't be there as a constant reminder of *his* failure. He was ashamed to admit that the thought had crossed his mind more than once. He'd also been aware that meeting Jennie after all these years would have been easier if Pippa wasn't a single mother with a baby on her hip.

He felt like an ogre when he realized how selfish those thoughts were, but he was only human. The point was he had to rise above those feelings. To use Leah's words, he had to *grow* from his *"mistake."* He just wanted Pippa back home. He missed her and loved her and wanted to be there to help in whatever way she needed him most.

What if she wants to stay with Devon? What then?

Matt gritted his teeth so hard a muscle worked in his jaw. Devon should never have agreed to let Pippa stay with him in the first place. What kind of young man was he to invite a single woman to live with him on a few days' acquaintance—even if they were distantly related? Matt blamed Devon far more than Pippa for his daughter's absence from home. Devon should have kept his nose out of Matt's family business.

Matt smiled grimly. There were ways to take Devon Flynn out of the picture, secrets Matt's mother had told him before her death, secrets Matt had kept because he saw no reason to give them up. Those revelations would give Devon enough issues of his own to deal with that he'd be happy to send Pippa on her way. He would wait and see what Pippa said today and then decide whether to reveal what he knew.

Chapter 19

PIPPA COULDN'T BELIEVE it had been four weeks since she'd left Kingdom Come. She'd missed her father, but she was more than a little anxious about seeing him again. She knew he wasn't happy about her decision to spend the past month at Devon's cabin. He was going to be even less happy when he found out she had no intention of returning to her grandfather's ranch. She loved her father, and it was hard to go against his wishes, but she was determined to hold her ground if he tried to talk her out of staying where she was.

She was seated at a picnic table with a red-checked tablecloth drinking iced tea and waiting to eat barbecue from an entire steer being roasted on an outdoor spit. A country band on a raised dais played raucous tunes that encouraged skirts to fly and boots to stomp on the dance floor in front of them.

Despite the calamity that might be right around the corner—or maybe because of it—Pippa was itching to jump up and join the dancers. She was wearing a pretty red dress, and Devon had surprised her this morning with a brand-new pair of

American cowboy boots, one of which was keeping time with the music under the table.

It was a good thing the front lawn at Kingdom Come was so immense, because Pippa estimated that three hundred people had shown up for the First Annual Safe Haven Country Barbecue and Dance. She was counting on the fact that she was sitting at a table in the center of the crowd with Angus and his sons to keep her father from making a scene.

Almost as soon as she'd arrived, she'd spied her father at a table on the other side of the lawn with her brother. Nathan had come running to her, and they'd shared a big hug. Then she'd pulled him onto her lap and they'd talked, something they'd only done on the phone since she'd been gone. But she'd remained on tenterhooks, because she knew it was just a matter of time before her father sought her out.

Pippa had encouraged Devon to go dance with one of the women who'd approached him, so he wouldn't be sitting there when her father confronted her. But he'd refused each of the women with a friendly smile, saying he was keeping Pippa company. "Come dance with me," he said when another woman had come and gone. "I don't want to leave you sitting here alone to go dance with someone else, and besides, I can see your toe tapping under the table."

Pippa laughed at being caught out. She'd watched couples dancing on television and had mimicked the steps, but those dances were nothing like what she saw people doing here. She dearly wanted to accept his offer but was forced to admit, "I don't know how to do those western steps."

"They're playing a waltz," he countered with a charming smile that made her insides dance, even though she was still sitting down.

"I've never done this with a partner," she confessed, her face flushing with embarrassment.

"I'll teach you." He took both of her hands in his, drawing her to her feet before leading her to the dance floor.

She'd seen the waltz performed in movies, and she'd secretly wished to be held in a man's arms and elegantly twirled around a dance floor. But dancing hadn't been a part of her life on a cattle station. She leaned close and said, "I don't want to make a fool of myself."

"You won't," he replied confidently.

"You seem very sure I'll be able to keep up with you."

He grinned. "Can you count to three?"

"Of course!" she said, surprised to find herself breathless before they'd even started.

"Then you can waltz." Without saying more, he placed one of her hands on his shoulder, put his hand at her waist, and took her opposite hand in his. "Now, count with me as you step—one two three, one two three."

Pippa realized Devon was using both his secure hold on her waist and his firm grip on her hand to guide her in the direction he wanted her to go. Before she knew it, she was following him—or he was leading her—gracefully around the dance floor. The full skirt of her empire-waisted sundress—the one she'd figured would hide her four-months-pregnant belly best—flared as he let go of his hold on her waist and twirled her under his upraised hand. She laughed, exhilarated by the music and the dance, as he caught her up again and took them on another turn around the floor.

Their eyes locked, and everything fell away except the warmth she felt in Devon's gaze and the strength she felt in his arms. When the music ended, he pulled her close for a hug. She hugged him back—until she remembered that her father might be watching her. She stepped aside, searching the crowd, and sure enough, spied him frowning in her direction. She wanted to postpone her conversation with him as long as she could, so she turned away and said, "I'm a little hungry. Why don't we see if that barbecue's done?"

She obviously hadn't fooled Devon. He glanced at her father and said, "Let's get you situated back at the table. Then I'll bring us both something to eat."

Pippa worried that her father might decide to get to her through Devon, and she didn't want him blaming Devon for something that was entirely her choice. It made sense to keep Devon by her side. That way she could head off her father if he tried that tactic. "I can wait to eat. Come back to the table with me."

When they got back to the table, they discovered someone had already brought prepared plates of food—barbecue, baked beans, coleslaw, and rolls—for everyone. Devon was just seating himself after adjusting her chair, when she realized her father had finally made his move. A moment later, he was standing right behind her.

"Hello, Pippa."

She turned in her chair so she was facing him, gripping the back of it as though she expected him to try to bodily remove her. His brow was furrowed, and she saw dark shadows under his eyes that hadn't been there before she'd left home. She felt her gut clench with concern for him. "Hi, Daddy."

"How are you?"

She tried to speak, but nothing came out.

"She's fine," Devon said.

To her dismay, her father's gaze shifted to Devon. "Pippa doesn't belong at some remote ranch in the mountains, especially with that wolf you keep as a pet in the house at night. She needs—" He cut himself off and refocused his gaze on Pippa.

She paled as she realized how close her father had come to inadvertently revealing her secret to everyone within hearing, including her aunt Eve, who'd come running—apparently to act as peacemaker—when her father approached the table. Pippa could guess what he'd started to say but hadn't.

She needs . . . to be taking better care of herself and her baby. She needs . . . to be closer to a doctor.

Her cheeks were hot, and she felt sick to her stomach. Without thinking, she put a protective hand over her baby. She was taking good care of both of them, but there was no way to say that to her father in such a public setting. She'd visited a doctor in town the week past, when she'd gone into Jackson for groceries while Devon was busy on the range. She'd learned that both she and the baby were healthy, and she'd started taking prenatal vitamins. If her father had drawn her aside, she would have told him as much.

She looked up at him, beseeching him for understanding. "Please, Daddy. I'm where I want to be."

Her father lowered his voice, but his tone was even harsher. "Come home, Pippa. You need to be with your family."

"She *is* with family," Devon said in a quiet voice. He laid a possessive hand on Pippa's shoulder and said to her father, "Sit down and stop making an ass of yourself, Matt. Pippa's old enough to decide what she wants to do with her life."

Pippa barely managed to keep her jaw from dropping. No one spoke to her father like that! Except, Devon just had.

Her father snarled, "Get your hands off her."

"Daddy, please don't do this!" Pippa cried.

She knew her father well enough to see that he was at the end of his rope. His eyes had narrowed and his fists were clenched. She'd known he was upset with her, but because he hadn't come after her, she'd assumed he'd reconciled himself to what she'd done. It was clear from his behavior toward Devon that she'd been very, very wrong. He'd bottled up his worry, and now it was about to spill out.

"Devon had nothing to do with this, Daddy. It was entirely my idea. I needed some time on my own. Devon just gave me a place to stay."

"He should have known better. He should have brought you home. He should have minded his own damn business!"

Devon's hand fell away as he rose. "Whoa, there, Matt. I only offered her—"

Her father suddenly took a swing at Devon.

Pippa cried a warning, but Devon had already dodged sideways, so the blow never struck him. Her father was gathering himself for another try when her grandfather arrived at the table and said, "That's enough."

Her father turned to King, his eyes tortured, his voice as rough as gravel, and said, "Butt out, old man! You've done enough damage to my life, don't you think?"

There it was again, the suggestion that her grandfather was responsible for her father's long-ago disappearance. She was still cringing from her father's attack on her grandfather when Angus said, "Don't worry, Matt. King won't be around much longer to bother you. He's about to go down for the third time."

"What is that supposed to mean?" King snapped.

"Even the *Titanic* can sink," Angus said with a smug smile. "Which is to say, you've invested in one risky venture too many." His voice turned nasty as he added, "I've been waiting twenty years for what's coming. I hope you suffer as much as my sister did when you drown in the shit that's coming your way."

Pippa's stomach was threatening to erupt, and she swallowed hard to force the bile back down.

Angus was going to destroy King? And King had no way to stop him? She'd heard about the animosity between Angus and King, but she'd never imagined the looks of hatred she saw on the two men's faces or the venom in their voices. She wanted to be gone from here, to escape to someplace where people didn't hate each other or hurt each other.

Devon's brother Connor suddenly appeared at Eve's side, put a reassuring arm around his wife's waist, and said, "What seems to be the problem, Matt?"

"Nothing that concerns you," her father retorted, his eyes darting from Connor to King to Angus to Devon and back again like a baited bear.

"You're all disturbing my guests," Connor said. "Folks are here to enjoy some barbecue and beer, so let's skip the fracas. You two old bulls—and you two young ones—can settle this another time."

Pippa grabbed at Connor's suggestion as though it were a tangled rope in a raging river. "Please, Daddy," she begged.

To her relief, her father's fists unclenched. "Fine," he said to Connor through tight jaws. But he turned to Devon and added, "If I find out you've touched so much as a hair on my daughter's head, I'll—"

"They're related, for Christ's sake!" Connor interrupted.

Her father looked straight at Devon and said, "No, they're not."

Pippa registered the stark look in Devon's green eyes as his brother Brian leapt up and said, "What the hell are you talking about?"

"Figure it out for yourselves," her father said.

Pippa had never made much of the blood connection between herself and Devon because they were only second cousins—his father was her father's uncle. But her father's comment made no sense, because that link did, in fact, make them related.

Pippa saw the malicious look King shot Angus—which seemed to confirm that the accusation her father had thrown out was going to create havoc for his rival—before both her father and her grandfather turned and stalked away.

Pippa realized that every male at the table had immediately jumped to the conclusion that Devon was the one without a connection to her, rather than the other way around. While no one had bothered to ask, Pippa knew for a fact that she was her father's daughter. That issue had been resolved when she was thirteen and had needed a transfusion. Her father had provided the blood.

Devon was looking to his father for an explanation, his face completely leached of color.

Angus's gaze remained focused on his hands, which were picking at the label on his ice-cold beer.

"Dad?" Devon said. "What did he mean?"

"He's just making trouble, stirring the pot to see what boils over," Angus said. But he never lifted his gaze from his bottle of beer.

Pippa could see that Devon was troubled by

Angus's refusal to deny her father's statement, which suggested that he wasn't Angus's son.

She tried to meet Devon's gaze, but it was still focused on his father. She felt her breath catch in her throat as she drew the only conclusion that seemed possible from Angus's continued refusal to refute her father's accusation.

Angus isn't Devon's father.

Chapter 20

I'M NOT HIS SON.

Devon was still reeling from Matt's revelation, which his father had refused to deny. All his life he'd feared the truth. Now he knew for certain that he was no relation to Angus Flynn. Which meant that his mother, the one he'd killed with his birth, had slept with another man. That certainly explained why his father had treated him differently all his life.

I'm some other man's bastard son.

Devon saw the looks of surprise and horror and disgust as each of his brothers reacted to the suggestion that their mother might have cheated on their father—and that Angus had apparently known about her betrayal. He felt only relief. Now he no longer had to live a lie.

And yet, with this new knowledge, his life had been irrevocably altered. His heart was pounding and his ears were ringing as though someone had just shot off a gun next to his head. His eyes were watering and his nose stung and he wasn't sure how much longer he could stand here without losing it completely.

Leah suddenly arrived at Eve's side—apparently unaware of the wreckage Matt had left in his wake—and said to her, "It's time you stopped playing peacemaker and started enjoying the party."

She took the beer out of Connor's hand, set Eve's hand in its place, and said, "Go dance with your wife."

Connor seemed willing to comply, but he paused long enough to say to Devon, "We'll discuss this later."

"No," Devon rasped. "We won't." His throat ached, and he was afraid that in another moment he wouldn't be able to speak at all. He reached out and grasped Pippa's hand, needing something to hang on to so he wouldn't fly into a million pieces. It was one thing to *think* he'd grown up with a father who wasn't related to him. It was another thing to *know* it.

He gritted his teeth to stop his chin from quivering, then focused his gaze on Angus and said, "As far as I'm concerned, the subject is closed." He turned to Pippa and, in a voice that revealed nothing of the turmoil he felt inside, said, "Would you like to dance?"

She quickly rose, as though she could see the cliff edge on which he was poised, and said, "Yes, I would. Thank you, Devon."

Without another word, he and Pippa left his slack-jawed brothers behind at the table. But they never reached the dance floor. Devon knew there was no way he could keep pretending in front of all these people that everything was fine when, in fact, he'd just been struck by a million volts of lightning.

He reversed course and headed straight for his truck.

"Devon, slow down!" Pippa said, tugging against his grasp on her hand. "I can't keep up with you."

He realized he was almost running and forced himself to relax his pace.

"Are you all right?" she asked.

"Hunky-dory," he said through tight jaws.

"What if my father made it all up? What if he doesn't know what he's talking about?"

"He knows, all right."

She frowned up at him. "You believed him? What makes you so sure he's right?"

Devon avoided the question, just kept moving toward his truck, pulling her along behind him.

"Devon, talk to me!"

He stopped and released his grasp on her hand, then balled his hands into fists because he didn't want her to see how badly they were shaking. "How did your father find out I'm not Angus's son?"

"I have no idea. I wouldn't be surprised if it's something he made up to piss you off so you'd throw me out."

"My father didn't contradict him."

"He shouldn't have to," Pippa said. "Why would you even consider such an outlandish suggestion?"

Devon met her gaze and said in a harsh voice, "I've told you why. I'm not like the rest of them. Angus doesn't treat me the same way as he does my brothers." He swallowed over the painful knot in his throat as he realized that Aiden and Brian and

Connor were actually his *half* brothers. "I've never felt like I belonged."

"Maybe it's because you're the youngest, and you never knew your mother."

"Maybe it's because I had a different father," he replied curtly.

Pippa's eyes looked as troubled as he felt. She didn't speak, just unballed one of his fists so she could take his hand in hers again. "Let's go home. Wulf will be hungry."

Devon huffed out a breath, then glanced over his shoulders at the table where the rest of his family sat. He didn't want to discuss his mother's affair with his brothers. He wasn't particularly interested in discussing it with his "father," either, except to force Angus to admit that that he'd been prejudiced against Devon all his life.

He was aware of Pippa's firm grip on his hand, keeping him grounded, keeping him in the here and now, but his mind was a jumble of thoughts. Who was his father? How had his mother met the man? Why had she engaged in an affair with him?

His mother had always been a mysterious figure in his life, but he was realizing just how little he really knew about her. Why had she stayed with Angus when she knew she was going to bear another man's child? Had she, perhaps, not known?

And why had Angus raised him, if he'd been so sure that Devon was another man's child. Did his biological father know of his existence? Was he out there somewhere? Might he want to meet Devon if he knew he had a grown son?

More importantly, do I want to meet him? I

don't know. He's nothing to me. He just provided the seed. What kind of man was he to have an affair with a married woman and then walk away without looking back?

Devon wondered just how much Angus knew, and whether he would tell Devon everything he did know if he asked. Was Angus certain who Devon's biological father was? If so, what had kept Angus from divorcing Devon's mother? And then Devon realized that divorce might have come later—if she'd lived.

Devon wasn't sure he wanted to know the answers to all of his questions. That didn't keep them from replaying endlessly in his mind, crashing around like an avalanche of boulders and causing his head to ache.

Devon realized that having Pippa stay with him—now that they weren't even distantly related—had become infinitely more complicated. But his feelings for her hadn't changed. Now, more than ever, he wanted someone in his life who loved him for who he was, someone whom he could love in return, someone he could rely on in his suddenly tumultuous life.

"Do you still want to stay at my place after what happened between me and your dad today?"

She shot him a curious look. "Do you mean because we're not technically second cousins anymore? I liked you before my father's revelation—and I like you now."

"But who is it you like?" he said bitterly. "Who am I now?"

She put her fingertips on his lips to silence him.

"You're the same kind, stong man you've always been. Having a different biological father doesn't change who you are."

She caressed his cheek as she looked deep into his eyes. "I can't imagine how I'd feel in your shoes. It must be . . ." She paused, frowned as she apparently searched for the right word, and finally said, "Upsetting, to say the least."

"Upsetting? Try life altering."

"You're missing the point," she said. "This revelation doesn't have to change how you live your life."

He made a sound in his throat but didn't contradict her.

"To prove my point, if you're willing for me to stay—in spite of how badly my dad acted toward you—I'd like to hang around a little longer."

"That sounds good to me," Devon said, kissing her fingertips and then taking her hand in his. "You're the one person in my life I can trust to be straight with me."

Devon watched a shadow cross Pippa's eyes. She opened her mouth to speak and then clamped it shut again. He wondered what it was she'd wanted to say. Something sympathetic? He didn't want her sympathy. Or her pity. He wanted her love. It was a relief to know she was going to be around so he could earn it.

Pippa sighed.

"Are you all right?" he asked, his lips quirking.

"I wish . . ." She let the words hang in the air.

"Yeah," Devon said, understanding how she could have second thoughts and regrets and wish she'd done things in her life differently, because he felt the same way himself. "So do I."

Pippa smiled and reached out to brush his forearm with her other hand in a gesture of friendship. "Thanks, Devon."

"For what?"

"For being you. And for putting up with me."

They'd reached his pickup, and he opened her door for her and helped her inside before crossing around the front of the truck and getting behind the wheel. "Believe it or not," he said as he buckled up, "once upon a time, I had to run away from home, too."

"Really?"

He surprised himself by smiling at the memory. "Angus had a fit when he found out I'd bought my ranch in the mountains. He told me I was crazy to live so isolated from other people. Told me I was just like—" He paused, struck suddenly by what his father's speech had revealed, something he hadn't understood at the time. "Angus cut himself off before he finished that sentence. He never said who I was just like." Devon's mouth flattened. "It must be *him* I'm like. My biological father."

He pounded the steering wheel. "Damn it! If Angus thinks I'm like *him,* it's because he knew my father. How could my mother have done something like that? She had Aiden and Brian and Connor one after the other and then, two years later, she had me. What the hell happened between my parents in those two years?"

"Maybe you should find your father—your biological father—and ask him."

Devon rejected the idea with a disgusted sound. "That man is nothing to me."

"Except it seems you're a great deal like him."

"How did we get on this subject?" Devon said irritably.

"We were wishing things could be different."

The silence between them grew oppressive. Pippa broke it by asking, "Do you think Angus has really figured out a way to ruin King?"

"How the hell should I know?"

Rather than snapping back at him, Pippa pressed her lips flat and turned to stare out the window.

Devon realized she had a very good reason for wanting to know whether King's empire was about to go belly-up. He chuffed out a breath of air and said, "Yeah, Angus might have figured out a way to do it. If he felt confident enough to talk about the trap he's set, it's a pretty good bet there's no way King can wriggle out of it. You're right to worry. Your dad might have come all this way for nothing. King might end up losing everything—including the ranch he promised to your father."

Pippa's head snapped back around. "You're kidding, right?"

Devon shot her a sideways look. "Angus has been pretty closemouthed about when the ax will fall, but he's been gloating that the day is coming when he'll finally have his revenge for his sister's death."

"Isn't there something King can do, or my father, to stop him?"

Devon shook his head. "I doubt it."

"What about my dad? He left everything behind to come here. What's he supposed to do?"

"I don't have an answer for that."

Pippa laid a beseeching hand on Devon's arm. "Is there any way we can find out exactly what Angus is planning?"

"What would you do with the information?"

"Tell my father, of course. So he can stop him."

He arched a brow. "You've run away from your dad, but you still want to help him?"

"He's my father. Despite ... everything ... I love him."

Devon dropped his hat on the bench seat between them and shoved a hand through his hair, leaving it askew. "I don't know, Pippa. I don't agree with what Angus is doing, but he's my father and—" Devon cut himself off. A muscle worked in his jaw. Angus wasn't his father. He'd made that clear all Devon's life. He didn't owe Angus Flynn a damned thing.

"All right," he said. "Let's do it. I've never supported Angus's desire for revenge. Let me see what I can find out."

Chapter 21

MATT HAD LOST hope that Pippa would come to her senses and return home. His unwed, pregnant daughter was no longer willing to listen to him. She needed the advice and counsel of her mother, which meant the sooner he got in touch with Jennifer Fairchild Hart, the better. His heart jumped at the thought of seeing the woman he'd loved since he was sixteen.

He had the best reason in the world—as though he needed an excuse—to contact her. However, in order to ask for Jennie's help, he would have to admit that he'd stolen their daughter and fled to Australia, keeping Pippa's existence a secret from her for twenty years.

By sunset on the day of the barbecue, he'd made the decision to head to Texas the next morning to speak with Jennie in person. His stomach did a somersault when he thought of what she might say, what she might do, when she realized the choice he'd made all those years ago. What if she refused to meet with him, to speak with him? He'd never really fallen out of love with her, probably because he'd never been allowed to say goodbye.

Was that all they would do? Say hello . . . and then goodbye?

Matt wanted so badly to have another chance with the woman who'd been the love of his life that his heart physically hurt whenever he thought of holding her in his arms. There had been years when he was free, but she was not. She'd been a widow for a year now, and he'd known that if he didn't reach for what he wanted, she would likely find someone else to love, and he would lose his chance.

And yet, he'd been in Wyoming for more than two months and he hadn't called, he hadn't written, he hadn't made the trip to Texas. He simply couldn't believe that, after all the loneliness and pain he'd suffered, and all the loneliness and pain he'd caused, fate would allow him to have his heart's desire.

He stopped halfway to the house and turned to King. "I need to leave the ranch for a few days."

"You can't go anywhere," King replied.

"Why not?"

"You heard what Angus said. That yellow-bellied cur finally has his knobby fingers around my throat, and I need you here when I talk to my banker and my investors this week."

"Investors?" Matt frowned. "In what?"

"A quarter-million acres of grassland I purchased in Brazil."

"What does that have to do with me?"

"I mortgaged Kingdom Come to buy it."

"Sonofabitch! You should have told me you were in way over your head when we spoke in

Australia. You signed a contract with me that stipulated—"

"Don't raise your voice to me."

Matt bit his tongue.

"The ranch will be yours," King continued. "Angus may think he can turn the screws and squeeze me out. But I'm not done fighting yet."

"What the hell were you thinking? A quarter-million acres? In Brazil?"

"I was planning to start a cattle operation, but the currency down there hasn't exactly been stable." He hesitated and said, "Then I had that cancer scare, and I put things on hold."

Matt halted in his tracks. "You have cancer?"

"It's in remission."

Matt eyed his father. He had mixed feelings hearing that King had been sick. He'd made a point of cutting his father completely out of his life. He wondered how he would have felt if he'd come home on his own someday and found King dead and gone. Would he have regretted missing the chance to confront him?

But his father looked hale and hearty now, and there were past transgressions he needed to atone for.

What other surprises—besides an astronomical mortgage—were out there waiting to ambush him? "What, exactly, is the problem with the land in Brazil?"

"The South American banker who made the loan cut off my credit. He wants his money." His eyes narrowed and his mouth flattened. "I don't know how Angus did it, but you can bet he was the one who convinced him not to give me an extension on the loan."

Matt's stomach churned. He'd known his father would cheat him in the end. He just hadn't expected King to be going down along with him. Disgusted, he asked, "What is it I need to be here to do?"

Matt was only half listening to King's convoluted explanation of his role in the upcoming negotiations, but it was obvious that he needed to be there. "Fine," he said, cutting him off. "If you'll excuse me, I have a call to make."

Matt had used the call as an excuse to get away before he said something he would regret. But as he headed for his room, he realized that he couldn't wait even another day to contact Jennie. Pippa's situation wasn't something that could be put on hold. She wasn't getting any less pregnant.

Matt had too many bad memories from Jennie's precarious pregnancy to believe that nothing bad could happen to his daughter. The longer he waited, the longer Pippa would be in danger if some mishap occurred on Devon Flynn's isolated mountain ranch, where medical help might not arrive in time. He hoped Jennie could provide the lever that would bring Pippa home.

He went to his bedroom and closed the door, then sat down on a chair near the bed with the phone in his hand, his elbows on his knees, his head down, aware that his heart was hammering a mile a minute and that he was having trouble catching his breath.

What if Jennie wouldn't take his call? What if

she still blamed him, all these years later, for the supposed death of their child? He'd kept track of her over the years, yet he'd never called her. Had she ever wondered where *he* was? Had she ever hoped that they would see each other again?

He tried taking a deep breath, but only got it halfway in before he huffed it out again. It was ridiculous to feel so nervous. He dropped his cellphone and clenched his fists to stop his hands from trembling. Then he picked up the phone from the floor at his feet and called the number that had been programmed into it for the past year.

The number he'd dialed was the home phone at Jennie's grandmother's ranch near Fredericksburg, Texas, west of Austin. Her grandmother had passed away and left her the ranch, and he could only suppose she'd wanted the privacy to grieve that she could have there.

A dozen thoughts ran through his head as the phone rang. What if she wasn't in? Should he leave a message for her to call? Or should he simply hang up? He figured the phone had caller ID, so if he hung up, Jennie would realize, when he called a second time, that he'd called once before and hadn't left a message. So he would have to leave a message if she didn't pick up. What should he say? And what if she listened to the message and didn't call back?

Matt realized he'd been listening to the phone ring for a very long time without any sort of answering machine picking up. Then he remembered that on a ranch, it might take a while to get to the phone, so he held on for one more ring.

At that moment, the call was answered and a female voice said, "Fairchild Ranch."

Matt's heart was in his throat, so for a moment he couldn't speak. He managed to croak, "Jennie?"

The silence on the other end of the line was so profound that all he heard was the pounding of his own heart.

"This is Jennifer Hart," she replied.

He had to clear his throat before he could say, "It's Matt." And then, because it had been twenty years, and because she might not have thought of him as often as he'd thought of her, he added, "Matthew Grayhawk."

"Matt."

Just his name. Nothing else. What had he heard in her voice? Surprise? Yes. Delight? Joy? Happiness? No. He felt frozen by what else he'd heard in that single word. Caution. Ambivalence. Wariness. Although, he couldn't imagine why she would think he would ever do anything to hurt her.

"It's been a long time," he said, aware he was walking through a minefield, and that saying the wrong thing could be deadly to his hopes of a reconciliation.

"How are you, Matt?" Her statement was as ordinary as his, as though they'd seen each other just yesterday. His answer needed to cover twenty years of living and a separation that had wrenched his soul from his body.

"How are you?" he said at last. "I heard about your husband's death. I'm sorry for your loss." He was sorry she'd been hurt. He wasn't sorry she was free. He wondered if she could make that distinction from the way he'd expressed his condolences.

"Why are you calling, Matt?"

Well, she wasn't going to beat around the bush, was she? She had a lot more courage than he did. He wiped the sweat from his brow, then swiped his hand on his jeans, stalling for time to come up with the right words to tell her everything he was feeling. In the end he blurted, "I need your help."

"Oh?" The caution was back in her voice. "Where are you?"

It was a logical question. He'd been out of touch with everyone he'd known for the past twenty years. "I'm at Kingdom Come."

"Did something happen to your father?"

Another logical question. His father's death or incapacitation was a good reason for him to have finally returned home. "King's fine. He offered the ranch to me if I'd come live here, so I came."

"Where have you been?"

"I was living on a cattle station in the Northern Territory in Australia."

"I always wondered how you disappeared so completely, as though you'd fallen off the face of the earth. I guess that explains it."

He felt encouraged that she'd wondered about him. But this meandering conversation wasn't getting him where he needed to go. He wished they were face-to-face. He didn't want to tell her this news on the phone. It was his own fault he'd waited so long, and now he had no choice.

On the other hand, this might be better—

especially if she wanted nothing more to do with him after all was said and done. He wasn't sure he would have been able to bear standing in the same room with her and having her send him away.

"There's something I need to tell you," he began. "Something I should have told you a long time ago."

"There's no need to say anything," she said, cutting him off before he really got started. "We were foolish children who lost something precious. It's over and done."

He wasn't sure if she was speaking of their love for each other or the child they'd supposedly lost, but it was the best opening he was going to get, so he took it. "Our daughter didn't die."

In the hush that followed, he imagined her brows deeply furrowed, her mouth open wide with disbelief, her hands trembling like leaves in the wind at the literal shock of such a statement. He heard a thump and wondered if her legs had given out. "Are you all right?"

He heard a gurgling sound, and then her frantic voice asking, "Where is she? How is she? How could this have happened?"

He wished he were there to take her in his arms and hold her and comfort her as he revealed the tale he had to tell. Maybe then he could keep her from hating him after he exposed the enormity of what he'd done.

"King told me that you died in childbirth and that our baby died with you. I went crazy thinking I'd killed you, getting you pregnant so young. I mourned for the loss of you and our child."

"My parents told me our daughter died," Jennie said in a voice that trembled. "I missed you terribly. I was . . . not myself . . . for a very long time."

For several moments, all he heard was the sound of breathing.

Then she said in a much calmer—but sharper—voice, "If our baby didn't die, what happened to her?"

"She went to a foster home."

"Was she eventually adopted? Where is she now?"

Matt's throat ached. His heart ached. He felt sick to his stomach. "She's with me. She's been with me for the past nineteen years."

An ominous quiet ensued, followed by the question, "How did that happen?"

"I didn't find out the truth—that neither of you were dead—until nearly a year after Pippa was born."

"Pippa?"

"It's short for Philippa." It was the name Jennie had wanted for their child, if it was a girl. It was from the Greek, meaning "lover of horses." Jennie had been horse crazy all her life.

"At first I couldn't believe it," Matt said. "I learned from my uncle Angus that you'd been told the same lie that my father had used to deceive me—that Pippa had died. Once I knew the truth, my uncle secretly helped me to establish paternity."

"Why didn't you say something to me? Why did you let me keep on believing that our child died at birth?"

He heard the torment in her voice and felt the

knot tighten in his stomach. "I wanted to tell you the truth. But I didn't dare."

"Why not?"

"Angus warned me against it. He said your parents might move Pippa somewhere else, somewhere I couldn't find her again, before I could prove I was her father."

"You should have told me anyway."

"I didn't know where you were!" he protested. "At least, not at first."

"But you knew before you ran away with her?"

"Yes, but—"

"You should have told me."

He spoke quickly, wanting her to understand the reasoning behind what he'd done. "I knew your parents didn't want you raising our daughter, because they'd lied to you about her being stillborn. But they obviously didn't want me to have her, either, because they dumped her in that foster home. Based on the lie my father had told me, I figured he was conspiring with your parents to keep both of us from raising our child.

"I couldn't take the chance that either of our parents would find out that I had Pippa and try to take her away from me. So I grabbed her and ran as far and as fast as I could."

"And left me behind!" she cried in an agonized voice.

That was the crux of his betrayal. He'd made the choice to escape with his child, rather than with the girl he supposedly loved more than life. And had wondered forever after if he'd made the biggest mistake of his life.

Jennie was crying now, choking sobs that tore his heart out. He waited, feeling sorry and guilty and wishing he'd been smarter about how he'd done this. He should have been there with her. He owed her the chance to strike out at him, to spurn him, to castigate him for what he'd done.

She choked back her sobs and said, "Why did you wait so long to tell me our daughter is alive? Why are you contacting me now?"

The two questions had very different answers. It was easier to answer the second one, so that's what he did. "Pippa's unmarried and pregnant. And in a dangerous situation."

"Dangerous?"

"She's living with one of the Flynn boys, Devon, in a remote cabin in the mountains. As far as I know, she hasn't seen an obstetrician yet, and I'm worried that if something goes wrong, she's a long way from a hospital."

"Do you have any reason to believe something will go wrong?"

"No, but . . ."

"But I had a difficult birth," she finished for him. "I was fifteen, Matt. She's . . ."

He waited for her to calculate the date and realize that they were only a month away from Pippa's twentieth birthday.

"She's almost twenty," Jennie said. "That's a big difference. Where is the father in all this?"

"He lied to Pippa about being married. He's out of the picture."

"So what is it you want from me?"

"I want you to talk to her, to convince her to come home."

"Does she even know I exist?"

Matt paused. Here was another decision for which he had to bear the responsibility. "I told her about you a month ago, after we returned to the States."

"So she never knew I was alive?"

Matt shook his head and then realized she couldn't see him. "No."

"She's known for a whole month that she has a mother, but hasn't called me or tried to contact me?"

Matt heard the disappointment in Jennie's voice. Or maybe it was despair.

"It seems pretty clear to me that Pippa doesn't want a mother she never knew existed interfering with her life," Jennie said.

"She asked about you as a child all the time. I just . . . I avoided the questions. I'm not really sure why Pippa didn't contact you herself. It could have something to do with the fact that she's unmarried and pregnant. She ran off about the same time I told her about you to go live with someone she hardly knows. She's always wanted a mother."

There was silence for a moment before she asked, "You never married?"

"I did. Twice. Neither marriage lasted long." He wanted to say that neither woman had measured up to his memories of her. That he hadn't blamed them for leaving him, because he knew the fault had been his. "I have a six-year-old son." He wanted to ask why she'd never had children, whether something had actually gone wrong when Pippa was born, but he didn't think he had the right. "The second marriage ended when Nathan was still a baby."

"I want to meet Pippa," she admitted.

"You can come here—"

"I will speak with Pippa," she interrupted, "to make sure she's taking care of herself and that she's happy where she is. But I don't want to see you. I don't think I can ever forgive you for what you did."

"Jennie—"

"I don't want to hear your excuses! I can understand why a boy of seventeen might steal a child and run. But a grown man could fix what a child could not. You could have found me when we were both adults. You should have given me the chance to be a mother to my child!"

There was a lot he'd done wrong. Getting Jennie pregnant, to start with. But his heart turned to stone at the thought of never seeing her again. He regretted more than ever his decision to have this conversation on the phone. "When can you come?"

"Did you tell her you were contacting me?"

"No."

"So she won't be expecting me?"

"Do you want me to call her and let her know you're coming?"

"I don't want or need your help. I can make arrangements on my own. Goodbye, Matt."

"Jennie—" But she was already gone. Matt stared at the phone, his heart broken. He might

have just ruined whatever hope he'd had of reconnecting with his lost love.

At least Jennie knew the truth now. That hur-
dle had been crossed. There was no telling what
might happen in the future if she established a relationship with their daughter. He refused to give up
hope.

Jennie was coming to Wyoming. Somehow, he
would find a way to see her and talk to her and
convince her that they belonged together.

Chapter 22

THE RIDE HOME with Devon was filled with quiet desperation. Pippa wasn't sure which of the two of them was more upset by what they'd learned at the barbecue. Her father and her little brother might find themselves out in the cold without a home if Angus made good on his vow to ruin King. And Devon might not be the son of the man he'd known all his life as his father.

They arrived at Devon's cabin to a joyous welcome from Wulf, but rather than stop to play with him as he usually did upon his return, Devon headed straight to the barn.

"I have to check on my animals," he said brusquely.

Pippa figured he needed time alone to think, and to absorb the truth about his birth father. She didn't try to stop him. She simply said, "I'll feed Wulf."

But when night fell and Devon still hadn't returned to the house, she went looking for him. She hadn't changed out of her dress, but she'd added a sweater, because the warmth of the day had disappeared along with the sun. She didn't want to intrude on Devon's privacy, but she was worried, so she grabbed two cubes of sugar, thinking she could use her work with Sultan as an excuse to show up in the barn.

She had to wedge her hip against Wulf to keep him from coming out the door after her. "Stay," she said, squeezing the door shut slowly so she wouldn't bang his nose. "We'll both be back soon, I promise."

She followed the dark path from the narrow, environmental lights on either side of the porch toward the glow inside the barn, wondering what she would find when she got there. What had Devon been doing to keep himself busy all afternoon?

When she opened the barn door, she saw that he'd turned on the single bulb in the center of the barn, leaving both ends in shadow. She peered at the area where the wild animals were kept in cages and saw no movement. She started to call out to him, but everything was so still and quiet, she felt foolish for coming here. Devon had obviously left the barn sometime during the afternoon and gone off somewhere to be by himself.

She might as well offer the stallion the sugar she'd brought. She walked silently down the center aisle toward Sultan's stall. She had no idea why she'd brought two cubes, when previously she'd never brought more than one. When she reached the stallion's stall, he was backed into the corner staring at her, his dark eyes liquid in the shadowy light.

"It's just me, Sultan. I brought you some sugar."

She set the two cubes on the top edge of the stall, six inches apart. Then she took a single step back and stood with her hands at her sides. Her voice remained calm and quiet as she murmured, "I know you've had a tough life, but that's all over now. I've brought you something sweet. Come to me. Come."

Maybe it was the fact that she was visiting Sultan at night, when she'd previously come only in daylight, or maybe all her hard work was finally paying off, but to her amazement, Sultan left the corner of his stall and took the few steps necessary to reach the stall door without rearing or stomping or laying his ears back. He stared at her, snorted once, then delicately lipped the sugar cube on the left into his mouth. A moment later, he retrieved the one on the right.

Pippa expected him to retreat, but he remained where he was. She slowly reached out her hand toward his nose, murmuring, "I will never hurt you. You're safe with me."

She was ready to pull her hand back if he tried to bite. She saw his withers quiver, as though he expected a blow, but he held his head still as her fingertips brushed his velvet nose. The touch lasted only a second before he jerked his head away and ran in a circle around the stall. But he didn't return to the corner. He stood in the center of the stall, his head up, his ears forward. He was out of reach, but not as far from her as he could get.

"You did it."

Pippa whirled toward the voice that came out of the dark. "Devon? Is that you?"

He pushed open the door of the empty stall opposite Sultan's and stepped out of the shadows.

"You scared the wits out of me!" she said in a voice made sharp by his sudden, unexpected appearance.

His hat was gone. His eyes were red-rimmed, as though he'd been crying, and he had straw in his hair, as though he'd been lying down in the stall.

Her heart went out to him. She took two steps and slid her arms around him. "I'm here," she said. "Everything will be all right."

She felt him shudder and tightened her hold around his waist. A moment later she felt his arms surround her.

"I must have fallen asleep," he said, his lips against her ear. "I woke up when I heard you talking. I thought it was . . ." He shook his head. "I wasn't sure who was speaking. But they were words I wanted to hear."

Pippa tried to recall exactly what she'd said that might have provided Devon solace. Then she knew. *I will never hurt you. You're safe with me.*

She pressed her nose against his throat. She would never hurt him. Not if she could help it. Right now she only wanted to provide comfort for his wounded heart. She kissed his throat beneath his ear, then his cheek, and when he turned his head, her mouth found his.

The exchange of kisses was tender, each of them offering the gentle touch of lips, but soon that wasn't enough. Devon's tongue traced the seam of her lips, and she opened to him.

He brushed the strap of her dress off her shoulder, and followed the falling bodice with his lips until her naked breast fell free. His thumb brushed the nipple, and she moaned as her body responded to his caress. A moment later he had the other strap off, and his mouth left hers and captured her breast.

Pippa didn't know what to do with her hands, she just knew his mouth and teeth and tongue were doing things to her that left her whole body trembling with need. She caught his head and forced his mouth back to hers, driving her tongue between his teeth, wanting to be joined with him, wanting it more than she'd ever wanted anything in her life.

He reached behind him and opened the door to the dark, empty stall and backed both of them into it. She glimpsed a striped saddle blanket laid out in the straw before the stall door closed. He lowered her onto it and followed her down onto his knees.

"Let me love you," he said urgently.

"Yes, yes, please."

Buttons pinged against the wooden stall as he yanked off his shirt. Then he reached for her dress to pull it off over her head, and she dropped back onto the rough wool blanket, naked except for a pair of bikini panties and her cowboy boots.

Pippa felt a momentary qualm, and then realized he couldn't see her body, at least not well, in the shadows. She kicked off her boots and toed off her socks. By then Devon had stripped himself naked and reached for her bikini panties, skimming them down her bare legs.

He thrust once and they were joined.

Pippa wasn't sure what she'd expected, but it wasn't what happened next.

Devon paused, his body touching hers from breast to thighs, with his weight braced on his arms. He nuzzled her throat and said, "I've wanted to make love to you since the first moment I laid eyes on you." He tenderly brushed a strand of hair away from her face. His face was shadowed above her, his eyes dark and mysterious. "Tell me what you like. I want to please you."

Pippa smiled, and then laughed with delight. She could tell Devon was smiling back at her, because his teeth gleamed white in what little light there was. "I like it slow and gentle." She kissed his lower lip. "And a little wild." And then she bit it.

He looked surprised. And then he laughed and kissed her back.

The lovemaking was both playful and carnal. Sensual and silly. Devon took his time, teasing and touching until her body was wired taut. Then he took her over the edge, falling with her until they lay together shattered and replete.

What happened next was best of all. Instead of abandoning her once he was satisfied, Devon spooned her naked body against his—her hips against his groin, his arm across her breasts, his warm breath against the back of her neck.

"This is nice," she murmured.

"Yeah," he agreed. "It is."

They lay quietly together, and Pippa was almost asleep when Wulf howled. Immediately, the stallion's hooves thumped against the walls of his stall, the owl hooted, and the fawn made a bleating sound.

Pippa abruptly sat up, realizing belatedly what

she'd done. She should never have made love to Devon without telling him first that she was pregnant. She'd felt compelled to comfort him, but she should have relied on her head, rather than her heart, to do it.

Devon sat up as well. She shivered with pleasure as he kissed her shoulder. If she didn't do something, they would be making love again. So far she'd been lucky. Devon hadn't gotten a good look at her body, nor did she think he'd spent enough time caressing her belly to perceive the changes her pregnancy had wrought. Her breasts were larger than they'd been a month ago, and more tender, but he couldn't know that.

The first time they'd made love, he'd been excited and easily distracted and committed to making the sex good for her. The second time he might notice things he hadn't observed before.

Pippa reached for her dress and pulled it on over her head.

"We should go," she said, searching for her socks and boots. "Wulf's going to keep howling until he knows we're all right."

When he realized she wasn't going to lie back down, he began searching out his own clothes and pulling them on.

Pippa stopped what she was doing to watch. He had a beautiful body, his flanks sinewy and lean, his belly flat, his shoulders and abdomen ridged with muscle. She enjoyed watching the fluid motion of muscle and bone as he stepped into his jeans.

He glanced over his shoulder and caught her watching and grinned. "Like what you see?"

She laughed as she stood and began threading her fingers through her hair to remove the straw. "As a matter of fact, I do."

Once he had his jeans zipped and snapped and his belt buckled, he crossed and pulled a strand of straw from her hair. She did the same for him. Their faces were close, and she saw that, although the tension had left his body, his eyes still looked haunted.

She stood on tiptoe to briefly kiss his lips. "Come on," she said. "Tomorrow *is* another day."

He laughed at her use of Scarlett's line from *Gone With the Wind*. He threaded his fingers with hers and shoved open the stall door. He stopped where he was and stared.

"What's wrong?" She leaned around him to look at whatever had caught his gaze.

Sultan's head was completely over the stall door, his nostrils flared as he stared at Devon.

"He's not running away anymore," Devon said quietly.

"He knows he's safe here."

Devon cocked his head at her. "Yeah. I guess he does."

Chapter 23

AS HE'D ACKNOWLEDGED the truth about his birth, Devon had run the gamut of emotions, from rage to resignation and back again, until Pippa had offered solace for his damaged soul. Once back in the house, they'd stayed up late into the night talking about Devon's mother, and the choices she and Angus had made. Mostly he'd done the talking, and she'd listened.

"We can't know why they did what they did," she'd argued. "People make mistakes."

But he hadn't been feeling tolerant. "I don't have to forgive either one of them." The more he ranted, the more unhappy Pippa had looked, so that when they'd finally gone to their separate rooms, he'd found it impossible to sleep.

Now that he knew he had a biological father out there somewhere who'd had an affair—or at least a sexual liaison—with his mother, he couldn't stop thinking about him. He'd stared into the darkness, his mind alive with questions.

This morning, he wanted answers.

Who was his biological father? Had it been a fling? Or had his mother been in love with the man? Where was his biological father now? Did he know about Devon? Did Angus know who he was?

At the crack of dawn, Devon left a note for Pippa and headed for the Lucky 7. When he stepped down from his pickup at the back door to the Flynn ranch house, he ran right into Brian. His older brother had been staying at the ranch when he wasn't on duty at the firehouse because his ex-wife had gotten their house in the divorce. Brian was still licking his wounds and hadn't yet bought himself another place.

"I thought you were off this week," Devon said.

"I am. I got called in to fight a forest fire in one of the national parks."

"It's awful early in the season for that, isn't it?"

"It was a dry winter, so there's plenty of kindling out there. And there's not enough snow on the ground anymore to slow down a fire—especially one that somebody set. What brings you here, little brother?" Brian asked.

"I came to get some answers."

Brian met his gaze and said, "You know it doesn't matter, right? You're my little brother, and I love you no matter what."

A sudden lump clogged Devon's throat. He swallowed over the painful knot and said, "Did you know?"

Brian grinned and punched him in the arm. "That you were a little different? I've always known that."

"You know what I mean."

"About Mom? No, I didn't."

There was a bitter twist to Brian's lips, and Devon recalled that his brother had divorced a wife who'd cheated on him. So maybe he understood a little of what their father must have felt.

"I knew Mom was unhappy for a while before you were born," Brian continued, "but I never knew why." He slipped an arm around Devon's shoulder. "I guess I do now." He suddenly flipped the brim of Devon's cowboy hat up with his other hand so Devon had to grab it to keep it from falling off.

"Hey!" Devon protested, freeing himself from Brian's grasp. "Cut it out."

"Good luck getting any information from Dad," Brian said. "If he hasn't talked about it for twenty-eight years, I don't expect he's going to let the cat out of the bag now."

"The cat's already out of the bag," Devon pointed out. "Matt took care of that."

"Yeah, I guess he did. Why do you suppose he revealed a secret like that?"

"He wanted to cause trouble for me so I'd send Pippa home."

Brian eyed him sideways. "Since the two of you left the barbecue together, I guess it didn't work."

"I love her."

"You barely know the girl. How can you be in love with her?"

"It just happened."

"Does she love you?"

"Not yet."

Brian whistled. "Good luck with that." He glanced at his watch and said, "Gotta go. Be careful, little brother." He reached out and flipped the brim of Devon's hat up again, this time managing to get it to fall completely off. He raced for his truck, laughing, and had the engine running by the time Devon retrieved his Stetson from the ground. Devon waved his brother goodbye with the hat and then put it on and pulled it low on his forehead.

He had some business inside with his father. Check that. Some business with the man who'd pretended all his life to be his father.

Devon left his hat and his coat in the kitchen and went searching for Angus. He found him sitting in his office behind his desk. The door was open, and when Devon knocked on the frame, Angus looked up and said, "I've been expecting you. Come in."

Throughout Devon's life, punishment had been meted out by his father from behind that desk. He wasn't about to stand in front of it like a child who'd misbehaved. He wasn't the one who'd done something wrong. He crossed to the wet bar, and even though it was early, poured himself a drink. "Do you want me to make something for you?"

"I'm not thirsty."

Devon took one sip and realized a drink wasn't going to make this conversation any easier. He set it down on the bar and turned to face the man who'd raised him. "Who is my father?"

"I am," he snapped.

The answer startled him. Had Matt been wrong? "Matt implied—"

Angus waved a hand to cut him off. "Biologically, you're not mine," he said. "But I brought you up, and you're as much mine—and as much a Flynn—as any of my boys."

The painful lump was back in Devon's throat. He hadn't realized how badly he'd needed to hear his father speak those particular words. But they didn't wipe out a lifetime of slights. "You didn't treat me the same."

"It wasn't for want of trying."

"What does that mean?"

"When she knew she was dying, your mother made me promise that I wouldn't hold what she did against you. But it wasn't easy. Every time I looked at you, I saw him."

"I look like him?"

Angus nodded. "But you're really just like her."

"What do you mean?"

"Your mother was always bringing home injured wild things and nursing them back to health."

Devon felt his eyes filling with tears and blinked to force them back. He swallowed hard and said, "Why did she do it?"

Angus took a deep breath and let it out. He met Devon's gaze without speaking for a long time but finally said, "Fiona paid me back for cheating on her by cheating on me."

Devon had never heard his father admit to any flaw in his character in the past, so he was astonished to hear him confess to infidelity now.

"You wonder why I hate King Grayhawk?" Angus said through tight jaws. "Well, you're a big reason why!"

The blood left Devon's face in a rush. "What?"

"That meddlesome sonofabitch told your mother

I had a mistress. Fiona asked me to end the relationship, and when I wouldn't—"

"You wouldn't?" Devon interrupted.

"Your mother decided to pay me back by having sex—in my bed—with a cattleman from Texas named Shiloh Kidd."

My father's name is Shiloh Kidd. He's a cattleman from Texas. He took advantage of my mother, which makes him a bad man. Or maybe not. Maybe my mother took advantage of Kidd, luring him into her bed to get revenge on my father.

"Why didn't you end your affair when Mom asked?" Devon asked. "Why would you risk your marriage for a mistress?"

"Because I love her."

Devon felt anger building at the enormity of his father's transgression against his mother, which had resulted, ultimately, in his birth. "You loved another woman—and kept her as your mistress—while you were married to my mother, and you have the nerve to blame her for having sex with another man?"

It suddenly dawned on him that his father hadn't used the past tense. "You *love* her? She's still a part of your life?"

"I still love her," Angus said.

Devon realized the subtle distinction in what his father had said. "If you love her so much, why haven't you married her?"

A flash of pain crossed Angus's face. Instead of replying to the question, he said, "In the beginning, there were reasons why Darcie and I couldn't get married and reasons why I had to marry your mother."

"Such as?"

"Nothing that matters now," he said, waving a hand to brush aside Devon's search for more answers. "It wasn't until after I married your mother that I realized I wasn't willing to give Darcie up. In the end, Darcie was willing to share me with your mother. We were careful. We were discreet. I loved your mother, never doubt it. I loved them both.

"Everything went fine for years—until King found out. He was furious with me for . . . for something I had done to him. So he made a point of telling Fiona what was going on."

Devon noticed that Angus had neglected to mention what it was he'd done to King. It must have been something heinous for King to retaliate by revealing to Devon's mother that Angus had a mistress.

Angus's voice grew harsh as he continued, "Your mother, understandably, wasn't willing to share me with another woman. She demanded that I give up Darcie. When I wouldn't, she slept with some stranger who showed up at the ranch and made sure I found them together."

Devon tried to imagine how much hurt and rage and pain his mother must have suffered to perform such a vindictive act. "So where is this mistress of yours now?" he persisted. "Why haven't you married her in all these years?"

Angus met Devon's gaze and said, "She doesn't want her son to know that I'm his father."

Devon's knees buckled, and he sank onto the

closest surface, which happened to be a leather chair. His voice wasn't quite steady when he said, "So I'm not the only half brother in this family." He looked into Angus's piercing blue eyes, wondering how he could have kept so many secrets for so many years. "If I found out the truth in the end," Devon pointed out, "it seems likely he will, too."

"Darcie married another man to make sure that never happens."

"You still love her, even though she's married to another man?"

"It's thanks to King that we've lived our lives separately. I hate King Grayhawk for what he did to my sister. But I despise him for what he did to separate me from Darcie and, in the end, from your mother."

"Yet you don't blame Darcie for marrying another man and concealing the fact that she bore you a son?"

"I've gotten pretty good at hiding what I'm feeling."

Devon thought that was the understatement of the year.

"Darcie didn't want her son ever to be called a bastard. I understood that." He met Devon's gaze with bleak eyes. "And I was married to your mother. So I had no choice but to accept Darcie's decision."

Devon had never imagined his father's love life was such a tangled web of deception and damage and loss. "Why are you telling me all this?"

"Because I hope my experience can save you from the same fate."

"I'm not in love with two women at the same time," Devon retorted.

"No, but the woman you're in love with is in love with another man."

Devon's heart stuttered. He hadn't imagined his father could say anything that would shock him more than the secrets he'd already disclosed. He felt like a rawhide rope was being cinched ever tighter around his chest.

When he could finally draw a breath to speak he said, "You're wrong. Pippa's not—" He cut himself off, trying to remember exactly what it was Pippa had said. *She'd been deceived by the man she loved, who'd turned out to be married.* She'd never said that she'd stopped loving him.

"His name is Tim Brandon," Angus continued. "He's the father of the child Pippa's carrying."

It was a good thing Devon was sitting down, because that statement would have flattened him.

No. She would have told me.

And then he remembered all the times last night when Pippa had started a sentence and then stopped. The guilty look on her face when he'd urged her to finish her thought, before she'd lowered her eyes . . . and remained mute. He'd figured she was having regrets about what had happened in the barn, and he'd stepped in to fill the silences and keep her from saying that she wished they hadn't made love.

But maybe that hadn't been it at all. Maybe she was feeling bad because there was something she should have told him a long time before now.

Something she sure as hell should have told him before they'd made love.

He turned on Angus, furious because he didn't want to believe it was true. But he couldn't think of any reason why Angus would lie to him about such a thing. "How could you possibly know all this?"

"Matt confided in me. Pippa's pregnancy is one of the reasons they left Australia. She was being treated like a pariah because she was carrying a married man's child."

Devon opened his mouth to say that if Pippa was pregnant he would have noticed the signs, since he wasn't blind, but closed it before any sound escaped. He remembered that Pippa had been nauseated a few mornings when she'd first come to stay with him. And he'd been surprised when they made love in the barn that her belly wasn't as flat as he'd expected it to be. He'd thought with an inward smile that the roundness he felt was the result of Pippa's eating so many of the oatmeal cookies she'd baked for him, because he'd told her they were his favorite.

Now he realized that the nausea had been morning sickness. And her belly had grown larger since she'd come to stay with him because a child— another man's child—was growing inside her.

"I'm sorry, son."

"I'm not your son!" Devon snapped, rising and heading for the door. All his life he'd wished his father would call him *son*. But not like this.

"Devon! Stop. Wait!"

Devon turned in the doorway and saw that Angus had risen from his chair and had a hand outstretched as though to offer succor. "I didn't need to hear your confession, old man. And I sure as hell don't need your help."

He'd turned to leave again when Angus called out, "Don't be a fool!"

Devon whirled on his father and snarled, "It's too goddamn late for that!"

Chapter 24

PIPPA HAD SLEPT late, because she'd spent several hours of the previous night sobbing with her face held against a pillow, so Devon wouldn't hear her. She'd felt sick with shame because she couldn't find the courage—even after she'd made love with Devon—to tell him about the baby.

She'd been on the verge of confessing the truth last night. But then Devon had made it clear what he thought about a man—he'd meant his biological father—who had sex with another man's wife. He'd continued—using Brian's wife as an example—with what he thought of a woman who would cheat on her husband, refusing to concede that there could be any set of circumstances deserving of forgiveness.

Pippa hadn't *known* Tim was married, but when all was said and done, he'd been someone else's husband. What would that make her in Devon's eyes? Especially since, not unlike his mother, she was carrying that married man's child?

She'd spent a sleepless night, determined to come clean in the morning and admit that she was pregnant, only to find a note from Devon on the kitchen counter telling her that he'd gone to see his father and expected to be back for lunch. She'd felt more relieved than disappointed that he'd left her behind.

She was feeding Wulf a late breakfast when she heard a knock on the door. She frowned, wondering who in the world it could be. It made no sense to answer the knock. There was no one she knew, including her father and Devon's brothers, whom she wanted to talk to, and besides, she wasn't dressed to meet company. Her eyes were gritty, her mascara smeared, her hair a mess, and she was naked under the long-sleeved white T-shirt she'd worn to bed along with a pair of Devon's long john bottoms.

Wulf's attention remained completely focused on the door. He growled, and his neck hairs hackled. Pippa realized that whoever was standing on the other side of that door, it wasn't someone Devon knew well, or Wulf wouldn't be acting so predatory. Which was when she realized that she was all alone and completely defenseless—and if Devon had followed previous habit, the door wasn't even locked!

She was reaching for the phone to call 911— not that anyone could get here in time to save her—when a female voice called out, "Is anybody home?"

Wulf immediately sat on his haunches, looked up at her, and whined.

Pippa was confused by the wolf's behavior, which suggested that he'd changed his mind, that whoever was out there was friend rather than foe.

In any case, knowing it was a woman, Pippa no longer felt physically threatened. She crossed to the curtained window and looked out to see if she recognized whoever it was.

She dropped the curtain immediately and pressed a fisted hand against her heart. She didn't know the woman, but she recognized her—because she saw many of the same features in her own mirror every morning.

Pippa forgot that she was wearing pajamas, that her hair was a mess, that her eyes were smeared with mascara. She ran to the door and jerked it open, her heart jackhammering in her chest.

She said nothing, just stared her fill, absorbing every detail of the woman she believed was her mother. The woman on the front porch was wearing a crisply pressed white shirt open at the throat and covered by a fringed black suede jacket, a black belt with a delicate silver buckle, ironed jeans, and black ostrich cowboy boots. Her hair was as blond as Pippa's, but it was shorter and swung freely just below her jaw. A few bangs fell onto her forehead, leaving her finely arched brows visible over dove-gray eyes the exact same shade as Pippa's.

"Pippa?" The woman attempted a smile, but her mouth wobbled and she stopped trying.

"Mum?" Pippa whispered.

The woman nodded as her eyes filled with tears. One slid down her cheek, and still she didn't move. At last, she cleared her throat and said, "May I come in?"

Pippa stepped back and pulled the door farther open. And then remembered Wulf. "Just a minute,

I need to—" But Wulf was sitting in the same place she'd left him, observing the two of them with a cocked head. Pippa realized Wulf must have heard something of her voice in her mother's, which was why he'd stopped bristling. And he must have sensed—or smelled—the biological connection between her and her mother, because he allowed Jennifer Hart to enter the house without moving a muscle to stop her.

"Is that a wolf?" her mother asked, freezing just inside the door.

"He won't hurt you," Pippa assured her. "Come here, Wulf," she said, calling the wolf to her side, "and meet my mother."

Pippa waited and watched as Jennifer Hart took the few steps to put her close enough to reach out a tentative hand. Wulf sniffed and then licked her fingers.

Her mother gave a nervous laugh as she retrieved her hand. "For a moment there, it looked like he was deciding whether or not I'd make a tasty dinner."

Pippa smiled. "I don't know why Wulf accepted me as a friend. I'm just grateful he did."

Wulf crossed to the buffalo robe on the floor in front of the fireplace and curled up with his tail over his nose.

Pippa was suddenly self-conscious about her appearance and shoved both hands through her hair in an attempt to get out some of the tangles. "I'm a mess. I overslept this morning," she said by way of explanation.

"I should have called ahead, but . . ." Her

mother smiled—doing a better job of it this time—and said, "I was afraid you would tell me not to come."

Pippa wondered what she would have done if she'd been given a choice about this meeting. She supposed the fact that she'd opened the door when she'd recognized her mother answered that question. "How did you know where to find me?"

"Your father called me yesterday."

Pippa stiffened. "And asked you to come talk some sense into me?"

Ignoring the agitation in Pippa's voice, her mother said, "I've been traveling all morning. I could really use a cup of coffee."

"How about a cup of tea instead?" Pippa suggested. She still hadn't figured out how to use Devon's automatic coffeemaker.

"Tea would be fine." Her mother followed her into the kitchen, dropping the sleek black purse that had been hanging by a strap from her shoulder onto the breakfast bar.

Pippa stopped what she was doing and turned to fill her eyes with the sight of the woman who'd borne her. "I know I'm staring," she said, "but I never even knew until very recently that you were alive. It's hard to believe you're real."

Her mother smiled, and this time her gray eyes were filled with warmth. "I'm afraid I'm doing the same thing. I thought you'd died at birth. I had no idea you existed until yesterday."

"I've known about you for a whole month. I just . . ." The reasons she hadn't contacted her mother were all tied up with her being pregnant.

She wondered if her father had revealed the truth to her mother. If he had, it hadn't kept her mum from coming to see her. And if he hadn't, she wasn't yet ready to admit how flawed a daughter she'd turned out to be.

Instead she said, "You must have been pretty shocked when my dad told you I was alive."

"Yes. I was," she admitted. "I wasn't going to come. I thought you wouldn't want to see me." She shrugged, looking chagrined. "In the end, I couldn't stop myself."

Pippa stood motionless as this stranger—who was her mother—reached out and brushed her bangs away from her forehead. Pippa's whole body was quivering with excitement and fear and joy and a dozen other emotions that were tumbling over one another as her mother touched her for the first time. When she held out her arms, Pippa walked right into them.

Pippa hugged her mother as tightly as she was being hugged in return. She heard her mother sob once, and felt like sobbing herself, but her throat was so constricted no sound could escape. She felt the caress of her mother's hand on her hair, and leaned back to look down at her, which was when she realized she was several inches taller.

"You're so short!" Pippa said with a laugh.

"You're so tall!" her mother replied with a grin. "Your father comes from a family of towering men."

Pippa grimaced at the mention of her father. "Is he coming here, too?"

Her mother sobered and shook her head. "He

doesn't know I'm here. Besides, I told him I don't want to see him." Her thumb gently brushed Pippa's cheek, and her eyes roamed over Pippa's face as though she still couldn't quite believe she wasn't dreaming. "I need a little more time first to get used to having a daughter."

"Does that mean you have a son?" Pippa asked.

"The senator and I never had any children."

Instead of remarking on the fact that her mother had apparently been married to an American politician, Pippa focused on the other question that came to mind. "You didn't want children?"

"I never got pregnant again after you were born."

Pippa wondered if that meant her mother wasn't able to have children, or that she'd taken precautions to be sure she wouldn't get pregnant again, but she didn't want to spoil this first meeting by asking that sort of question.

"I would like a chance to get to know you better. I'd love for you to come stay with me at my family's ranch in Texas."

Pippa was stunned by the offer. And relieved. And confused, because she should be jumping at it, yet found herself hesitating. It didn't take much soul-searching to realize that, as much as she wanted to spend time getting to know her mother, she wanted to stay with Devon more.

Now what? Especially since she had no idea how Devon was going to react when he discovered she was pregnant—and that she'd been keeping her plight a secret from him since the day they'd met. Pippa felt sick to her stomach—and not because she was pregnant. She wondered if it was already too late, if she'd already ruined any chance she'd had of a life with Devon by lying from the start.

Now her mother had offered to have her come to Texas so they could get to know each other. Would Devon understand why she wanted to go if she walked out of his life right now? How she needed to spend time with her mother? Surely he would, since he'd admitted last night how curious he was about his own biological father.

Or would he simply think she was running from him, unwilling to face his judgment when he finally learned—as he must eventually—that she was carrying Tim's child?

Pippa took a step back from her mother and said, "I should make us that tea."

Her mother leaned back against the kitchen counter and watched as Pippa plugged in the electric teapot Devon had bought as a surprise for her earlier in the week. Which reminded her that he might be returning at any moment.

"Would you mind watching the teapot while I get dressed? Devon's supposed to be back in a little while, and I don't want him to find me still wearing my pajamas."

"Sure."

Pippa could feel her mother's eyes on her all the way to Devon's bedroom. She felt almost guilty shutting the door. It wasn't as though she wasn't coming right back out again in a couple of minutes. She just needed some time alone to adjust to the fact that *her mother* was standing in the next room.

Pippa wished she knew whether her father had

revealed her pregnancy to her mother. Would her mum still be willing to have Pippa come and live with her if she knew *everything*? Or was that why she'd come—to rescue her pregnant daughter?

Pippa had never felt so torn and confused. She wanted to spend more time with her newfound mother, but she wasn't sure she wanted to go all the way to Texas to do it. Especially when it meant leaving Devon behind. But what if Devon wanted nothing to do with her when he learned the truth?

Pippa's stomach had been cramping a little ever since she'd woken up, and it had gotten worse after her mother appeared at the door. She'd thought it was simply the stress of knowing she was finally going to tell Devon the truth, followed by the excitement of meeting her mother for the first time. But when she pulled off her long johns and saw several spots of bright red blood, she realized it was something a lot more serious—and potentially devastating.

For a moment she couldn't catch her breath. She tried not to panic. If there had ever been any doubt that she wanted this baby, she knew the truth in that moment. Because all she could think about was getting to a hospital where they could find out what was wrong and save her baby.

Pippa dressed hurriedly, grateful that her mum had shown up at the door, because without her mother's arrival she might have been in dire straits. She would have had no way to get to a hospital except to call for someone to come get her, which might have delayed her getting help until it was too late.

When she flew out of the bedroom a few minutes later, she was dressed in what she'd been wearing lately to conceal her pregnancy—a T-shirt covered by one of Devon's wool shirts over half-zipped jeans and her new cowboy boots.

She walked straight to the teapot and unplugged it, then turned to her mother and said, "Can you drive me to the hospital?"

"Of course! What's wrong? Is it the baby?"

Well, that answers that question, Pippa thought, relieved that her mother both knew the truth about her pregnancy and had apparently accepted it. "Yes. I'm spotting. Please, can we go now?"

Pippa was grabbing her jacket when her mother said, "Do you want to call your father?"

"No." She was too afraid he wouldn't be saddened by this loss. He might think it was a blessing in disguise. He might even say such a thing out loud. She would hate him forever if he did.

"What about Devon?" her mother asked.

Pippa froze. Did she want to call him? And tell him what? That she might be losing a baby he knew nothing about? "No," she said, moving toward the door.

"Will he be worried if he comes back and finds you gone?" her mother persisted.

He would likely think she'd gone for a walk, at least for a while. When she didn't return he would worry. He might start making phone calls—maybe even to her father. Heaven knew what her father might reveal in such a conversation. She wanted to be the one to tell Devon she was pregnant. She shuddered to think how he would feel if he got the news secondhand.

"I'll leave a note," she said.

It was easier to announce that she would leave a note than to decide what to write. What should she say?

I'm spotting and I might lose my baby—oh, did I mention I'm pregnant?—but my long-lost mother showed up this morning—perfect timing—so she's taking me to the hospital.

Pippa giggled at the absurdity of such a note and realized she was on the edge of hysteria.

A moment later her mother was by her side, her arm around her waist holding her close. "Take a deep breath."

"I don't have time—"

"A deep breath," her mother insisted.

Pippa took a quick breath and huffed it out. "Satisfied?"

"Another," her mother said. "Deeper. Slower."

Pippa followed her instructions and realized her thundering heart was no longer galloping quite so fast. She looked into her mother's eyes and said, "I'm scared, Mum. I'm scared I'm going to lose my baby."

Her mother's arms folded around her like angel's wings and she whispered, "Whatever happens, sweetheart, I'll be there with you."

Pippa found the words comforting beyond measure. She didn't understand why she was so glad to have this stranger who'd given birth to her by her side when she was keeping her father—who'd loved her all her life—at a distance.

Her mother took the pen from Pippa's trembling hand and wrote on the top sheet of the notepad: *Gone to the hospital.*

She dropped the pen, stuck the blue sticky note in the center of the breakfast bar, and said, "Let's go."

Chapter 25

DEVON FUMED ALL the way home. It was bad enough that his father had been lying to him all his life. It hurt even worse to discover that Pippa hadn't trusted him enough to tell him something pretty damned important about herself. Good Lord. A baby! He was having trouble separating his anger over her deception from his feelings for Pippa, especially now that he knew having her in his life meant raising another man's child.

It wasn't just the news that Pippa was pregnant that had him so upset, it was the suggestion his father had made that Pippa still loved the bastard who'd gotten her pregnant and then abandoned her. What if he was right? Pippa had admitted to him that she wasn't in any hurry to fall in love because she didn't want to get hurt again. But he'd never imagined she could still be holding a candle for a married man who was beyond her reach.

Devon took an extra second outside his front door to calm down, to remind himself to listen to what she had to say before he said anything to her that he might regret.

When he opened the door at last, he found

Wulf standing there waiting for him. The wolf shoved his nose against Devon's hand, and Devon gave him a scratch behind the ear. "Where is she?" he asked, knowing Pippa must have heard his truck door slam, and at the same time feeling the emptiness of the house.

"Pippa?" When she didn't answer, he figured she must be in the barn. He turned around and went back out again, making sure Wulf stayed inside, reassuring him, "I'll be right back."

A quick search of the barn revealed that Pippa wasn't there, either, although Sultan stuck his head out—that was a first—to greet him. "Hello, big guy," he said, keeping his distance because he wasn't sure the stallion wouldn't bite his arm off if he got too close. "Where is she?"

Sultan turned to look toward the door.

"She's not with me. I thought she would be here with you."

He risked reaching a hand out to the horse, but Sultan backed away. "Yeah, I know. You want her, not me. Where the hell is she?"

The mount Pippa usually rode was still in its stall, so she hadn't taken off on horseback. Maybe she'd decided to take a walk. If so, he figured she wouldn't have gone far. He'd be better off waiting for her at the house than trying to find her.

He headed back to the house feeling even more disgruntled. The worst part of this whole mess was that he had no idea what she might do when he confronted her and demanded the truth.

Hell, he wasn't sure what he was going to do himself.

When he got back inside the house, he stood there for a moment feeling antsy and anxious. Pippa would probably be hungry for lunch when she got back, so he might as well fix something. He headed to the kitchen, which was when he spied the blue note in the center of the breakfast bar.

Gone to the hospital.

His blood ran cold. *The baby.* Something had gone wrong with the baby. Why hadn't she called him? He smacked his head. Because he supposedly didn't know there *was* a baby.

Then it dawned on him that he'd left Pippa here without any way to get to the hospital. *Oh, my God,* he thought. *If anything has happened to her or the baby because she had to wait for paramedics to get way out here, I'll never forgive myself.*

He was out the door again a moment later, gunning the engine and racing for the hospital in Jackson. "Please be all right. Please be all right."

He grabbed his phone from his pocket and called Pippa's cell. The call went to voice mail. He debated whether to leave a message, but she didn't know that he knew about the baby, and he didn't want to start that conversation on the phone. So he simply said, "I'm on my way. Call me when you get this message."

Chapter 26

PIPPA WAS APPALLED when her father entered her hospital room only minutes after she'd gotten there herself. "How did you know I was here? And how did you get here so fast?"

"King is president of the hospital board. The hospital administrator called to let him know his granddaughter was on the way, and King told me so I could come and make sure you're okay. Are you?"

His face looked too worried for Pippa to send him away. "The spotting has stopped," she said, "and they gave me something to make sure it doesn't start again. Honestly, there's no reason for me to be in this bed." She pursed her lips. "They must be worried that Grandpa King will sack everyone in the place if something happens to me."

"Maybe so," her father said, his tight jaw relaxing at her effort to make light of the situation. "How do you feel?"

"I'm fine, Daddy. You shouldn't have come."

He'd been standing by the door, but he closed the distance between them and reached out to take her hand, his thumb caressing the back of it. "Now you see why I didn't want you staying at that cabin in the middle of nowhere."

Pippa pulled her hand free, irritated that he was back on his high horse. "Devon would have been home soon. And anyway, Mum showed up and gave me a ride to the hospital."

"Your mother's here? In Jackson?" He looked like he'd been poleaxed.

Pippa nodded. "She just showed up at Devon's house. She's parking her car. She should be here in a minute, if you want to talk to her."

Beads of sweat popped out above her father's upper lip, and he thrust a nervous hand through his hair. "I didn't think she would come," he muttered.

"She told me she talked to you yesterday." Pippa wished she'd been a fly on the wall. That must have been an absolutely fascinating conversation.

"Did your mother say anything about what her plans are now that she's here?"

Pippa hesitated, then admitted, "She asked me if I'd like to come stay with her in Texas." It dawned on her that if she went, she would end up separated not only from Devon but from her father, since he had to remain at Kingdom Come in order to fulfill his bargain with King.

"What did you decide to do?"

"I haven't given her an answer yet. We left for the hospital right after that, and we didn't talk much in the car."

They were interrupted by a commotion in the hall. Her father crossed to the door to see what was going on.

"What's happening?" Pippa asked.

A moment later Devon appeared in the doorway, a stout female nurse dogging his heels.

"I tried to tell him that only family is allowed in here," the nurse said to her father. "He wouldn't listen."

"I need to see Pippa," Devon said.

"Let him in, Daddy."

Her father turned to the nurse and said, "Thank you. I'll take it from here." The woman made a *hummph* sound and walked away.

Devon only had eyes for Pippa as he entered the room.

"You've seen her. Now leave," her father said.

"I'm not going anywhere until I talk to her. Pippa?"

Seeing the muscles in her father's shoulders and arms bunch for combat, she quickly shoved the sheets away and shifted her bare feet over the edge of the bed. "Please leave, Daddy. I need to speak privately with Devon."

She saw a pained expression cross his face before he said, "Fine." On his way out he stopped in front of Devon and said, "If you do anything to hurt her—in any way—I'll make you regret it the rest of your life."

He stalked out the open doorway, and Devon shoved the door closed behind him.

"Get back in bed," Devon snarled as he turned

toward Pippa. "Or do you want to lose that bastard's baby."

Pippa's face flamed. "How dare you say such a thing to me!"

"When were you planning to tell me you were having some other man's kid?"

Pippa's mouth dropped open. She'd left a message that she was going to the hospital, but she hadn't said why. "How did you find out?"

"Matt told my father, and he told me. Believe me, it was a helluva way to get the news. You had plenty of chances, Pippa. Why didn't you tell me yourself?"

"It was none of your business."

"Are you kidding me? You've lived with me for a month. We've spent every minute together. We made love."

"That was a mistake."

His eyes narrowed. "If you say so. But I thought at least we were friends!"

"You're not bloody acting like it! All you've done since you walked in here is snarl at my father and yell at me."

"You should have told me the truth."

"I told you I couldn't get involved. I told you I wasn't free to fall in love."

"Because you're still in love with that jerk in Australia?"

"Tim? I *loathe* Tim."

She saw a flicker of something—maybe relief— in his eyes before he said, "So why couldn't you tell me you were pregnant?"

"I'm about to have a child whose father I hate.

I've been terrified that I won't be able to love my baby—a baby my father has urged me to give away because keeping it might ruin the rest of my life. I have feelings for you that I don't want to have, considering the turmoil my life is in, and I didn't—and still don't—have a clue how you might feel about raising another man's child. I told you I only wanted a *friend*," she cried. "I didn't want to hurt you, and I didn't want to get hurt."

"Then you shouldn't have lied to me."

"Getting dumped by the man you love when he finds out you're carrying his child isn't something you want to go around blabbing to the neighborhood."

"I'm not just some guy in the neighborhood," he said angrily. "I thought I was more to you than that."

"You are. You've been exactly what I needed. You've been a good—a great—friend."

The light went out of his eyes when she refused to acknowledge that far more than *friendship* had existed between them. Pippa's heart was beating hard in her chest, and she threaded her fingers together so tightly her knuckles showed white. She'd been so glad to see him when he'd shown up at the door. She'd wanted his arms around her. She'd wanted his reassurance that everything would be all right.

But nothing was going the way she'd hoped. What did he want from her? Why was he so angry to be labeled her *friend*? Even when they'd joined their bodies, no words of love had been spoken. They'd returned to the house and spent the evening in front of the fire talking. She'd loved the closeness she'd felt toward him when they made love in the barn, even though there'd been nothing loverlike about their behavior the rest of the evening.

One mistake—one lie of omission—and he was acting as if the world had come to an end.

Devon's eyes roamed her face as though he were taking one long, last look before saying good-bye forever. Pippa shivered. She didn't know how to ask him for the comfort she needed when he was standing so stiffly on the other side of the room.

When he spoke again, his voice sounded calm and detached, as though he'd taken an emotional step back. As though he were something *less* than a friend. "I don't see you wearing an oxygen mask or connected to a bunch of machines. Should I assume you and the baby are out of danger?"

"We're both fine, thank you for asking." She heard the sarcasm in her voice, but she was confused by his behavior. If he didn't want anything more to do with her, he should just say so and leave.

"I'm glad you got here in time to avoid any more serious consequences."

"My mother showed up at your cabin," Pippa said. "She gave me a ride to the hospital."

He looked adorably startled. "Your mother?"

Pippa bit the inside of her cheek. This was no time to be thinking how adorable Devon looked. "My father finally told her I hadn't died at birth. He also told her that I was pregnant, and she came to offer me a place to stay."

"With her?"

Pippa nodded. "On her family's ranch in Texas."

"Are you going to take her up on it?"

"I haven't decided." Pippa wanted Devon to ask her to stay now that he knew she was pregnant. But the offer didn't come.

Instead he said, "I suppose you want to spend time with her, now that you've met her at last."

"Yes, I do." *But I'd rather stay with you.* It dawned on her that Devon hadn't touched her since he'd entered the room. That he was still standing where he'd been when he shut the door on her father. *I don't have the plague, I'm just pregnant.*

"I guess that's it, then." He stuck his hands in his back pockets. "When are you leaving?"

"Is that all you're going to say?"

"What do you want me to say?"

If you don't know, I'm not going to put words in your mouth. She'd imagined many times what Devon might do when he found out she was pregnant. This was not the outcome she'd been hoping for. He hadn't crossed the room to take her in his arms and comfort her. He hadn't asked her to stay with him until the baby was born, to see how their relationship might develop. He hadn't declared his love and offered to take her home with him when she left the hospital. It seemed he was going to let her head to Texas without saying a word to stop her.

Pippa was fighting tears, and she needed Devon gone before she broke down completely. "Go. Get out!"

Devon turned and left without another word.

Pippa sat frozen in place. Devon had walked out of her life as though she meant nothing to him. Which was when she realized how much he meant to her. "Oh, my God," she whispered. "I love him."

Chapter 27

JENNIE HAD MISSED seeing her daughter grow up, and it was terrifying to think that now that they'd been reunited, Pippa might be taken away again. She'd called ahead to the hospital and been instructed to bring Pippa to the emergency room entrance, where an orderly was waiting to rush her daughter inside. The fear in Pippa's eyes as she was wheeled away reminded Jennie of herself as a pregnant teenager.

She'd wanted to stay with her daughter, but the orderly had made it clear she couldn't leave her car where it was. She drove around to valet parking, but the valet wasn't there, and she fought tears as she looked in vain for a parking spot. In desperation, she parked the car on the street a block from the hospital and started running back. Her daughter needed her.

Every step of the way, Jennie was overwhelmed by memories—good and bad—of that terrible fall day when she'd discovered she was pregnant and the eight insane months that had followed. She remembered the early days, when she and Matt had found such joy in the child growing inside her . . .

the later lonely months, when her parents had separated them . . . and finally, the jubilant moment when her daughter had been born—and the dreadful tragedy of her supposed death.

Jennie had never forgiven her parents for keeping Matt from her side while she was grieving the death of their daughter. Her feelings for him had gone through many permutations that sad summer, as she both questioned why he hadn't found some way to get in touch with her and missed him with every fiber of her being.

Since Jennie was only fifteen, her parents had been able to control every aspect of her life. After her baby was born, they'd kept her isolated from everyone she knew in Jackson, especially Matt, by living on a ranch in a remote part of Wyoming and schooling her at home. She'd run away several times, but since she didn't know how to drive, and didn't have the money for a bus ticket and had to resort to hitchhiking, she'd always been caught before she got very far.

A year had passed before her parents relaxed their vigilance enough for her to contact Matt. She discovered that he'd disappeared without a word to her or, apparently, anyone else. It wasn't until she'd spoken with Matt's cousin Aiden that she discovered that Matt had searched for her like a crazy man for months without success. He'd only stopped when he was told that she'd died along with their daughter.

Jennie had been furious when she'd learned how her parents had continued to manipulate their lives. It had taken a long time before she was herself again. Once she was old enough to leave home, she'd moved to Texas to live on her grandmother's ranch, and to this day, she was estranged from her parents. All her life she'd wondered what had happened to Matt and grieved for the loss of the boy she'd loved, along with the daughter who'd died.

And then, yesterday, after twenty long years without a word, he'd called.

Jennie was still reeling from Matt's admission that when he'd discovered their daughter was still alive, instead of doing everything in his power to contact her and share that wonderful, amazing news, he'd taken their baby and run.

He'd stolen her chance to be a mother. He'd deprived them of a life together. He'd made all the choices and given her none.

How many times had she dreamed of what it might be like to see Matt again someday, to laugh with him and make love with him? The doctors had told her there was nothing physically wrong with her to keep her from having another child. The reproductive problem, when she'd married at last, had been her husband's. He'd refused to adopt—he'd wanted his wife free to act as a political hostess—so they'd never had children.

Meanwhile, all those years she'd despaired of having a child to hold to her breast, Matt had been raising their daughter without her. It was a bitter pill to swallow. Her heart ached in a way it hadn't in twenty long years.

She entered the emergency room breathing hard, sweat streaming down her back under her jacket. She did a quick search of people in the room and didn't see Pippa. She approached the nurse's desk and said, "I'm looking for Pippa—Philippa—Grayhawk. Do you know where she is?"

"She's been taken to a private room."

"Already? Is there some paperwork I need to fill out?" Jennie hesitated, then added, "I'm her mother."

"The hospital administrator was here and took care of everything."

"What? Why would he do that?"

"King Grayhawk is the president of the hospital board. When I saw the Grayhawk name and realized that she was Mr. Grayhawk's granddaughter, I called him immediately."

"I see." What Jennie hadn't counted on, what she'd forgotten in all the years she'd been gone, was how much influence King Grayhawk wielded in Jackson Hole.

As Jennie raced down several corridors, trying to remember the confusing directions to Pippa's room she'd been given, she suddenly found herself face-to-face with Matt.

He stepped into her path, forcing her to stop.

She felt her heart leap and clenched her hands until her fingernails bit into her palms to keep from reaching out to touch him. She should have realized King would tell Matt his daughter was here. She felt off-kilter because she should have made that mental leap and hadn't, and therefore had been caught completely by surprise.

Matt's eyes were just as blue, but now they were decorated with crow's-feet at the edges. His jaw was still firm, but he had a scar on his cheek that hadn't been there twenty years ago. His hair was black, and as shaggy as ever, but it was threaded with silver at the temples. His face bore a five o'clock shadow even though it was early afternoon, making him look a little dangerous and unapproachable. And his body . . . He had a man's broad shoulders, which narrowed to a slim waist, a flat belly, and long, long legs. He towered over her, making her feel . . . like the girl she used to be.

Luckily, resentment came to her rescue, keeping her from falling into his arms and forgiving all. "Get out of my way, Matt. I'm here to see my daughter."

"She's fine. The baby's fine."

"You can't know that already."

"The spotting's stopped. They're giving her medication to prevent any further cramps."

"I want to see her."

"Devon's with her right now."

"How did he know she was here?"

"He saw the note you left at the house."

"How could he possibly get here before us?"

He shrugged. "Drove fast and took a shortcut, I guess. Once he got here, Pippa pretty much threw me out. I left, because it was clear he wasn't going anywhere until he talked to her, and I figured they have a lot to discuss."

Jennie realized he was babbling because he was nervous. It was something Matt had done when he'd first asked her out on a date. She'd found it endearing then. She found it annoying now. Or rather, she found the fact that she found it endearing to be annoying. "I told you on the phone I didn't want to see you."

"There hasn't been a day since I took Pippa and ran that I didn't wonder whether I'd done the right thing."

"And that's supposed to make what you did okay?"

"At least give me a chance to explain." He took her arm and began leading her down the hall.

Jennie would have jerked free, except a doctor and a nurse appeared, and it was ingrained habit, learned from years as a political wife, to never, ever make a scene. A few turns later they were inside the empty hospital chapel, which was lit by warm sunshine streaming through rainbow-colored glass.

As the door closed behind them, Matt led her to a bench close to the altar, let go of her arm, and said in a surprisingly gentle voice, "Sit, Jennie. Please."

She sank onto the bench, and a moment later he sat down beside her.

"I want another chance with you."

She hadn't expected him to speak so frankly. Her heart was beating fast, and her mind had gone blank. "Why would I agree to that?" she asked at last.

"Because we have unfinished business."

"What we have is a grown daughter. I don't need *you* to have a relationship with *her*." Jennie heard the bitterness and resentment in her voice and realized that she'd revealed more of her feelings than she'd intended. But once she'd started, everything came pouring out. "You cheated me.

You stole my chance to be a mother to my daughter."

"Your parents did that."

She glared at him. "They lied to me because they wanted what they thought was best for me. You stole something far more precious. You betrayed the love I thought we felt for each other."

"I'm sorry."

"That's not enough! Your apology can't turn back the clock. It won't give us back the years we lost." It took her a second to realize what she'd admitted. That she'd missed him. That she'd yearned for him. That she'd dreamed of the future together that had been taken from them.

"I'm not talking about trying to recapture the past," he said. "I want a life with you now."

"I don't know you. Or love you. I knew and loved a sixteen-year-old boy."

"I'm the same person, just a little older and a whole lot wiser."

"It's too late."

"It doesn't have to be," he argued. "I've never stopped loving you, Jennie. There hasn't been one day we've been apart that I haven't thought of you."

"You had our daughter to remind you of me. I, on the other hand, had nothing to remind me of you."

When he flinched, she knew she'd hurt him. She'd wanted to wound him. She'd wanted him to feel the pain she'd endured all these years without him. But she was out of practice fighting back. Out of practice letting her emotions run wild. She'd lived such a . . . controlled . . . existence as a senator's wife. It felt good to say exactly what she thought.

"I don't want a second chance with you, Matt. Thanks, but no thanks. I'll be leaving at the end of the day, and if Pippa agrees to come, I'll be taking her with me."

Matt blanched. "I suppose I deserve that. But I hope you change your mind about taking Pippa so far away."

Jennie felt a spurt of guilt, but quashed it. "You took her to another continent! You had her for nearly twenty years. It's my turn."

She wanted time to get to know her daughter. She was more than happy to provide the refuge that Pippa had apparently sought when she'd fled her father's house and moved in with someone she barely knew.

"Why not stay here with me?" Matt suggested, ignoring the animosity she hadn't been able to keep out of her voice. "There's plenty of room at the ranch."

"I need to go home."

"Why?"

"If you must know, I'm running for my late husband's Senate seat."

The shocked look on his face soothed a raw place she hadn't known existed inside her. *See how far I've come without you? You disappeared, and I moved on with my life.*

Then he said, "What's your campaign manager going to say when he finds out your unmarried pregnant daughter—a daughter no one has ever heard of before—just moved in?"

She knew Matt was desperate to keep Pippa with him, and it seemed he was playing hardball. One of the things that had made Jennie such a good prospective candidate was the pristine life she'd led. Her youthful indiscretion had never seen the light of day. But as Matt had just pointed out, if she brought Pippa home, that would change.

A Bible verse flashed through her mind. *Let him who is without sin cast the first stone.* And she had her answer for Matt. "I think the voters in Texas will understand and forgive a twenty-year-old mistake made by a fourteen-year-old girl."

Matt's shoulders sagged, and she knew she'd won.

Now all she had to do was convince Pippa to come live with her.

Chapter 28

MATT WATCHED JENNIE pause at the door to Pippa's room, as though she were gathering her composure before entering, and realized he couldn't let things end like that between them. His pulse was still racing, and his stomach was still doing loops. He'd known Jennie was somewhere in the hospital, but it was clear that she'd been surprised—okay, shocked—to see him. His heart had jumped at the sight of her, and he'd known that, for him, nothing had changed. He was as much in love with her now as he had been the day she'd bumped into him in the gym.

Jennie had only grown more beautiful in the years they'd been separated, but the vivacious girl he'd known was now encased in a hard shell of reserve. Her gray eyes had been cautious and her posture rigid. Her soft curves and long legs had been concealed by an expensive suede jacket and ironed jeans with a sharp crease down the front. That cold, aloof lady wasn't his Jennie. That was Jennifer Fairchild Hart, the senator's widow.

But he'd seen flashes of the girl he'd loved. Boldness. Impertinence. Defiance. Just enough to believe that she was still in there. Just enough to offer him hope.

There had to be some way to convince Jennie to give them a second chance. She wouldn't have been so angry if she weren't hurt. And she wouldn't have been so hurt if she didn't care. Matt was convinced that he and Jennie could reignite the love that had lain dormant between them all these years. All he had to do was figure out a way for them to spend time together and fan that spark into flame.

The problem was he had to stay at Kingdom Come for the next year, and she was committed to a Senate race in Texas. The strict terms of his agreement with King required him to be on the premises. Of course, his father hadn't exactly stuck to the terms of their agreement himself, so maybe there was some leeway for Matt to spend time in Texas with Jennie, if that turned out to be his only alternative.

As Matt watched, Devon exited the room and stopped to exchange a few words with Jennie. Then Jennie entered the room, and Devon started down the hall.

Matt intercepted him and asked, "How's Pippa?"

"She's got her mother now," he said flatly. "She doesn't need me."

"If you think that, you're a fool."

Devon looked affronted. And then thoughtful.

Matt hadn't wanted Pippa staying with Devon because they were two young, attractive people, and it would be the most natural thing in the world for them to get romantically involved. He'd been afraid that whatever feelings Devon developed for his daughter would change once he discovered that Pippa was pregnant, and his vulnerable daughter would get her heart broken again. It seemed his fears might have been well-founded.

"Do you care for her?"

"That's none of your business."

"She's my daughter. Ensuring her happiness is every bit my business. Answer the question."

Devon looked Matt in the eye and said, "Yes. I have feelings for her. But Pippa and I have only known each other a month, and her mother's asked her to go live with her in Texas."

Matt tensed. "Is she leaving?"

"She hasn't made up her mind."

"Did you ask her to stay?"

Devon shoved his hands into his front pockets. "No."

"Why not?"

"I told you. She has her mother now."

"Is it the baby?" Matt asked.

Devon looked startled. "What do you mean?"

"Is it that you don't want Pippa if she comes with another man's child?"

Devon's brow furrowed. "I just found out about the baby today." His mouth turned down. "From my father."

Matt thought that failing to tell Devon about the pregnancy had been a mistake on his daughter's part. But maybe Pippa didn't care as much for Devon as he cared for her. Or maybe she liked him so much she'd kept her pregnancy a secret for fear it would drive him away. He would need to speak to his daughter to find out one way or the other. Or maybe her actions would speak louder than words. It would say a great deal if she left Devon to go to Texas with her mother. But why stay unless Devon made it clear that he wanted her?

He eyed Devon speculatively. "Are you going to fight for her?"

"What does that mean?"

"Are you going to tell Pippa that you want her here with you?"

"She's made it plain from the start that all she ever wanted from me was friendship."

"That was likely because she hadn't gotten over that sonofabitch breaking her heart. Not only that, she was hiding her pregnancy from you, and she probably didn't want to be dishonest about what she could offer in return." Matt was putting a lot of words in his daughter's mouth, but he knew Pippa, and those were both valid reasons why she might not have given Devon any indication that she had stronger feelings for him. "Did Pippa give you any reason to think that she might feel more for you than friendship?"

Did you make love with my daughter?

Devon pursed his lips and made a thoughtful sound in his throat. "Yes, but . . ."

"But what?" Matt felt outraged on Pippa's behalf. How could Devon make love to her and then not fight to keep her? It reminded him too much of the shoddy behavior she'd gotten from Tim. But Devon didn't look like the villain in a melodrama. Far from it.

He met Matt's gaze again, his eyes troubled. "I think I have to let Pippa make this decision."

Matt knew too well how someone—with the best intentions—could make the *wrong* decision, as he had all those years ago with Jennie. "Are you sure you don't want to say something to her about your feelings?"

Devon shook his head. "I can't. Not yet. Not now."

"For what it's worth, I think you're making a mistake."

"Maybe so. But if I've learned anything from Pippa in the month I've known her, it's that she speaks her mind. If she wanted to stay with me, she would have said something."

Matt had no doubt that Pippa had told Devon exactly what she thought about everything *except* her innermost feelings. It was one thing to talk freely with a *friend*. It was something else entirely to lay your heart bare to someone you loved. Matt's experience with Jennie, and with his two wives, had taught him that. His marriages might not have suffered the fate they had if he'd been willing to admit to either wife the true circumstances of his flight from Wyoming. But he'd kept the knowledge of his heartbreak—and his unhealed heart—to himself.

"Look," Matt said, "if Pippa decides to go to Texas with Jennie, it's going to happen in a hurry. You're not going to have much time to change your mind."

"I'm not going to change my mind," Devon said stubbornly.

"Suit yourself," Matt said. "But don't say I didn't warn you."

"Warn me?"

"If you truly love my daughter, you're going to regret this decision the rest of your life."

Chapter 29

"So you were going to say goodbye to the horse, but not to me?"

Pippa whirled at the sound of Devon's voice, spooking Sultan. The stallion took a sudden step back from the stall door, shaking his head and snorting, and Pippa turned back to soothe him. "It's all right, boy. Everything's fine." She waited until the stallion closed the distance enough that she could run her hand down the side of his neck, and then opened her hand so he could gently take the cube of sugar she held there.

She pressed her cheek against the stallion's and rubbed his forehead murmuring, "No one's ever going to hurt you again. Your days of being afraid are over."

They were words she needed to hear herself. But from the tone of Devon's voice when he'd entered the barn, she wasn't likely to hear them from him. She turned at last to face him.

He stood in the center of the barn, his hip canted, his hands stuck deep in his back pockets. His mouth was clamped tight, and a muscle worked in his jaw.

She felt shut out. Pushed away. Rejected.

But wasn't that exactly what she'd done to him? She'd snuck over here when she'd believed Devon would be gone, hoping to collect her things and leave without ever having to face him. She was ashamed of her behavior, but she could see she hadn't been wrong. Devon wasn't going to make this easy. This was the very scene she'd been hoping to avoid.

"I saw your luggage on the bed in the house. I take it you're heading to Texas to stay with your mother."

"I am."

"Were you really planning to leave without explaining . . . anything?"

"Like what?"

"Like why you lied to me about the baby."

"I never lied," she countered. "I just didn't tell you everything."

"Including one pretty damned important thing!"

His eyes dropped to her belly, and Pippa laid a protective hand over the child growing in her womb.

"You should have told me you were pregnant. I got ambushed by my father—Angus, I mean—who relished telling me something I should have heard from you. There's no way I would have—"

"I know I should have told you about the baby before we had sex," she admitted, cutting him off.

"Was that what it was to you? Sex?"

It had been far more. But she was leaving town with her mother, so what was the point of dwelling on a budding flower that had been snapped off before it ever had a chance to bloom? "You needed comfort. That was the way I chose to give it."

He snorted, a sound showing displeasure not unlike Sultan's. "So the first chance you have to run, you're taking off like a scared rabbit."

"That's not fair! It's my *mother*. I've wanted a mother all my life. I want to get to know her. Why shouldn't I spend time with her?"

"What about me?" His hands had come out of his back pockets and were bunched into fists at his sides.

She took a hitching breath and discovered that all the air seemed to have been sucked out of the barn. His gaze was so intense that she was tempted to take a step backward. She didn't know what to say. And regretted what came out of her mouth as soon as she said it. "I'll miss you, of course."

"Of course." He said it with sarcasm, with an angry sneer on his face. "What happens now, Pippa? Are you going to keep the kid? Are you going to raise it at your mother's ranch in Texas? Tell me. I'd like to know."

"Yes, I'm going to keep my child," she said, responding to his anger with anger of her own. "Why wouldn't I?"

"What if it's a boy? What if the kid looks just like that sonofabitch who took advantage of you?"

"Now you sound like my father."

"I'm sure as hell not any relation to you. I think your father settled that! I'm not even sure I'm your friend anymore."

Pippa felt as though he'd speared her in the heart. She felt wounded by his utter rejection of everything they'd shared. But she had no one to blame but herself. She was the one who'd kept him in the dark. She was the one refusing to give an inch now. Why couldn't she tell him how she felt? Why couldn't she admit that her feelings for him went far deeper than friendship?

But if he was so anxious for her to stay, why didn't he ask her to stay? Why did she have to be the one to risk getting hurt? What if he was only angry because he'd been duped, and was actually relieved that he'd escaped getting caught in a pregnant woman's net.

"What's your plan when the kid turns out to look like that Tim guy?" he said. "I'd like to know."

"Don't you think I've struggled with the knowledge that I hate Tim, and yet I'm going to have his child? That I'm scared I won't be able to love my baby if it looks anything like him? Nevertheless, I'm determined to give my child the very best life I can—which means being the very best mother I can be."

"I notice there's no father in this picture you're painting."

"Are you volunteering for the job?"

There was a long, uncomfortable silence before he said, "Nobody's offered me the job."

If that was a cue for her to speak, Pippa missed it. Another silence ensued while she stared at him, her heart thundering in her chest, and he stared back, the knuckles of his bunched fists turning white.

At last she said, "What do you want from me?"

"Nothing. Not a goddamn thing. Goodbye,

Pippa. Have a good life." He turned and stalked from the barn, leaving her standing there alone. He stopped at the door and turned back to her. She thought he was going to speak, but he merely searched her features as though to imprint them, so he wouldn't forget how she looked.

Pippa's throat was swollen nearly closed, but she managed to say, "Hooroo."

Then he was gone.

When she returned to the house to retrieve her luggage, he was nowhere to be found. Before she left, she dropped to her knees and hugged Wulf, who licked her face. As she walked away from the house, the lump in her throat was so huge it threatened to choke her. She realized she didn't want to go. As much as she'd always wanted a mother, she wanted Devon more.

But she couldn't stay where she wasn't wanted. He'd had his chances, and he'd let her go. He was the one who'd left the barn. Without hugging her goodbye. Without a single human touch to suggest that he'd ever wanted more from her than the brief friendship they'd shared.

Pippa swiped at the tears that fell on her cheeks and brushed at her eyes so she could see to drive. Her interlude in the Wyoming mountains was over. She had to move on with her life. She had a mother to get to know and a child to raise. And a whole life to live without Devon Flynn.

Chapter 30

PIPPA CRESTED A rise in the Texas Hill Country on horseback and turned back to watch her mother canter her horse the short distance to join her. She surveyed the grassy valley dotted with mesquites and live oaks and said, "It's so beautiful here. I don't know how you can stand to leave."

"Duty calls," her mother replied. "I can do a lot to help folks if I'm in Washington."

Pippa had been staying with her mother for a month, and during that time, her mum had frequently left the ranch for political fund-raisers and a myriad of meetings that were apparently necessary for her election to her husband's Senate seat.

"But you don't seem happy about it," Pippa blurted.

Her mother looked startled, and then rueful. "I have to admit I was looking forward to all of this political maneuvering a lot more before I knew I was going to be a grandmother. I never realized what fun it would be to have a daughter."

Pippa felt flattered until her mother added, "Or did I miss all the hard parts?"

Pippa laughed. "Only someone as good at

being a mum as you are could believe this isn't one of the 'hard parts.'" She sobered and added, "It's been so nice having someone I can talk with. Someone who can help me sort out everything in my head."

Her mother brushed away a strand of hair that had blown across Pippa's cheek and tucked it behind her ear in much the same way as her father had when she was a child. She'd noticed that her mother often found excuses to touch her, as though she couldn't quite believe that Pippa was real.

Pippa had been surprised at just how many things she and her mother had in common, even though they'd never laid eyes on each other until four weeks ago.

Neither of them could stand ketchup on their eggs, something her father loved. Neither of them liked pickles. Neither of them liked mayonnaise. They both loved horses and horseback riding. They both would rather wear jeans than a dress—even though her mother admitted that she'd spent her entire marriage to the senator without once donning a pair of Levi's in public.

And they both loved to read. Pippa had found that the way to the wide world outside her father's cattle station was through books. Her mother had used books to escape a life that she'd chosen but apparently hadn't enjoyed all that much.

"So is everything clear in your head now?" her mother asked, searching Pippa's face for the signs of distress that had been there when she'd first arrived in Texas. "Do you know what you want to do next?"

"Yes." One word, but it had taken her the better part of the month she'd been with her mother to be able to say it. Part of her decision about the future involved moving back to Wyoming.

"You know you're welcome to stay with me as long as you like."

Pippa nodded. She saw the yearning in her mother's eyes and recognized the restraint that kept her from saying that she never wanted Pippa to leave. Pippa might have stayed, except she'd realized that once her mother was elected—and she had no doubt she would be—and went off to Washington, she'd be all alone at the ranch. Despite her differences with her father, she missed him, and she missed her little brother. They were her family.

But they weren't the only ones she missed.

Devon had never left her thoughts. She regretted not admitting how much she cared for him, regretted diminishing the intimacy they'd shared. But apparently, he didn't feel the same way. He hadn't once called since she'd been gone, and she'd been too proud to ask her father about him when she'd spoken to him on the phone.

They'd brought lunch with them, and both women dismounted, loosened the cinches on their saddles, and then tied their horses on a line so they could munch grass, before retrieving the saddlebags that contained everything they needed for their picnic.

"You've never told me how you met and married Jonathan Hart," Pippa said.

"There's not much to tell," her mother said as she spread a blanket in the shade of a nearby live oak.

"I'd still like to hear about it." Pippa dropped to her knees on the blanket, grateful for the shade from the hot Texas sun, which reminded her of summers in the Northern Territory. She began passing out food, one ham and cheese sandwich for her, one for her mother, one bag of potato chips for her, one for her mother, one chocolate chip cookie with pecans for her, one without nuts for her mother.

Her mother opened a can of soda for each of them and balanced them carefully on the uneven ground.

When Pippa had arrived in Texas, almost the first question she'd asked her mother was how her parents had met. She'd been delighted with the story. She'd cried when she heard how they'd been torn apart and how awful it had been for her mum when she'd supposedly lost her newborn daughter.

Pippa had the feeling that her mother had glossed over how painful those days had been. She'd been envious of the love it seemed her very young parents had shared, and she'd wondered if they could ever be reunited. It was another reason she was heading back to Wyoming. She was determined to get her father and mother back together . . . and see what happened.

Pippa was curious to know more about what had happened to her mother during the years her parents had been separated, how her mother had picked up the pieces and moved on after losing someone she cared about, because it was something she was struggling with herself.

Once they were settled and Pippa had taken her first bite, she said, "Will you tell me how you met Jonathan? How you fell in love? I really want to know."

"I was attending the University of Texas in Austin, and Jonathan Hart was speaking on campus."

"You were a student?"

"A graduate student," her mother said. "I was one of the hostesses for a reception held after Jonathan's speech. He was a state representative at the time. We started talking at the reception, and he asked me to go for coffee afterward. We talked all night. I found him . . . fascinating. He had so many hopes and dreams for the future. He planned to run for the U.S. Senate when his term as state representative was up."

Pippa was watching her mother closely, so she saw a wry smile come and go. "What was that smile about?"

Her mother met her gaze, and the wry smile reappeared. "He needed a wife to run for the Senate. It turned out that I fit the bill."

"That doesn't sound very romantic."

"He was charming. And handsome. And smart and funny. He was everything any woman could have asked for in a husband."

Pippa frowned. "Except you didn't love him."

Her mother didn't contradict her. Instead she said, "I admired him. I respected him." She hesitated and then admitted, "I didn't think I could ever love anyone the way I'd loved your father. Marriage to a man with all of Jonathan's qualities seemed like a good idea at the time."

"But if you didn't love him—"

"Why did I stay with him?"

Pippa nodded as she picked up her soda and took a drink.

"Life is all about compromises. We were good friends. We gave each other pleasure." Her mother flushed at the admission. "Jonathan was faithful to me—as far as I know—and I was faithful to him. We made a good political team. Life was satisfying, with one exception."

"What was that?"

"I never had any more children."

Pippa decided to ask the question that came to mind, even though it might be a difficult for her mother to answer it. "Was it because you couldn't?"

She shook her head. "Jonathan didn't want children. It was the one thing we argued about. Divorce wasn't impossible—although it would have caused a few problems for Jonathan politically. Perhaps I could have found another husband who wanted children as much as I did. But I told myself I had a great deal to be thankful for in my marriage. And it isn't that easy to find someone like Jonathan. He was a very special man."

"Except he didn't want children." Pippa felt angry on her mother's behalf. "It sounds like you did all the giving, and he did all the taking."

Her mother winced. "Perhaps I gave too much.

But I wasn't unhappy. It was a better marriage than most."

"Are you suggesting I should give up on love and make a practical marriage with someone who wants to be a father to my child?" Pippa asked bluntly.

Her mother looked troubled. "Is that what you got from the story of my marriage?"

What worried Pippa was the thought of her mother never falling in love again. Of her mother having settled for "a better marriage than most." What if that was one of the ways she was like her mum? What if she never fell out of love with Devon? She couldn't imagine a life like the one her mother had described. It felt . . . empty.

Her mother deserved better than that. She deserved the life that had been stolen from her all those years ago. But that meant getting her parents back in the same place. Although they'd apparently spoken to each other at the hospital, Pippa hadn't seen them in each other's company even once before she left Wyoming. That didn't bode well for any sort of future together.

She'd actually broached the subject of a reconciliation to her father, but he'd said, "Let it go, Pippa."

She glanced sideways at her mother. Maybe she'd been asking the wrong parent. "Have you thought about getting back together with Daddy?"

Her mother was startled into laughter. "What?"

"You said you never fell out of love with him."

"My life is fine the way it is, Pippa. Besides, too

much time has passed. Your father and I don't have much in common anymore."

Pippa opened her mouth to argue further, but her mother said, "The subject is closed."

Pippa had learned that there was more than one way to skin a cat. She would find a way somehow, someday, to get her parents back together. That is, after she fixed her own life.

"When are you leaving?" her mother asked as she began gathering up plastic wrap and napkins.

"Soon," Pippa said.

"I love you, sweetheart. I've loved having you here."

Pippa grinned and scooted over to hug her mother. "Good. Because I'll be here a couple more weeks."

She needed more time to plan. More time to figure out how she could make her life—and her parents' lives?—turn out happily ever after.

Chapter 31

DEVON HAD SPENT every day of the past six weeks ruing his decision to walk away from Pippa in the barn. He knew now that he'd made a terrible mistake, but he had no idea how to undo the damage he'd done. Pippa was long gone, living at the Fairchild Ranch in Texas.

He'd relived both his talk with Pippa at the hospital—and his parting from her in the barn the next day—a hundred times, wondering if Matt had been right about where he'd gone wrong.

At least he'd had an excuse at the hospital for not thinking straight. He'd arrived at the door to Pippa's hospital room with his heart in his throat, terrified that something dire had happened to her, only to find her sitting up in bed looking cute as a button in a hospital gown.

His first impulse had been to cross the room, take her into his arms, and kiss her silly for scaring him so badly. At the last second, he'd stopped himself, recognizing that a lover's embrace might not be welcome. Unfortunately, he hadn't offered her a friendly hug, either.

Once it was clear that she was all right, his feeling of ill use for being left in the dark about her pregnancy—which he'd put on the back burner when he'd thought her life might be in danger— had returned with a vengeance. Why hadn't Pippa trusted him enough to share her secret? She could have saved him that awkward scene with his father by telling him herself. He'd felt like a fool for not noticing—or rather, for ignoring—the signs of her pregnancy, which in hindsight had been blatantly evident.

He'd been further disheartened when Pippa kept insisting, despite their sexual interlude in the barn, that they were no more than friends. *Friends* who hug? Maybe. *Friends* who kiss? Maybe. *Friends* who have sex? As Pippa would say, not bloody likely! But if she'd worn blinders where his feelings were concerned, he was at fault for not tearing them off. He should have said something. He should have made it clear sooner that he'd fallen in love with her.

But when would have been the right time to speak? A man didn't declare his love when a woman purposefully kept him at arm's length.

Then she'd dropped her mother's sudden appearance at his cabin into the conversation. He'd put himself in Pippa's place, imagining how he would feel if his biological father showed up at the door. He'd want to spend time getting to know him. He'd added Pippa's particular situation—her pregnancy and the fact that she was estranged from her father—and realized that her mother's offer of a place to stay must have seemed like the answer to her prayers. How could he compete with a long-lost mother?

He couldn't. So he hadn't tried.

The next day, he'd stood by without stopping her when she'd collected her things from his cabin, fed Sultan a sugar cube, uttered a soft "Hooroo," and walked out of his life.

But he was beginning to think, as Matt had warned, that his decision to let Pippa leave without telling her how he really felt about her was the biggest blunder of his life. How was she supposed to know he loved her when he'd never said the words?

On the other hand, maybe it was better this way. Maybe she was never going to be ready to love or trust another man. Maybe all this pain he felt would have been a lot worse if he'd taken the leap and told her how he felt and then discovered that she couldn't return his feelings. Especially since loving Pippa meant raising Tim Brandon's child as his own.

Devon tried to remember exactly how he'd felt at the moment he'd learned that Pippa would be giving birth to another man's baby. And not just any man, but a man who'd treated her so shabbily. Shock. Disappointment. Dismay. All he could think was *What if she has a son, and he looks like his father? Am I going to have a reminder of that despicable man around the rest of my life?*

If he married Pippa, the answer to that question was a resounding yes.

Then he'd realized that Pippa must be dealing with these same quandaries herself. No wonder she'd needed time away from her father to think.

He could also understand better why Matt might have encouraged her to give up the child.

But from everything he'd seen and heard, Pippa seemed committed to keeping the baby. Which meant that if Devon wanted her in his life, he was going to have to accept the child and become its father.

It hadn't taken him long to realize that—irony of all ironies—he was faced with the same dilemma his own father had faced. The child was bound to have some features that weren't Pippa's, features that would remind him every day that she'd once given her heart—and her body—to another man.

At least he had his own experience as a child—aware that he was somehow different from his siblings and that he was being treated differently by his father—to help guarantee that the same thing never happened to Pippa's child. It had taken only a small step further to realize that if he could love Pippa's baby, then maybe his father had been telling the truth about loving him. He'd found that the most comforting—and reassuring—thought of all.

But thinking about Pippa was no substitute for talking to her or holding her in his arms or making love to her. He'd missed her dreadfully since she'd been gone. He'd wondered about how she and her mother were getting along and worried about how she was feeling.

When a month had passed, he hadn't been able to stand the distance any longer, and he'd called her on the phone. It had been one of the most stilted conversations of his life.

"Hello, Pippa. How are you?" It had been hard

to get the words past the horrible constriction in his throat.

"I'm fine. How are you?"

"I'm doing okay." I'm in agony, but thanks for asking.

"How are Sultan and Wulf?"

"Sultan misses you. Wulf, too." I miss you most of all. I wish we could be together to see the baby grow. *"Are you feeling all right?"*

"I'm feeling fine, Devon."

"And the baby?" You aren't having any more complications? You're healthy and the baby's healthy?

"The baby's fine. Growing and moving a lot."

"It's good to hear your voice."

"It's good to hear your voice, too."

He kept waiting for her to say something about the life she'd left behind in Wyoming. That she missed the smell of the evergreens and the sight of trumpeter swans gliding on the pond. That she missed Wulf's eerie howl or Sultan's dark eyes and darker soul. That she missed *him.*

She remained reticent, answering the questions he'd asked but not posing any of her own. He'd finally ended the torture for both of them by saying goodbye. He'd listened long enough to hear a forlorn "Hooroo" before dropping the phone in the cradle and his head in his hands.

He thought maybe that had been his lowest moment.

Lately, he'd realized that if he didn't do something soon it was going to be too late. It was bad enough that he'd waited six weeks. If he wanted

Pippa in his life, he was going to have to take the risk of telling her how he felt.

He even had an excuse to go to Texas. His biological father had a ranch not far from where Pippa was staying. He tried to imagine what it would be like to hug her now. She was five and a half months pregnant, and her body would have changed to reflect the child growing inside her. When Connor's late wife Molly was carrying their first child, he'd watched enthralled as the impression of a tiny foot moved across her abdomen. He wanted to be around when that happened to Pippa.

Devon made a frustrated sound in his throat. He should never have let her leave the house when she'd come to get her things. She'd given him plenty of opportunities to tell her not to go.

She'd said, "I'll miss you."

How much more of an opening did a man in love need?

It was past time he did something about getting her back.

He began throwing clothes into a suitcase, his heart pounding in his chest. He was going to Texas to get Pippa and bring her back, and he wasn't going to take no for an answer.

He stood up abruptly and stared at himself in the mirror. He had a stop to make first at a ranch in South Texas. Maybe he should find out who his father was before he became a father himself.

Chapter 32

WITHIN A MATTER of hours after making the decision to go after Pippa—and to meet his biological father along the way—Devon found himself standing on the back porch of a ramshackle ranch in South Texas. He'd entered the property through a sagging metal gate marked with a large K—for "Kidd," he supposed—the last name of his biological father. It was a long drive from the front gate to the back door, and he saw a few—very few—red Santa Gertrudis cattle on rugged grassland dotted with mesquite and sagebrush.

The ranch house was a disaster. The roof of the back porch was canted like a horse on three legs, and he'd stumbled and nearly fallen trying to avoid a broken step. A rusted-out pickup sat in the backyard, which was filled with weeds a foot high.

What kind of people lived here? He couldn't imagine his mother having anything to do with anybody who lived in such a hovel. Yet, if he had the address right, these were his relations.

He took a deep breath and let it out, then knocked on a door with a torn and curling screen.

When no one answered, he called out, "Hello! Anybody home?"

A cheerful female voice called back, "We're in the dining room. Come on in!"

Devon followed the voice through a small kitchen strewn with clothes and books and cluttered with tack that should have been in the barn. He lived in an all-male household, but his father had insisted they pick up after themselves and had hired enough help to keep the house clean and straightened. As he looked around at the mess, he was having trouble imagining the sort of people who could live like this.

He turned a corner to find a crowd of young people standing around an older man seated at a dining table with a birthday cake sitting in front of him. The cake was covered with burning candles, and he was just about to blow them out.

He looked up at Devon, and the smile froze on his face.

The laughing group around him had equally broad smiles on their faces as they called out to the man in front of the cake.

"Blow out the candles, Dad!"

"Quick, before they melt!"

"We're going to be eating wax instead of cake, if you don't hurry."

"Need some help, old man?"

That last comment caused the man seated at the table to respond, "Who are you calling an old man?" before he turned back and, with a single *whoosh*ing breath, blew out the conflagration on the cake.

Devon counted and realized there were five people standing behind the man he believed was his father. Not a single one looked a bit like Devon. Or like the man sitting at the table, for that matter. He would have thought he'd come to the wrong place, except there was one person in the room who bore a striking resemblance to him.

The man sitting at the table was getting up.

One of the boys—he was in his early twenties, Devon guessed—said, "Hey, Dad, you need to cut the cake."

"You cut it," the old man said. "I need to speak with our visitor."

Shiloh Kidd hadn't taken his eyes—his intense gray-green eyes—off Devon.

Devon felt as though all the air had been sucked out of the room. What he saw coming toward him was himself in thirty years. He hadn't seen a trace of himself—or his father—in the five kids still circled around the cake. But the man walking toward him had Devon's lean torso, the same height, and even his sun-streaked chestnut hair, something Devon had always believed came from his mother.

"Hello," Kidd said. "Do I know you?"

Devon had to clear his throat to speak. "I believe you're my father. My biological father, that is."

A deep frown furrowed Shiloh Kidd's brow before he said, "Come with me." He turned and headed down a dark, narrow hallway that ended in a bright, sunlit room full of bookcases and containing a battered desk. Instead of sitting behind it, Kidd turned and leaned his hips back against the front of it. He crossed his arms and said, "What makes you think you're my son?"

"My mother was Fiona Flynn."

Kidd's weather-beaten face paled. He rose to his feet, his arms dropping to his sides, his fists bunched. "Fiona? How is she?"

"She died when I was born," Devon said bluntly.

He was surprised by the sudden tears that rose in Kidd's eyes before he said, "I'm sorry to hear that."

"So you admit you knew my mother."

"We were childhood sweethearts," Kidd admitted.

"And lovers sometime after that," Devon said in a harsh voice.

Kidd nodded. "Your mother never told me about you."

"What happened?" Two words asking the questions that had gone unanswered all of Devon's life.

Shiloh Kidd sighed and gestured toward two tall-backed armchairs covered in cracked brown leather. "Have a seat."

Devon hesitated, then realized he wasn't going to get his answers any faster standing up. He took the chair closer to the blackened fireplace and left the other for his father.

"Does Angus know?" Kidd asked.

Devon nodded.

Kidd closed his eyes in acknowledgment of the pain he'd caused Devon and his father before opening them again. "I wanted to marry Fiona, but her father needed money. She married your father to save her father's ranch."

"That's ridiculous!" Devon said. "That sort of thing only happens in novels."

Kidd lifted a sardonic brow. "Where do you think writers get those sorts of ideas? She married him, and her father got a settlement." He rubbed his temples. "It didn't do much good, though. Grady Garrett gambled away the money, and it was only by the grace of God and a lot of hard work that Fiona's brothers held on to the ranch. But by then it was too late for me to get her back. She was already pregnant with her first child."

Devon was remembering what his father had said to him—that there were reasons he couldn't marry Darcie and reasons he needed to marry Devon's mother. "I can understand why she might marry my father. Why would my father want to marry her?"

"She was beautiful enough to take your breath away," Kidd murmured. "But that wasn't the reason."

"Why, then?"

"You won't believe me when I tell you. It's something else out of a book."

"I'm listening. Why did he marry her?"

"To acquire a world champion Santa Gertrudis bull."

Devon frowned. "What does a bull have to do with anything?"

"That bull was her dowry. Fiona's dad figured that if he married Fiona off to a rich man, he'd have an endless supply of money. Angus's father wanted that bull—and Fiona's dad wasn't selling. The only man who was getting that bull was Fiona Garrett's husband."

"Are you telling me Angus Flynn married my mother so my grandfather could own a world champion bull?" Devon said incredulously.

"Yep."

"We don't have any Santa Gertrudis cattle on the Lucky 7. We raise Black Angus."

"The bull died in transit from Texas to Wyoming."

"I'm confused. So why bother getting married."

"The bull wasn't shipped until your mom delivered her first child. Old man Garrett wasn't taking any chances that Angus would back out of the marriage before he had a reason to support Fiona forever after."

Devon couldn't believe Angus would have kowtowed to his father that way. Then he remembered something else Angus had said. *I loved both women.* Somewhere along the line, his father must have fallen in love with his mother.

"Do you know if she ever loved Angus?" Devon asked.

"From the moment she laid eyes on him," Kidd said sadly. "I didn't stand a chance."

"Then why—"

"Why did we end up creating you?"

Devon's throat ached. He settled for nodding.

"She was hurt by what your father did—cheating on her with another woman. I was in town for a cattlemen's association meeting in Jackson. She found out and invited me to the house. I think she just wanted a friend to talk to. But all that pain came spilling out."

Kidd's eyes had turned very green and looked as sharp as cut glass. "I wanted to kill him for hurting her like that. But she was still very much in love with him. I only meant to comfort her. We never intended for what happened to happen." His shoulders rose and fell with resignation. "The timing was bad. Fiona regretted what she'd done. And I knew she was never going to come back to me, so I had to let her go. If I'd gotten out of there a few moments sooner, Angus would never have been the wiser."

"Except I got born."

"Even then he might not have suspected." Kidd lifted a sardonic brow. "A lot of men are raising kids that aren't their own blood without knowing it."

"Like you?" Devon said.

Instead of being insulted, Kidd smiled. "Absolutely. I've got five great kids. Not a drop of my blood in any one of them."

"They're all adopted?" Devon said.

"Wife couldn't have kids, and we wanted a family," Kidd said. "Found every one of them a different way, but love them all the same."

"They seem happy," Devon said.

"They are. We are. Don't have much." Kidd's smile became a grin, and he spread an arm wide. "As you can see. But we're happy as larks. Got me a champion bull-riding son and a champion calf roper, a daughter who's a champion barrel racer

and another who bakes first-place pies, and a son
who can make you cry when he plays the fiddle.
We've got enough cattle to get by and everybody
gets along. What more could you ask?"

Here was more proof, if Devon needed it, that
families weren't born, they were made. It was up to
him to be a good father to Pippa's child and help
make their home as happy as this one seemed to be.

"Would you like to meet my family and have a
little birthday cake?"

"Sure."

Kidd rose and took two steps toward the door,
before he turned back and said, "Would you mind
if I give you a hug?"

Devon felt tears sting his nose and fill his eyes.
"I wouldn't mind at all."

His father opened his arms and Devon stepped
into them, fighting tears as he hugged his father
tightly and was hugged back. A few moments later
the older man let go, swiped at a tear that had
fallen on his cheek, and said gruffly, "It's nice as
hell to finally meet you. Welcome to the family."

"Thanks," Devon choked out. He tried to
imagine what life would have been like growing
up in this poor—but apparently happy—mix-and-
match family. Very, very different.

At that inopportune moment, his phone rang.
Every single time it had rung over the past six
weeks he'd hoped it was Pippa, but it never was.
He considered letting it ring without answering,
but what if she'd finally called? "I have to take
this," he said.

"I'll leave you to it," the older man replied as

he left the room. "See you in the dining room when you're done."

Devon pulled the phone from his pocket and saw it wasn't Pippa on the line. It was Aiden.

"Where the hell are you?"

"Texas," Devon replied.

"How soon can you get back here?"

"What's the rush?"

"Brian was smoke jumping in Yellowstone, and his plane went down."

Devon's heart shot right to his throat. "Is he all right?"

"He's missing."

Devon's knees buckled, and he dropped onto the nearest chair. "What happened?"

"The rest of the smoke jumpers got out fine," Aiden continued, "but a wall of fire engulfed the plane before Brian jumped. The other jumpers said it simply disappeared in the flames."

"Are you saying Brian's plane went down in the middle of the goddamn fire?"

"We don't know that for sure. Right now the fire is burning too hot for anyone to get close enough to tell exactly where it crashed."

Devon shuddered at the thought of his brother being consumed by fire. It was a danger Brian had lived with all of his professional life, but it didn't make it any easier for Devon to accept.

Brian had once explained to him that, after the horrific firestorm in Yellowstone in 1988 that had destroyed nearly a million acres of forest, very few fires in the park were allowed to burn themselves out, which had been previous park policy. Now every fire was fought. But that meant underbrush had been collecting for nearly thirty years, creating a lot of kindling for the next time lightning—or some human with a match—started a blaze.

"How long has this fire been burning?" What Devon really wanted to know was how big the fire was—whether it had been growing for days . . . or weeks . . . or perhaps been out of control for a month or more.

"Two weeks. It's big, Devon. It involves a part of the park that wasn't affected by the disaster in '88." He huffed out a breath and added, "This monster has been growing, leaping over firebreaks faster than firefighters can carve them out. Brian was jumping with a hotshot crew out of Idaho, trying to head off the fire before it moved into another section of the forest. The plane took a dive, and he was just . . . gone."

"Doesn't Brian have a two-way radio? Or a plain old cellphone? Isn't he wearing some kind of equipment he can be tracked with?" Devon asked.

"Yeah. All of the above, I think. But none of it seems to be working."

Devon's heart sank at the most logical reason for Brian's lack of communication. *His gear isn't working because it got burned up in the fire. Along with Brian.*

"Connor and I are heading to Yellowstone to help in the search," Aiden said. "Do you want to come along?"

"Hell, yes! Don't wait for me. I'll find you when I get there."

"One more thing. Taylor Grayhawk was piloting the plane, so Leah's coming with us."

He hissed in a breath at the depth of this disaster, which had apparently struck both Grayhawks and Flynns. It was difficult to wrap his head around the fact that Taylor and Brian might both be dead.

Devon forced himself not to think the worst. Taylor was an experienced pilot who'd been dropping smoke jumpers for as long as he could remember. Maybe she'd maneuvered the plane beyond the fire before it went down. And Brian was an exceptional firefighter. He knew a lot about surviving against all odds in a fiery inferno.

It surprised him that Leah was coming with them instead of going to Yellowstone on her own or with her sisters. It certainly wasn't typical Grayhawk-Flynn behavior to join forces. Then he remembered that Leah and Aiden had once dated. She must have asked him for a ride, and under the circumstances, it made sense.

"Do you think anyone's told Pippa what's going on?" he asked.

"I assume Matt called her, but you might want to contact her yourself."

"I think I will."

Devon needed to get back to Jackson as quickly as possible, which meant postponing his visit to Pippa. There were things he needed to say to her in person, he didn't dare broach on the phone. But he welcomed the excuse to talk to her, even if it was about a Grayhawk with whom she hadn't been on the best of terms and a Flynn she'd only met once.

As soon as he disconnected the call with Aiden,

he dialed Pippa's number, not allowing himself a chance to have second thoughts.

"Fairchild Ranch."

"Pippa?"

"Devon, is that you?"

She sounded glad to hear his voice. He bit back all the things he'd practiced to say in person—how he loved her and wanted her back and knew he could love her baby as though it were his own. Instead, he said, "Taylor was dropping a bunch of smoke jumpers on a fire in Yellowstone and her plane crashed. She's missing, along with my brother Brian. He was smoke jumping and didn't get out before the plane went down. I just thought you should know."

"Thank you, Devon. My father already called."

"Oh." He hung on to the phone, unwilling to end the call and lose contact with her again.

"Do you have any news about them?"

"No. I'm headed to Yellowstone now."

"Is that singing I hear? Whose birthday is it?"

Devon realized the five kids in the other room were singing "Happy Birthday" to his father. "My father's."

"You're celebrating Angus's birthday? Now?"

"It's my biological father's birthday. I'm at his ranch in Texas."

"You're in Texas, and you didn't come to see me?"

A long silence ensued while Devon tried to figure out how to turn a conversation that had begun by conveying information about the uncertain fates of his brother and her aunt into the call he should have made to Pippa a long time ago.

Her voice sounded anxious as she said, "Is there something you're not telling me?"

There were a lot of things he hadn't said to her. Things he would have preferred to say in person. But it seemed he wasn't going to get the perfect opportunity to open his heart to her. Would she believe that he'd been planning see her after he left Shiloh Kidd's ranch? Or would she think he'd intended to go right back home again? The time had come to fish or cut bait.

He took a deep breath and said, "I love you, Pippa. Think about that while I go hunt for Brian and Taylor."

He didn't say goodbye. He just hung up the phone.

Now she knew. The next step was up to her. If she loved him . . . Devon refused to speculate on what she might do. Once he and Aiden and Connor found Brian—and they would find him—he would go see Pippa and ask if she was willing to spend the rest of her life with him.

Then he realized he hadn't said a word about the baby.

Chapter 33

PIPPA'S MOUTH WAS still agape when she realized the phone was dead. When she'd heard Devon's voice, she'd been afraid something might have happened to her father, who'd been headed to Yellowstone to help fight the fire. Devon's announcement that he loved her was shocking—and wonderful. She just wished he'd said how he felt about becoming an instant parent to another man's child. But he must know that she and the child were inseparable.

The baby moved inside her, and Pippa put a protective hand over her belly. It was time to go meet her future instead of waiting for it to come to her.

She turned to her mother, who was working at a desk in the kitchen, and said, "I need to go back to Wyoming."

"Have they found the missing plane?" her mother asked, removing a pair of reading glasses.

"Not yet. But I want to be there when they do."

"Who was that on the phone?"

"Devon. He said he loves me." Pippa still felt a little dazed.

Her mother rose and crossed the room, folding her arms around Pippa. "Oh, darling. I knew that boy would figure out how he felt sooner or later. I'm glad it was sooner."

"Sooner?" Pippa said. "It's been six weeks."

"Believe me, that's no time at all."

Pippa was reminded of the sorrowful months her mother and father had been separated. Her mum had waited *twenty years* to see her lost love again. So maybe six weeks wasn't so long after all.

"You're lucky to be able to share these final months of your pregnancy with Devon," her mother said, tucking a curl behind Pippa's ear. She laid her other hand tenderly on Pippa's belly. At that moment, the baby kicked.

Pippa looked at her mother's startled face and laughed.

"Devon can experience fun moments like that," her mother said, laughing along with her. "And he can be there when your baby's born. That is, if you want him there. You've told me how Devon feels about you. You haven't said how you feel about him."

Her mother put an arm around Pippa's waist and led her toward the living room, where the two of them settled onto a comfortable couch. A cool evening breeze was blowing through the open windows, and Pippa grabbed a blanket to cover her bare feet. There had been too many poisonous spiders and snakes in Australia to run around barefoot, but it turned out her mother rarely wore shoes in the house, and Pippa had picked up the habit.

Pippa had sat on this couch and discussed her

life growing up in the Australian Outback, her stepmother, Irene, her brother, Nathan, her work whispering brumbies, her ill-fated romance with Tim Brandon, and her experiences with Beowulf and Sultan. She'd never spoken about Devon.

"I made such a fool of myself with Tim," she began, "that I kept Devon at arm's length so I wouldn't get hurt again. I kept telling myself—and Devon—that I only wanted a friend. I'm not sure when my feelings changed, but they did. I thought about saying something to Devon when I went to his cabin to pick up my things, but he looked so forbidding, I didn't."

"So you know he loves you, but he has no idea how you feel?"

"Too right." Pippa wondered where Devon had found the courage to lay his heart before her like that, when she'd never been brave enough to be equally vulnerable. Even now she quaked when she thought of telling him she loved him. Especially since Devon hadn't said a word about the baby.

He knew she planned to keep it, which meant he must have thought about becoming the father of Tim's child. Saying he loved her likely meant he was willing to take the baby along with her. But accepting the presence of another man's child in your home and actually being a good father to it were two different things.

What if Devon said he would cherish her baby and love it as his own . . . and then didn't? What if he honestly believed he could accept another man's child . . . and then couldn't? If she had to leave Devon someday in the future for the sake of her child, she would be leaving her shattered heart behind.

"When do you want to go?" her mother asked.

"I should call Daddy and see if he can send King's jet to pick me up."

"I have a jet available that can take you back to Jackson."

"Thank you, Mum," Pippa said.

"Where are you planning to stay when you get there?"

Pippa realized Devon was on his way to Yellowstone and was likely to remain there until Brian and Taylor were found. She would rather not stay at his cabin alone. "At Kingdom Come, I guess." She hesitated, then said, "There's plenty of room at the ranch. Why don't you come with me?"

Her mother looked startled. "I couldn't do that!"

"Why not? I'm sure Daddy would be glad to see you. Maybe you'll fall in love again."

"I have a life—and responsibilities—here in Texas, and your father's tied to Kingdom Come, at least for the next year. What would be the point?"

"Your love story with Daddy seems so sad. I wish there were some way for it to have a happy ending."

Her mother's mouth curved in a smile, but her gray eyes remained somber. "Not all fairy tales end happily ever after. I'm so glad we've gotten to know each other, that I've had a chance to be your mother and for you to be my daughter."

Pippa felt her throat swelling closed. It sounded almost as if she were saying goodbye forever.

"I'm only going to Wyoming," she said. "It's not the end of the world."

Her mother reached out, and a moment later they were hugging each other tight.

"You'll always have a home here if you ever need one," her mother whispered in her ear. She leaned back and brushed the tears from Pippa's cheeks. "And I hope you'll invite me to visit now and then to get to know my grandchild."

"I will," Pippa promised.

As they hugged again, Pippa realized that she'd just met her mother, and here she was walking out of her life. It didn't seem fair for them to have found each other and then be separated again so soon. But Devon's life was in Wyoming. And her life was with Devon.

She cocked her head and asked, "Do you really want to run for the Senate? I mean, if you weren't doing that, you wouldn't have to stay here in Texas. You could come to Wyoming and live close to me and Daddy and your brand-new grandchild."

"There are things that Jonathan began that I want to finish."

"Couldn't someone else do it? Now that I've found you, I don't want to lose you."

Her mother laughed. "You won't. I'll visit and you'll visit and we'll stay as close as we are now."

Pippa conceded that she wasn't going to change her mother's mind. At least not today. That didn't mean she couldn't do her best to figure out a way to get her mother and father back together. She knew that part of what had brought her father back to the States was the chance to reunite with his lost love. Now that her mother knew the worst of what her father had done, they could begin to build a new relationship as adults. She just needed to get her mother back to Wyoming.

The baby would solve that problem in the short term. With any luck, her mother wouldn't win that Senate seat. And then, well, anything was possible.

Chapter 34

"SHE'S WONDERFUL, DADDY. I can see why you loved Mum so much."

Pippa's description of her time with Jennie made Matt want to drop everything and go to Texas to see his former love. But he couldn't leave until Taylor was found—one way or the other. He'd come home from Yellowstone long enough to make sure Pippa was settled at the ranch, but he was heading back this afternoon.

The charred wreckage of the smoke-jumping aircraft had been found in a burned-out area of the forest, but no bodies had been recovered. Apparently, Taylor and Brian had escaped before the plane hit the ground, or at least before it burned. The forest fire was still raging too fiercely, and the winds were whipping the fire into a frenzy that was too unpredictable, for a wider search to be safely launched.

The discovery of the plane in a large burned-out area had led the authorities to conclude that they were looking for remains, rather than living souls. Collective wisdom said there was no way Brian and Taylor could have moved faster than the wildfire, especially since it was likely one or both of them had been injured in the crash.

The fact that none of Brian's communication gear was working also lent weight to the conclusion that Brian, along with his equipment, had been consumed by the fire. Since he was presumed to have Taylor with him, she must have been burned to death as well. It was just a matter of time, the authorities had announced to the news media, before their charred bodies would be found.

Aiden had taken violent exception to that announcement, and Connor and Devon had been vocal in agreeing with him. But there was nothing any of them could do about a further search until the fire was under control, and it was still burning ferociously.

Pippa interrupted Matt's grim thoughts when she asked, "Have you seen Devon?"

"Last time I saw him, he and Aiden and your aunt Leah were clearing brush to create a firebreak."

"Was he close to the fire?" Pippa asked.

Matt saw the fear in her eyes and said, "This is not like the bushfires in Australia."

"It's not?"

Bushfires were one of the great dangers in Australia, especially when pushed by the wind, dashing across the dry grassland, torching everything in their path at speeds up to twenty-two kilometers per hour. Matt and Pippa had barely outraced a bushfire when Pippa was eight. Dark clouds of smoke had caused tears to stream down her sooty face, and her hair and eyebrows had gotten badly singed by flying embers before they'd finally made it to the river and safety.

Matt wasn't sure whether the forest fire in Yellowstone was more or less dangerous than an Australian bushfire. But since Devon was a long way from the flames, he wasn't going to put visions of Devon getting burned to death in Pippa's head.

"How long before the fire is out?" Pippa asked.

Matt shook his head. "No idea. It was still leaping firebreaks when I left. They're asking for more volunteer firefighters, so I guess it must be pretty bad."

"I tried calling Devon, but I couldn't reach him," she said, chewing anxiously on a fingernail.

"Most likely he's too busy to answer his phone or check his messages. I'll hunt him down and have him give you a call. By the way, does he know you're here?"

"I didn't tell him I was coming. I wanted to surprise him."

Matt smiled. "You certainly surprised me. What made you decide to come back?"

"Devon told me he loves me."

Matt's smile disappeared. "And the baby?"

Pippa stuck out her chin pugnaciously. "He knows I'm pregnant. And he loves me."

Matt's first instinct was to protect his daughter. Then he remembered how Jennie's parents had made all the decisions for them. And how badly that had turned out. Pippa had been telling him all along—by running away, for a start—that she was determined to make her own choices and live with the pain if she was wrong. It was time to step back and let his daughter decide what she wanted to do with her life.

"He's a good man," he said at last. "If you ever need me, Pippa, I'm here."

He saw the moment when she realized he wasn't going to fight her anymore. Tears filled her eyes, and she threw her arms around his neck. "Thank you, Daddy. I love you so much!"

Matt would have answered, but his throat was too swollen to speak.

Chapter 35

DEVON, HIS TWO older brothers, and Leah were taking a break, faces covered with soot, bodies streaked with sweat, clothes singed, gloved hands blistered, muscles protesting sixteen hours straight of extreme physical labor. Leah had gone with Connor to retrieve food and drink for the four of them. Devon had been impressed at her resilience. She'd worked as hard as any of them.

As Devon watched, a batch of fire retardant was dropped from a low-flying plane in the final moments before official nightfall, which was 10:03 p.m. Steam and white smoke rose into the air. A moose clambered up a slope to his left, and a badger waddled along a dirt track where firefighting machinery was parked as though he owned it.

His visit to his biological father seemed like a dream that he still hadn't woken up from. When he'd explained the situation in Wyoming to Shiloh Kidd, his biological father had urged him to go help. Devon had promised to return someday soon to spend more time with him, but he'd seen from the look in Kidd's eyes that he didn't believe him. Devon planned to prove him wrong.

"So the fire is finally under control?" he said to Aiden.

"That's what I was told."

"How soon can we start searching?"

"I've had helicopters looking all day while we've been working," Aiden replied, "overflying a search grid in each section of the forest as the fire was controlled, leading out from where the plane went down."

"Nothing?" Devon already knew the answer to his question, because Aiden would have said something if any sign of his brother and Leah's sister had been reported. But he kept his gaze focused on Aiden, hoping against hope.

"They spotted most of Brian's firefighting gear piled up as though he'd dumped it there in a hurry."

"But no bodies?" Devon persisted.

"No bodies," Aiden said in a hoarse voice. "We'll need to get in on the ground to make sure . . ."

Devon swallowed over the ache in his throat. He could never remember seeing his older brother so choked up. He might only share a mother with his brothers, but he'd grown up loving them, and that hadn't changed. Devon refused to believe that Brian's body was lying burned beneath his gear. He knew Brian had survived. He just couldn't imagine how he'd done it. "What happened to them?" Devon asked. "It's like they disappeared into thin air."

Aiden focused his gaze on the thousands of acres of blackened, barren landscape—and the two million acres of thick green forest beyond that. "They're out there somewhere."

"Now what?" Devon asked.

"We eat. We sleep. We search again tomorrow."

Devon felt a hand on his shoulder and turned to find Matt looking as filthy and exhausted as he felt himself. "Hi, Matt. You look like shit."

"You don't look much better. I've been hunting for you half the day."

Devon felt his stomach clench. *Something's happened to Pippa.* Then he realized that was ridiculous. Matt would be with his daughter if something was wrong, not here fighting a fire. But he could imagine no other reason why Matt would have been looking for him. "What's up?"

"Do you have a minute?"

Devon realized he must want to talk about Pippa after all; otherwise, he would have said whatever he had to say in front of Aiden. "Sure." He turned to his brother and said, "Don't eat my sandwich. I'll be right back." Then he walked aside with Matt, nearly getting run down by a panicked coyote with a patch of fur burned off its back that was darting across the road.

"Pippa's at Kingdom Come," Matt announced.

"What?"

"You heard me. She seems to think you love her."

"I do love her." It was easier to say the words to Pippa's father than he'd expected.

"What about the baby?"

Devon shrugged.

Before he could say that he knew the baby came along with Pippa, Matt had grabbed handfuls of his shirt with both fists, and Devon felt Matt's spittle on his face.

"You sonofabitch. How can you say you love Pippa and dismiss her child with a shrug?"

Aiden shouted, "Hey! What the hell's going on over there?"

"Butt out!" Matt snarled.

Devon realized the mistake he'd made, gripped both of Matt's wrists, and said, "I'll love the baby, too—because it's Pippa's."

It took Matt a moment to realize what Devon had said. He let go and shook his head in disgust. "Why the hell didn't you say so in the first place?"

Devon's lip curved in a chagrined smile. "I forgot I was speaking to my kid's grandfather."

Matt looked stunned, as though it had just occurred to him that he was going to be a grandpa.

Aiden hurried over to them, and Devon put himself between his brother and his future father-in-law to prevent any further misunderstanding from escalating into violence.

But it wasn't Matt whom Aiden wanted to speak to. He stopped in front of Devon and said, "A new fire's started in the Bridger-Teton National Forest. If they can't put it out, it could threaten your cabin."

Devon had cut a firebreak around his property, but his cabin was literally surrounded by forest, and a gust of wind carrying flying embers could easily set his home ablaze. "Any idea how close it is to my place?"

Aiden shook his head. "I don't have coordinates yet. They're sending firefighters from this blaze to put out that fire before it can grow. But you'd better get home, so you can move your stock if it becomes necessary."

Devon turned to Matt and said, "Don't let Pippa leave. I'll be coming to get her." And then he ran for his truck.

Chapter 36

PIPPA WAS TOO excited to sit still. She felt useless because her pregnancy kept her from helping to fight the fire. Everyone else at Kingdom Come had something to do or somewhere to be except her.

She'd only ever been at odds with Taylor, but she empathized with her grandfather, whose face had looked bleak during the long hours of futile search for her missing aunt, and with Victoria, who'd been so overwhelmed by the disappearance of her twin that she'd collapsed in tears. Her grandfather had gone to Jackson, where he could help organize—and get the latest updates on—the search for Taylor and Brian. Before Leah had left to help fight the fire and search for her sister in Yellowstone, she'd suggested that Victoria stay with Eve so she wouldn't be alone, and had sent Nathan along with her so he could play with Eve and Connor's two kids.

The Grayhawks had banded together in this time of trouble, but Pippa hadn't been a part of it. She knew they hadn't excluded her on purpose, but it hadn't made her feel any less alone.

There was a place where she belonged. And someone with whom she belonged. She'd felt happy living with Devon. She loved the life they'd led on his ranch. She wanted desperately to see him, to have his strong arms close around her when she told him that she loved him, too. That would all have to wait while he fought the fire that might have claimed his brother's life.

However, she knew the first place Devon would go when all was said and done. He'd head home to check on Beowulf and Sultan and his menagerie of wounded animals. Pippa realized she could see him that much sooner if she borrowed her father's pickup and drove to Devon's cabin.

She was on the outskirts of Devon's ranch when she noticed smoke on the horizon. This smoke was different from the haze that covered most of Jackson as a result of the fire in Yellowstone. This smoke billowed, and she saw an occasional flame. She felt a shiver run down her spine.

Ever since she and her father had narrowly escaped that wildfire in Australia when she was a child, Pippa had harbored a deathly fear of her clothes and hair catching on fire. Her natural instinct was to turn around and go in the opposite direction. But the thought of Wulf or Sultan or any of Devon's menagerie burning to death kept her foot on the accelerator.

Pippa gunned the engine, anxious to get to Devon's home in a hurry. Right now it looked like the wind was driving the fire away from his place, but that could change. As she hit the brakes and skidded to a stop at his front door, she heard Wulf howling inside. She was glad Devon didn't lock his door. She shoved the exuberant wolf away so she could squeeze inside and a moment later was on her knees beside him.

"Everything's all right," she said, smoothing the ruffled hackles on Wulf's back. He was clearly excited to see her, licking her face and bouncing around. "The fire's a long way from here. We're safe if we stay inside the house."

Then she realized that the animals in the barn must be equally agitated. "Wait here. I'll be right back."

Before she left the house, sugar cubes in hand, Pippa thought about calling Devon to tell him a fire was burning in the forest nearby. But he was an hour and a half away. What could he do from there that she couldn't do, since she was right here? Besides, she might be worrying him for nothing. The fire could burn itself out, or the wind could take it in the opposite direction, and she would have made him leave the fire in Yellowstone—and the search for his brother—for nothing.

She watched the direction of the distant smoke as the wind swirled around her. Which way was it blowing now? She saw charred ashes floating in the sky, but no burning embers.

She'd been gone for six weeks, but the instant she spoke, Sultan's head appeared over the stall door. "There you are," she said, smiling at the sight of his ears tipped forward in welcome. "I have something for you."

Pippa held out her hand and Sultan lipped the sugar into his mouth, all the while watching

her with calm—rather than wary—eyes. Pippa
smoothed a hand over his nose, then let her other
hand wander up his jaw. She smiled when he lowered his head so she could more easily scratch behind his ears. "You like that, don't you?"

She slid her arm around his neck as she moved
his forelock away from his eyes. "You're such a
beauty. I hope I won't need to test your trust by
trying to lead you out of this stall."

If the fire came in this direction, Pippa could
simply release Sultan, but there was no guarantee
he would escape. It would be better if she could
load him onto a horse trailer and drive him out of
here. But she wasn't sure whether that was feasible,
since she'd never even put a halter on him.

Maybe she ought to try that now.

She left Sultan and found a halter, holding it
out so he could see it as she returned. He became
restless again, turning in circles, but she stood patiently at the stall door, waiting for him to return.
At last he stuck his head out and stood, his ears
flicking back and forth, his nostrils flared, his dark
eyes focused on her.

"I know you must have had a halter on before,
so you know this won't hurt a bit." The halter circled his nose and had straps running up either side
of his jaw which connected to a strap that went
over his head behind his ears and buckled on the
side. A lead rope could be attached to a metal ring
under his jaw. "Easy peasy," she said as she slipped
the halter over his nose, then laid the strap over his
head, before buckling it on one side of his jaw.

When she was done, Sultan shook his head,

testing the halter, but he didn't retreat from the door.

"See? That wasn't so bad. Now if I need to get you out of here in a hurry, we're all set."

Pippa went to check on the animals in the cages at the other end of the barn. They were all different from the ones that had been there before she left. She was shocked to see a skunk and wondered how Devon had been able to treat it without getting sprayed. He was also helping out a blue jay, a possum with babies, and a fox. The fox surprised her, because it looked exactly like the picture on the "F is for Fox" page in a book her father had read to her as a child. Somehow she hadn't expected the fox to be quite so red, or its face to be framed with such distinct white and black fur.

Pippa had just made a plan for how she could lift and carry each of the cages to her pickup, if and when she might have to evacuate, when she heard a car door slam. She looked out and saw Devon's truck, then caught sight of him entering the house. She left the barn on the run—or as much of a run as she could manage.

She met him coming down the front steps as she was going up. "Have they found Brian and Taylor?"

"What the hell are you doing here? Don't you know there's a fire headed this way? You could have been trapped!"

Pippa was stopped in her tracks by the anger in his voice. A second later he picked her up in a crushing hug and said, "Thank God you're safe!"

She suddenly realized his anger had actually

been fear for her safety. She wrapped her arms around him in return, but gasped, "Devon, I can't breathe."

He loosened his hold on her enough to search her eyes and said, "I didn't mean to hurt you. Are you and the baby all right?"

"We're fine."

He pulled her close again, laid his cheek against hers, and said, "I can't believe you're here. I was on my way to get you and the baby when I heard about Brian and Taylor."

"Are they all right?"

He leaned back and said, "The fire is out, but Brian and Taylor have disappeared like the morning mist."

"How is that possible?"

He released her, but then took her hand and twined their fingers together. "I have no idea. I came home because I heard about the fire here in the Bridger-Teton forest. They've sent a bunch of firefighters from the Yellowstone fire to put it out, but I couldn't tell on the drive in whether it's coming this way or not."

"The wind keeps shifting," Pippa said, as she turned and searched the air above the surrounding forest.

"Let me look at you," Devon said, taking her other hand and turning her to face him, his eyes eating her hungrily. "You look so . . ." He laughed and said, "Big."

She made a face.

"And beautiful," he added. "Very beautiful," he said in a softer voice.

"I love you, Devon."

He smiled his lopsided smile, his eyes crinkling as he met her gaze. "I've been waiting a long time to hear you say those words, my friend."

Pippa laughed.

He took her face in his hands and kissed her tenderly on the lips. Then he looked into her eyes and said, "I love you, Pippa." He put his hand on her swollen belly, leaned down, and whispered, "I love you, too, Sprite."

Pippa felt her heart swell with gratitude at Devon's gesture. She had all the answers she needed. And a whole lifetime of *friendship* to look forward to.

She was reaching for Devon's hand when he suddenly said, "Wait!"

Pippa froze. Had he changed his mind? Was he having second thoughts?

"Listen. Do you hear it?"

"Hear what?" Pippa listened, but she wasn't sure what it was Devon had heard.

His arms circled her from behind, his hands resting on her burgeoning belly. He kissed her on the neck and murmured, "Rain."

Epilogue

PIPPA COULDN'T BELIEVE eleven days had passed without any word of Brian or Taylor's fate. Her grandfather was beside himself. Angus was in mourning. She was amazed at Aiden and Leah's continued dedication to the search. Neither of them seemed willing to give up. Both seemed convinced that *somehow*, although Pippa couldn't imagine how, Brian and Taylor had survived the fire.

"One of them is hurt," Leah had speculated. "It has to be Brian. Otherwise, he could carry Taylor out. You wait and see. Both of them will be back with a story to tell."

Pippa wasn't so sure. A thorough search of the burned area had revealed no sign of them. And eleven days was a very long time to be missing. If one of them was injured badly enough to keep them from moving around for that long, what were the chances that whoever was injured could have survived without professional medical attention?

Pippa covered the male arms that enfolded her in bed with her own and said, "It seems wrong to feel so deliriously happy when everyone else is so sad."

"I have something to ask you, Pippa."

"What is it?" she murmured, half asleep.

"Will you marry me?"

It was a heroic feat, but Pippa managed to turn her nearly seven-months-pregnant body over so she was lying flat on her back, her head elevated on a pillow so she could see Devon's face. "Say that again."

He looked very serious as he leaned over to kiss her. Then he said, "Will you be my wife?"

"You want to marry me before the baby's born? It will have your last name if you do that."

"I know," he said. "It's what I want. You haven't answered my question. Will you?"

"Yes, my very dear friend. I will."

Devon leaned down far enough to whisper to her belly, "Hear that, Sprite? You're not going to be a Grayhawk. You're going to be a Flynn."

Pippa laughed. "She's going to be the spitting image of her mother."

"*She?* It's a girl?"

Pippa nodded. "I found out when I was staying with my mother. I only tell you because there seems to be a dearth of little Flynn girls."

"Connor has one."

"Yes. And now *you're* going to have *two*."

The dazzled, dumbfounded look on Devon's face made her laugh. Pippa kissed him sweetly and said, "Did I neglect to mention that twins run in my father's family?"

Acknowledgments

I owe a great debt to my friends Sally Shoeneweiss, Barb McCleary, Gloria Skinner, and Billie Blake Bailey, who keep me inspired and support me when I'm struggling to get words on the page, and my sister Joyce, for her advice on arranging commas and syntax.

I also want to thank my public relations and marketing assistant, Nancy November Sloane, who makes it possible to stay in touch with my readers and still write.

I want to thank you, the readers, for sharing your kind thoughts with me and making it easier for me to keep the seat of the pants to the seat of the chair so you'll always have another book to read.

And last, but by no means least, I want to thank my friends at Penguin Random House, who make my book read like a better writer than I am wrote it, put a stunning cover on it, and then sell it to devoted readers in great numbers. Gina, I appreciate all your support. Shauna, you have the patience of a saint and the perfect editorial touch. I could never do this without you. And Sarah, you are a blessing. Thanks for all your help.

LETTER TO READERS

Dear Faithful Reader,

While you're waiting for Brian and Taylor's story, *Surrender,* to hit the stands, I'll be looking forward to hearing your theories about what happened to them. I've included an excerpt from *Surrender* at the end of this book.

Those of you who've been reading my historical Mail-Order Brides series of Bitter Creek novels, *Texas Bride, Wyoming Bride,* and *Montana Bride,* will be delighted to know that I'll be writing the final book in the series, *Blackthorne's Bride* (Josie's story), next!

You can contact me, sign up for my e-newsletter, and enter contests through my website, www.joanjohnston.com. You can also like me at facebook.com/joanjohnstonauthor, or follow me at twitter.com/joanjohnston. I look forward to hearing from you!

By the way, if you enjoyed this novel, it's connected to more than thirty-five other books in my Bitter Creek series, which begins with my contemporary novels *The Cowboy, The Texan,* and *The Loner.* If you'd like to read more about Libby and North Grayhawk, check out *The Next Mrs. Blackthorne, A Stranger's Game,* and *Shattered.*

Enjoy!

Take care and happy reading.

Joan Johnston

Taylor and Brian's story heats up in the next
installment of *New York Times* bestselling author
Joan Johnston's sizzling contemporary
Western romance series, where power, money,
and rivalries rule—and love is the best revenge.

Surrender

Coming soon from Dell

Continue reading for a special sneak peek

DOES YOUR LIFE *really flash before your eyes when
you know you're going to die?* Taylor Grayhawk
was a great pilot, but there was nothing she could
do with both engines flared out. A whirlwind of
fire had engulfed her Twin Otter as she flew over
Yellowstone National Park dropping smoke jumpers to fight the raging inferno that had been burning for the past two weeks. She turned to stare over
her shoulder at the single smoke jumper who hadn't
made it out of the plane.

"You can still jump," she said over the eerie
rustle of the wind in the open doorway at the rear
of the plane.

"Not without you," the jumper called back.

"I don't have a parachute."

"We can share mine."

Taylor calculated the odds of getting to the
ground hanging on to Brian Flynn by her fingernails—
and whatever other body parts she could wrap
around him. He was wearing a padded jump jacket

and pants made of Kevlar, the material used for bulletproof vests. It was bulky, to say the least. She imagined herself falling—sliding down his body—into the flames below and shuddered.

"I'll take my chances on getting the plane to the ground in one piece," she said, turning back to the control panel to see how much lift she could manage without the engines. Not much. She searched in vain for a meadow—any opening in the trees—where she might crash-land the plane.

She regretted leaving the ground without the spotter who usually came along to gauge the wind, fire activity, and terrain. He might have been able to steer her away from the catastrophic encounter with fire that had occurred.

Or maybe not. Maybe taking off without waiting for the overdue spotter had saved his life. She doubted anyone could have anticipated the sudden tornado of flame that had shot up hundreds of feet into the air from the forest below.

"This plane's headed straight into the fire," Brian said from the doorway. "We need to jump now, while there's still time to hit a safe clearing. Get over here, Tag. Move your butt!"

The use of her nickname—from her initials, Taylor Ann Grayhawk—conjured powerful, painful memories. Brian had dubbed her with it when he was a junior and she was a freshman at Jackson High.

Taylor felt the plane shudder as the right wingtip was abruptly shoved upward by a gust of hot air, and knew that time was running out. In a voice that was surprisingly calm considering the desperation she felt inside, Taylor reported their position on the radio, along with the fact that she'd been unable to restart the engines.

"I'm putting us down in the first clearing I find," she told the dispatcher.

"Roger," the dispatcher replied. "Good luck."

The problem was that she didn't see a clearing large enough to land in without going in nose first. Survival was questionable. Disaster seemed imminent.

Two words kept replaying in her mind: "What if . . . ?"

What if their fathers, King Grayhawk and Angus Flynn, hadn't been mortal enemies? What if Brian's elder brother, Aiden, hadn't caught Brian making love to her after the junior prom? What if her fraternal twin, Victoria, hadn't made it clear that if Taylor didn't stay away from Brian, to her mind just one more of "those awful Flynn boys," she would never speak to her again?

Brian had become a firefighter and married someone else. She'd become a corporate pilot and gone through several futile engagements. They were both free now, but Brian's divorce a year ago had left him so heartsore and gun-shy that he was likely never to fall in love again.

None of that mattered now. Very likely, she and Brian were going to die in the next few minutes. What made her heart ache was regret for what her life might have been like if only . . .

"Tag?"

She looked over her shoulder at the tall, broad-shouldered man who'd been forbidden fruit when

they were teenagers. She'd run her fingers through his thick black hair, holding on tight as they made love. His piercing blue eyes had seen past her movie-star-beautiful, confident, blond-haired, blue-eyed exterior to the abandoned child inside who desperately wanted to be loved.

She'd grown up with an older sister as a mother, after her own mother had run off with one of her father's cowhands. Her wealthy father had been mostly absent, serving two terms as Wyoming's governor in Cheyenne while he left his four daughters back home at his ranch in Jackson Hole.

Because of the animosity between their families, she'd started out determined to seduce Brian Flynn—and dump him. It would be fair repayment for all the nasty things he and his three brothers had done to her and her three sisters. His heart was supposed to end up broken, not hers. She hadn't planned on liking him. Brian was the first boy to offer affection in return for the sex she'd been offering to any boy who gave her a kind look—and some whose looks weren't so kind—hoping to find someone who would care about her.

"I'm not leaving without you, Tag," Brian said. "Get out of that seat and get your beautiful ass over here!"

Their eyes met, and she felt the past flooding back. All the things she should have done . . . and hadn't. All the things she shouldn't have done . . . and had.

The thought of a future with Brian almost had her rising. But there was too much water under the bridge. Or water over the dam. She'd been disap-

pointed too many times by too many men. Some people are lovable, and some are not. She was just one of those people who wasn't destined to find a man who could love her. Brian Flynn had had his chance. She no longer believed in the possibility of any kind of happily-ever-after. Her life was liable to end in an altogether gruesome way.

"You go," she said, turning back to peer through the windshield in search of the clearing she knew had to be there somewhere.

A moment later she felt a strong hand gripping her arm, yanking her out of her seat.

"I am not, by God, going to take the blame for leaving you behind, you stubborn brat!"

The plane shuddered, and the wings tipped sideways.

"Let me go!" she cried, reaching back toward the controls to attempt to right the plane. But he pulled her inexorably toward the door, which was already tilting upward at an angle that might keep them both from escaping.

Taylor jerked free and rushed back to her seat, grabbing the control column and bringing the plane back to level. She glanced over her shoulder and said, "Just go, Brian! Someone has to keep the plane steady so you can get out the door."

"I'm not going anywhere without you, Tag. Get that into your head. So you can either join me in getting out of this plane, or we can both go down with it in flames."